The Spook
in the Stacks

Also available by Eva Gates

The Spook in the Stacks

A LIGHTHOUSE LIBRARY MYSTERY

Eva Gates

CROOKED LANE

NEW YORK

Published in the United States by Crooked Lane Books, an imprint of The Quick Brown Fox & Company LLC.

Crooked Lane Books and its logo are trademarks of The Quick Brown Fox & Company LLC.

Library of Congress Catalog-in-Publication data available upon request.

ISBN (hardcover): 978-1-68331-580-3
ISBN (ePub): 978-1-68331-581-0
ISBN (ePDF): 978-1-68331-582-7

Cover illustration by Joe Burleson.
Book design by Jennifer Canzone.

Printed in the United States.

www.crookedlanebooks.com

Crooked Lane Books
34 West 27th St., 10th Floor
New York, NY 10001

First Edition: June 2018

10 9 8 7 6 5 4 3 2 1

To "SAVE OUR COZIES." You know who you are and you did it!

Chapter One

My colleagues burst through the library doors, weighted down by gravestones, skeletons, and a giant black spider.

I've never been a big lover of Halloween, mainly because, frankly, I don't consider being scared at all fun.

Clearly, in that I am in the minority.

Ronald dropped a gravestone on the floor. It bounced as it hit the white and black marble tiles. "RIP" was scrawled across the front.

"That's grisly," I said.

"Where's your sense of fun?" Ronald said.

"I don't have one," I replied.

"Why does that not come as a surprise to me?" said Louise Jane McKaughnan.

If there's a Halloween version of the Grinch, I'm it. Against the wishes of Bertie James, our library director, Louise Jane had managed to convince the board of the Bodie Island Lighthouse Library that a special Halloween exhibit was a good idea. My role today was to ensure that if we had to decorate the lighthouse, it would fall somewhere in the bounds of good taste, if such a thing can be applied to Halloween. Bertie put her foot firmly down at fake blood and gore, missing body parts, scary music, and zombie-costumed volunteers leaping out from under the spiral iron staircase, yelling, "Boo!"

All of which Louise Jane had suggested.

Even normally sensible Ronald Burkowski, the children's librarian, and Charlene Clayton, our research librarian, had leapt eagerly into the spirit of the thing. The grave markers and spiders' webs were for the second-floor children's room, and Charlene had said she'd print out some legends of ghostly happenings in the waters off the Outer Banks in the days of sail.

Louise Jane, not a library employee, but an excessively over-eager volunteer, had wanted the exhibit to be all about the supposedly haunted happenings at the Bodie Island Lighthouse, in which our library was situated. The last thing Bertie wanted was word to get around that the building might be haunted. She warned Louise Jane to keep her ghostly tales generic. Louise Jane had reluctantly agreed, recognizing that she had no choice. Now, she smiled at me and shifted the large cardboard box in her arms. I didn't trust Louise Jane, and never less than when she smiled. Tall, scrawny, and flat chested, with a thin face, piercing eyes, and sharp chin, she always put me in mind of a circling shark. Or, today, a grinning skeleton.

"And this," she said, "is the pièce de résistance." She put the box on the table in the center of the room. With an air of great expectation and some ceremony, she unfolded the flaps and opened the box. She reached in with both hands, paused to ensure we were all watching, and slowly pulled out a model sailing ship. She glanced at us, her smirk indicating that she was anticipating praise as well as astonishment.

For once, she got it. "Wow!" Ronald said. "Look at that detail."

"Beautiful," Bertie said.

"Where on earth," I asked, "did you find it?"

"A little something my grandmother's had in the back of her closet for ages," Louise Jane said. "Among her . . . special things." Ronald moved the empty box, and taking great care, Louise Jane gently placed the ship on the table. It was, I had to admit, an extraordinarily beautiful piece. About three feet long, the hull was constructed of individual wooden planks, above which were fitted the decks, the quarterdeck, and bridge, and above that every post and spar and section of sail was in place. The figurehead, a buxom, longhaired woman, was so lifelike, she might be about to burst out of the bow of the ship. Tiny sailors scurried about the deck or climbed the rigging. A man stood at the wheel while the captain watched. A black cat sat at the captain's feet.

Charles, one of the library's most valued employees, hissed and moved as though to swat the tiny cat.

Louise Jane shrieked. "Keep him away."

I scooped Charles up. I tapped his nose. "That is not a toy. Do you understand?"

He blinked. I decided to take that as agreement, and I put him down. Charles, named in honor of Mr. Charles Dickens, was a beautiful (and didn't he know it) Himalayan. He strolled away with a flick of his fluffy tail.

I turned my attention back to the model. "It's . . . unusual."

The ship was a perfect miniature, no attention to detail

missing. It appeared to have been in a fierce battle. Gaping holes, as if blasted away by miniature cannonballs, dotted the hull, and the sails hung in tattered, ripped sheets. I peered closer. The miniature sailors, dressed in loose white pants and striped shirts, were skeletons. I shuddered, and Louise Jane preened. *"Rebecca MacPherson."*

"Who's she?" I asked.

"A ship." Louise Jane settled into lecture mode. "She was sailing these waters, not far from this very spot, as it happens, back in 1754, when—"

"Opening time," I said. "I'll get the door."

Which is how, on Thursday, October 25th, the Bodie Island Lighthouse Library came to be open ten minutes before the regular time of nine o'clock.

The day was cold and wet, bringing thoughts of winter soon to come, and the library was busy. The decorations, the *Rebecca MacPherson* in particular, were a huge hit with our patrons. The excited squeals of children as they caught sight of papier-mâché tombstones, spider webs made of string, and plastic insects drifted down from the second-floor children's library. Next week, Ronald would be hosting Halloween parties, and the children had been told they could come in costume if they wished. Ronald had come to Nags Head from New York City many years ago to take up a new career as a children's librarian. He was great at it, and he truly looked the part, with a wild mop of white hair curling around his collar, thick glasses, and a mischievous grin. Never mind the kids—knowing Ronald and his background in theater, I was looking forward to seeing what sort of outfit he'd appear in.

I hadn't been in favor of turning our respectable library into Halloween Central, but even I had to admit that it was proving popular with our patrons, and Ronald and Charlene were getting a big kick out of it. I was even finding my own thoughts turning to what I might wear. I am far too mature to dress in a silly costume, but I still have the elaborate Victorian hat I'd worn over the summer as part of our special Jane Austen exhibit. I should be able to find some extravagant earrings from a second-hand jewelry store to accompany the hat. Not only was the staff going to dress up on Halloween for the amusement of our patrons, but tomorrow night we had a special meeting of the library's classic novel book club, and Louise Jane (of course) suggested everyone dress as a character from the classics.

It was going to be a busy week. On Saturday afternoon, Louise Jane would be giving a public lecture on the ghostly history of the Outer Banks, as well as two talks on Wednesday as part of our Halloween festivities.

The Thursday morning preschool story-time group started to arrive. Little children, most of them dripping with rainwater, ran up the spiral stairs, calling to Ronald that they were here. Smiling parents followed them in and either browsed the stacks or took seats around the magazine rack for their weekly gossip. Several of the mothers, and one young father, exclaimed over the *Rebecca MacPherson*.

The front door opened, and three people—an elderly man and a much younger man and woman—blew in on a gust of wind and a bucketful of rain.

Today, I was working at the circulation desk. My name is Lucy Richardson, and I'm the assistant librarian here. I've only been at the Lighthouse Library a few months, but I fell in love with it on my first day. I'd worked in the Harvard Libraries for several years and enjoyed it there, but when my engagement broke up (meaning, when it never happened), I fled my hometown of Boston for the Outer Banks and the comforting arms of my favorite aunt. Aunt Ellen isn't one for indulging petulant nieces, and she introduced me to her friend Bertie James, who happened to be searching for a new assistant librarian at the time.

I looked up and gave the new arrivals a smile. "Good morning. Welcome."

They furled umbrellas and shook water off their shoulders.

"Thank you," the older man said. He was in his early eighties, I guessed, tall and slim, with deep brown eyes, full lips, strong cheekbones, and a mane of gray hair. The young woman was probably a late-in-life-daughter or his granddaughter; the resemblance was strong. "Sorry to drop in unannounced," he said in a voice that indicated he wasn't sorry in the least, "but I'm hoping to have a chat with Albertina James, the library director, if she's available."

Charles leapt onto the circulation desk. The young woman squealed. "Oh, he's beautiful. May I pet him?"

"He'd like nothing more," I said.

Charles stretched and preened.

She reached out and gave him a tentative pat on his back. He rubbed against her arm, and she smiled. The younger man smiled at her. He was quite handsome, with clear gray eyes, black hair curling slightly at his collar, high cheekbones, a trace of dark stubble, a chiseled jaw.

I picked up the phone. "I'll check with Ms. James. Can I say who's calling?"

"I'm Jay Ruddle," the elderly man said. He looked as though he expected me to recognize the name. I didn't. "This is my granddaughter, Julia, and my assistant, Greg Summers."

"Hi." Julia spoke from under a waterfall of bangs, and Greg said, "Pleased to meet you."

The phone was picked up at the other end, and I said, "Bertie, there's a gentleman here to see you. Mr. Jay Ruddle?"

Bertie gasped.

"Are you okay?" I said.

"I'll be right out."

I opened my mouth to tell our visitors Bertie would be here in a moment, but I needn't have bothered. She must have broken an Olympic record in her dash down the hall. She burst into the main room, eyes wide with excitement.

"Mr. Ruddle." She thrust her hand forward, and he took it in his. "Welcome to the Bodie Island Lighthouse Library. This is such a pleasure. How can I help you?"

"I might be able to help you, Ms. James." His voice was deep and slow and full of memories of the Outer Banks. "May I introduce my granddaughter, Julia, and my personal assistant, Greg Summers?"

"So pleased to meet you, Ms. Ruddle, Mr. Summers." I don't think I've ever seen our calm, laid-back, yoga-instructor director quite so excited. She was almost dancing on her toes. Even Charles looked excited. Charles never gets excited, except when a mouse manages to find its way between the stacks. He meowed loudly, and Julia laughed.

Bertie led the way to her office, calling over her shoulder for me to make tea or coffee.

"No refreshments, thank you," Jay said. "We had a late breakfast."

Greg followed them, but Julia continued to fuss over Charles. "This is a Himalayan, isn't it? I adore cats, but Grandfather doesn't care for them, so I was never allowed to have a pet when I was growing up. Maybe it's time now."

Charles rubbed against her arm, and she smiled. She had her grandfather's strong features, but on her they were softened enough to be feminine. She wore no makeup, her hair hung limp to her shoulders, and she was dressed in slightly baggy black trousers and a well-worn sweater. Her eyes were not her grandfather's brown, but a beautiful soft blue.

Footsteps clattered on the staircase. Children, clutching their book selections, burst into the room, and parents stood up to greet them. Ronald followed his little charges and stood at the door, saying goodbye.

"Good story time?" I asked.

"They're so excited about Halloween, it was hard to get them to pay attention." He smiled at Julia. "Hi."

She dipped her head and murmured a response. "That's a beautiful model ship over there. May I have a look?"

"Of course," I said. We'd strung a couple of strands of colored string around it and attached a small sign saying "Do not touch." Julia wandered over and stood with her hands behind her back, studying the ship. Charles settled on the returns cart and set about washing his whiskers.

"I need to talk to Bertie for a couple of minutes," Ronald said. "Is she free?"

"Not right now. She has a visitor. Someone named Jay Ruddle."

Ronald's eyes opened wide.

"What?" I asked. Julia had her back to us. I pointed to her and mouthed, "Granddaughter."

Ronald leaned toward me. Instinctively I leaned in also. He spoke in almost a whisper. "Does Charlene know?"

"Know what?"

He jerked his head toward the back hall.

"About our visitors? I don't think so."

Ronald crossed the floor in a few steps. He held his hand out to Julia. "Ms. Ruddle. I'm Ronald Burkowski, children's librarian. Do you like our ship?"

She accepted his handshake. "It's marvelous. The detail is incredible. The *Rebecca MacPherson*, right? Went down off this coast in the late eighteenth century under the command of Captain Thaddeus Clark. All hands lost, as I recall."

"You know a lot about it," Ronald said.

"North Carolina nautical history is one of my grandfather's passions in life. Hard for me not to pick a few things up. Do you suppose this is a reimagining of the *Rebecca MacPherson* as some sort of *Flying Dutchman*? I don't know that I've ever heard it's rumored to have become a ghost ship."

"Someone's fancy, I suspect," Ronald said.

"It might have been inspired by the *Flying Dutchman*," I said. I happened to currently be reading (or plowing through)

Washington Irving's *Bracebridge Hall*, which mentioned the legend of the lost eighteenth-century ship and its dead crew, doomed to sail the seas forever, portending disaster to all who saw it.

The door opened, and Theodore Kowalski, impoverished rare-book collector, self-appointed literary scholar, and staunch library supporter, burst in, shaking rain off his black umbrella.

"Lucy," he said, in a crisp English accent, "do you have a copy of . . ." His voice trailed off. Julia and Ronald had turned to see who'd come in.

Theodore stared, open-mouthed. I doubt he was staring at Ronald, who he knew perfectly well. Julia gave him one of her shy smiles and dipped her head. Theodore tripped over his own feet in his rush to get across the room. The *Rebecca MacPherson* was saved only by the quick intervention of Ronald, who put his arm out to catch the flailing man.

Theodore's cheeks flamed red. He laughed in embarrassment. "What have we here? A model ship. Looks very—oh, are those skeletons?"

"We were saying," Julia said, "that the ghost element might be fake, but the model itself is historically accurate, down to the last spar and the details of the sailors' uniforms. What remains of them, anyway."

Speaking of fakes, Theodore, who we often called Teddy, wore his usual regalia of Harris Tweed jacket and paisley cravat. A pipe was visible in his breast pocket, and the scent of tobacco trailed behind him. I knew he didn't smoke, and I also knew he was Nags Head born and raised, despite the clothes and the English accent he put on in a failed attempt to sound serious.

Theodore smiled at Julia through a mouthful of small, stained teeth. She smiled back. Her teeth were in perfect condition and almost blindingly white. Ronald glanced at me and raised one eyebrow. I tried not to laugh.

"Theodore Kowalski meet Julia Ruddle," Ronald said.

"Delighted," Teddy said.

At that moment, Bertie and her guests came into the main room.

"Ready to go, honeybunch?" Jay asked.

"I was admiring this ship," Julia said. "Isn't it beautiful?"

"Sure is."

"At the Bodie Island Lighthouse Library," Bertie said, "we take the preservation of the history of the Outer Banks very seriously. We're mainly a public library, but our research department is top notch."

"Is that supposed to be the *Rebecca MacPherson*?" Jay peered closer.

"I think it is," Greg said. "It's got the right number of cannons, and that's her figurehead." He put his hand on Julia's arm, and she made no attempt to move away. Theodore noticed, and his back stiffened.

"It's a Halloween exhibit," Bertie said. "Something fanciful to amuse the patrons."

"Seems to me that if you wanted a fanciful ship, you shouldn't have interfered with a piece of Outer Banks history," Greg said.

"I—I . . . ," Bertie said.

"Don't be so serious all the time, Greg," Julia said. "It's just for fun."

"Quite right. Fun," Theodore said.

"There's fun and then there's misrepresentation. Don't you agree, Jay?" Greg said.

"I can't say I'm comfortable with it."

"We . . . we . . . ," Bertie said.

"But," Jay continued, "most people won't recognize *Rebecca* at first glance. I assume you're planning to use the model ship to educate your regulars on the history of the Age of Sail, Ms. James?"

"Absolutely. It will be a valuable learning tool for the time it's here. We don't own it. It belongs to one of our . . . uh . . . patrons."

Bertie James, of all people, had come over all tongue-tied. *Who were these people?*

"Thank you for your time. We'll talk again tomorrow afternoon," Jay said.

Julia smiled at Theodore. "It was nice meeting you."

He turned the approximate color of a ripe tomato. "The pleasure was all mine."

"Whatever," Greg said. He took Julia's arm. "Let's go."

The three library employees and the book collector stood in a circle, watching them leave. The moment the door slammed behind them, I said, "Is someone going to tell me what's going on?"

"I have to call Charlene right now," Bertie said. "She doesn't have much time." The library director hurried away.

"Time to do what?" I asked. "Who is that man?"

"Jay Ruddle is a multi-millionaire and an Outer Banks native. He's lived in New York for a long time, but he's known to have a keen interest in North Carolina history," Ronald said.

"Oh. I wonder why he was here."

"I don't know, but I can take a guess. His collection of Outer Banks historical documents is, they say, without compare. Charlene will know more, but it's been rumored that he's looking for a home for his collection."

"A home? Like, a library?"

"Yup."

"Wow. Do you suppose he's considering giving it to us?"

"Why else would he come here and put Bertie in such a state?"

"Isn't she charming?" Theodore said.

"Not the word I'd use," Ronald said. "I like Bertie a great deal, but I've never considered her charming."

"Julia. I meant Julia."

"Charming. And rich," Ronald said. "She's Ruddle's only grandchild."

"Totally without pretext or airs," Theodore said.

"If Greg is Jay's assistant," I said, "he might be the one who manages the collection."

"Well, I, for one, didn't like him," Theodore said. "He's a nasty piece of work. You can't trust those handsome men with their fake charm further than you can throw them."

Chapter Two

"That would be a heck of a coup," Stephanie Stanton said. "Make sure you have a good lawyer go over the papers."

"A good lawyer?" I said. "How about you? You're a good lawyer."

"Not me. Not my field. I can recommend someone, if you like."

Steph was one of my best friends. Five-foot two, pale-skinned, red-haired, and freckled, she was a defense attorney, junior partner to my uncle Amos, a tiny ball of energy and, sometimes, righteous indignation.

"Early days yet," I said. "We're in competition with another institution, or so I was told." The moment Jay Ruddle left, Bertie had called Charlene to ask her to come into work on a matter of great urgency. When Charlene arrived, still dressed in paint-splattered clothes, we were all called into Bertie's office, where she told us that Jay Ruddle was searching for a home for his collection, and the Lighthouse Library had made the short list. Charlene was struck speechless.

Jay planned to return tomorrow to continue the conversation, and so Bertie and Charlene would be working long into the night to put a proposal together.

"Steph's right," my cousin Josie said. "Families can take strong exception to charitable donations, and the library does not want to get into a public fight."

Grace nodded. "My mom still talks about when Old Man Farquarson left that patch of undeveloped land for a bird sanctuary, and all the trouble it caused." Grace Sullivan and Josie had been best friends since kindergarten. I'd been pleased that they'd made room in their friendship for me when I came to live here. Stephanie had joined our circle a bit later, when she returned to her hometown of Nags Head after her mother was injured in a car accident. Between the tiny Steph and the willowy Josie, Grace and I were the medium-sized ones. "What's wrong with leaving land for a bird sanctuary?" I asked.

"Nothing, as far as I'm concerned. But his three sons had plans to sell it to a developer who wanted to put in a golf course and five-star resort."

"Although," Steph said, "in the library's case, the man himself is giving away the property, not mentioning it in his will. Obviously, there's much less chance for a legal dispute if he's still around. Did he seem in possession of all his mental faculties to you, Lucy?"

"Totally," I said.

"Then you should be okay. But you still want to run everything past a lawyer before signing anything. You can be sure he'll have top-notch legal advice."

My three close friends and I try to get together once a week for dinner to catch up on each other's news. Tonight, at Grace's suggestion, we were having a special end-of-season treat at Owens', one of the Outer Banks' top restaurants. Like many places in the area, Owens' would be closing soon for the winter months, so we all agreed that we deserved to indulge ourselves. We usually went to Jake's Seafood Bar, owned, not coincidently, by Josie's boyfriend, Jake Greenblatt.

The restaurant wasn't full tonight, but the hum of conversation and gentle laughter drifted through the main room. Candlelight glowed, wine glasses sparkled, and marvelous smells filled the air. When we came in, I'd said hello to Diane Uppiton and Curtis Gardner, sitting at a table for two in a dark corner. They'd pretended to be pleased to see me but, as usual, Diane's eyes filled with suspicion and a touch of dislike.

Diane and Curtis were members of the library board. You'd think that anyone who joined a volunteer board would have the interests of the library first and foremost. In this case, you would be wrong. Diane's late husband had been the chair of the board. They'd been going through a bitter, highly public divorce at the time of his death, and she still resented everything he'd cared about. Including the library. Curtis didn't care about the library one way or another, but he'd soon taken up with Diane and was enjoying the largesse of her inheritance.

"I have some news," Josie said, taking a sip of her wine. She tried to make the comment sound off-handed, but her beautiful, cornflower-blue eyes sparkled with such joy, I immediately guessed what the news was.

"You've decided to close the bakery and run away to sea?" I teased.

"What? Why would I do that? You know I love the bakery." My cousin owned Josie's Cozy Bakery, which had rapidly become a Nags Head institution. To prove that life was totally unfair, despite owning a bakery and being a pastry chef, at five foot ten Josie was model thin and strikingly lovely. But she was anything but spoiled. Between Jake's restaurant and Josie's bakery and café, the two of them worked mighty hard feeding hordes of famished tourists and starving Bankers. I couldn't begin to imagine how they did it. In season, she worked seven days a week, getting up at four to start the baking. Jake put in equally long hours, but on an opposite schedule, often only falling into bed well after midnight. Their idea of a date night was Josie sitting on a stool in the restaurant kitchen, helping to chop vegetables. But they seemed to thrive on it, and they were very happy. I was happy for them. I adored my cousin, and Jake was a real sweetheart.

"Never mind, Lucy," Steph said. "We all know it's Josie's secret dream to run away to sea. Like Tiffany Featherstone did in *Ruby Passions* when she pretended to be a man to flee the clutches of the evil Lord Blackheart."

"I never," I said. "What the heck is a ruby passion anyway?"

"It's a book I've been reading. Grace passed it on to me."

"The author didn't really name a character Lord Blackheart, did she?" I kept one eye on Josie, knowing that teasing could only go on for so long before it became unpleasant.

"That wasn't his real name," Steph said. "It's the nickname Tiffany gave him. I don't think he was a real lord either—do you remember, Grace?"

"It wouldn't have been much different. I don't read

bodice-ripper romances for the subtlety." Grace laughed. "Enough. Poor Josie's about to explode. Spill, sweetie. What's your news?"

Josie beamed. She was a beautiful woman in any circumstances, and tonight she had a glow from within that lit her up. "Jake proposed."

Although that didn't come as a surprise to any of us, we let out a collective squeal and leapt to our feet. We hugged Josie and then folded ourselves into a circle and hugged each other. The other diners and some of the wait staff watched us with a smile.

"When's the date?"

"Do you have a ring?"

"Can I be a bridesmaid?"

The waiter came over. "Everything okay here, ladies?"

"We need a bottle of champagne," Grace said. "My treat."

We sat back down and eyed the bride-to-be expectantly.

"We haven't set a date yet," Josie said, "but it will be sometime over the winter, when business is slow. I don't have a ring because we want to put what money we have into building our businesses, and as for bridesmaids, I haven't decided about that yet. We're going to have a small, plain wedding. Family and a few close friends. Of course, you're all invited."

"That's so marvelous," I said.

"I'll drink to that," Grace said as a chilled bottle of champagne, an ice bucket, and four crystal flutes arrived at our table.

"Congratulations, Josie," the waiter said as he poured.

When the glasses, full of dancing bubbles, were handed around, I lifted mine in the air. "To Josie and Jake."

"Happiness forever," Grace said.

We drank. The diners at the next table applauded, and Josie blushed prettily, grinning from ear to ear.

Over our main courses—shrimp and grits for me, steak for Grace, the stuffed flounder for Stephanie, and scallops on pasta for Josie—we chatted about weddings, good and bad, we'd been to over the years. The excitement had died down, and the restaurant patrons returned to their own meals. The champagne was finished, the waiter was clearing our plates—scraped clean, and we were shaking our heads over the offer of dessert, when three people walked into the room: Jay Ruddle; his assistant, Greg; and his granddaughter, Julia.

They were shown to a table, and napkins were unfurled. Waiters descended with menus and pitchers of water. Jay made a show of an intense study of the wine list while consulting with the waiter. Julia buried her head in her menu while Greg studied the room. Another waiter brought Owens' special tray of crackers and Melba toast with restaurant-made, traditional North Carolina pimento cheese spread, and Julia gave him a shy smile of thanks.

"Speak of the devil," I said to my friends. "That's Jay Ruddle himself."

"Who's that with him? His granddaughter and her husband?" Steph asked.

"Granddaughter and the curator of the collection," I said. "He's advising Jay on choosing a location for the artifacts."

We turned our attention back to our coffee. "Now that we're up to date on my love life," Josie said, "what about yours, Lucy? I haven't seen Connor around much lately. What's happening there?"

"Nothing," I squeaked. "I mean, all's fine."

She gave me a look. "If you say so."

"I do. It's the election, you know. Busy, busy." Connor was the mayor of Nags Head, running for a second term. I'd told him Thursday night was my regular girls' night out, so I couldn't be *too* disappointed that he hadn't contacted me today. Truth be told, I didn't know if I was disappointed or relieved. I wasn't accustomed to the dating game, and my feelings these days were a mass of contradictions. I liked Connor—I liked him a lot. But I was afraid. What I was afraid of, I couldn't say, not even to myself.

"Has he asked you to help with canvassing or stuffing envelopes or anything?" Grace asked.

"I've done some of that. It was fun," I added weakly. Yes, it had been nice to be with him when he spoke to voters, to know that I was helping him with something important. But it wasn't the same as spending time *together*. We aren't married—we don't even live together—so he couldn't treat me as a politician's wife, sharing not-very-secret smiles and adoring glances, and holding hands.

Josie reached over and patted my hand. "Give it time, sweetie. He's more than just busy with the election. He's stressed too. The polls are showing that Doug has a shot at beating him."

Grace snorted. "I can't imagine what's wrong with people. Connor's been a good mayor. He's tireless on behalf of the community. Everyone he meets likes him."

"But Doug has the catchy slogans," Josie said. "He'll fix everything, and it won't cost the taxpayers a penny. Isn't that what he says?"

"He'll give you a magnet for your fridge—can't forget that."

"You get a lot more than a magnet if you put up a lawn sign or help with phone calls," Steph said.

"You mean, like a bribe?" Josie looked shocked.

"He's paying for canvassers is what I hear."

"That doesn't surprise me. That Doug Whiteside is—" I broke off mid-sentence. Curtis Gardner had gotten to his feet. His face was set into hard, angry lines as he watched Jay Ruddle enjoying his evening.

"Don't . . ." Diane said.

Curtis ignored her and approached the new arrivals, hand outstretched. A look passed over Jay's face before it settled into a forced smile.

"Jay! It's been awhile!" Curtis's voice was loud enough to have heads turning.

Jay stood up. The two men shook hands.

"How you been?" Curtis asked.

"Well, thank you. Don't let me interrupt your dinner." Jay sat back down. He put his napkin on his lap. The action was rude and dismissive, but Curtis didn't seem to take the hint.

"What are you looking at?" Josie asked me.

"Trouble, looking for a place to happen," I answered.

"I've been trying to contact you," Curtis said.

"I've been busy," Jay replied.

"So it would seem. But as you're here now"—Curtis plopped himself down in the fourth chair at their table; Julia's eyes were open wide, and Greg perched on the edge of his seat, ready to move—"we can discuss our business."

"I never discuss business over dinner, and certainly not in

the presence of my family. I never did, but even more so now that I'm retired. If you have concerns, contact the office during business hours." Jay turned his attention to the wine menu and the hovering waiter. "I'm going to have a steak, so a Spanish Rioja would be good. Julia, do you know what you want yet?"

Curtis leaned forward, putting himself in Jay's space. "Look. You might say you're retired, but everyone knows you're the one pulling all the strings. I need to know what you think you're up to, and I need to know now."

Greg got to his feet. "Time for you to leave, buddy. Call the company office in the morning like Mr. Ruddle said."

"I keep calling!" Curtis yelled. "I leave message after message, but no one ever calls me back."

Jay sipped from his water glass. The hostess hurried over to their table. "Is everything all right here?"

"No, it is not," Greg said. "This gentleman refuses to return to his own table."

Diane downed the last of her wine and got to her feet. She wobbled slightly on her stiletto heels as she crossed the room. She plucked at Curtis's sleeve. "Come on, honey, let's go."

He shook her off. "I want an answer."

"Sir," the hostess said, "if you don't return to your table, I'll have to call security."

Jay Ruddle slowly turned his upper body toward Curtis. He spoke in a low hiss that somehow could be heard throughout the entire room. "Have you never heard of the expression 'Silence was the loud reply'?"

"What's that supposed to mean?" Curtis said. His words were slurred, and his hands were shaking.

"It means that you are a foolish little man who got himself in way over his head." Jay looked at Diane for the first time. A sneer crossed his face. "Probably to impress a foolish woman."

"Hey," she said.

"Perhaps you should call the police," Jay said to the hostess. "That way they can take care of two matters at the same time. Business is business, Gardner. If you can't manage your stores, don't blame the competition. You make any more threats and I'll see you in court."

Greg had rounded the table, and he stood behind Curtis's chair. He made no move to touch the man, clearly not wanting to give anyone cause to file a complaint.

"Sir?" the hostess said. "Please come with me."

Curtis stood up so quickly, his chair toppled backward. It would have hit the floor had Greg not been standing there.

Everyone in the room was no longer pretending not to notice.

"Men like you think you own everyone and everything. Well, you don't own me, Ruddle. I'll see you dead before I hand over my company to the likes of you." Curtis turned and stormed out of the room.

Diane, in her too-tight skirt and too-high heels, tottered in his wake.

"That was better than a night at the movies," Josie said.

"Or a Lord Blackheart novel," Grace said.

Chapter Three

I have the world's best commute.

I live on the fourth floor of the library building in a charming (although tiny) apartment I call my Lighthouse Aerie. Most days I'm the first to arrive at work, but on Friday morning, by the time I descended the spiral iron stairs, Bertie and Charlene were huddled around the computer at the circulation desk.

"Morning," I said.

Charlene lifted an arm and gave me a backward wave. Bertie didn't even do that.

"It looks impressive," Bertie said.

"We have the advantage of local and public. You should press that."

"Press what? Why?" I said.

Bertie blinked. "Oh, good morning, Lucy. Is it opening time already?"

"Soon. How long have you two been here?"

"Hours," Charlene said. "And we didn't leave until almost ten last night. We're working out our plan of attack."

"Do you think we have a chance?"

Bertie leaned back, giving her shoulders a good stretch. "I'll put the coffee on. You fill her in, Charlene."

The academic librarian grinned at me. Her ever-present earbuds hung around her neck, but, to my infinite relief, the sound was switched off. Charlene was devoted to rap and hip-hop, and nothing could convince her that the rest of us didn't want to enjoy her music. "Jay Ruddle is an Outer Banks legend. His father owned a small furniture store in Nags Head, and when he died, Jay took it over and built it into a mega-chain. He hasn't lived in North Carolina for a long time, but the old-timers still talk about him. Some pride in 'local boy done good'; some resentment at his success, which some say wasn't entirely aboveboard."

I'm not an Outer Banks local, although my mother was born and raised in Nags Head. She moved to Boston when she married my dad. We came here for vacation every year, visiting Mom's sister Ellen, Josie's mother. The Outer Banks—OBX as it's affectionately known—has always had a special place in my heart. When I was looking for a new start in life, where else would I go but into the arms of my beloved aunt and to my favorite place in all the world?

"Jay Ruddle is known for his passion for Outer Banks history, nautical history in particular," Charlene said, "and the money to indulge it. He has a particularly excellent collection of maps, captains' logs, and letters and other documents from the sixteenth to eighteenth centuries. His collection is private, but he opens it to historians and other interested parties regularly. I was lucky enough to go on a tour a couple of years ago. Amazing stuff."

"And he wants to give it to our library? That's fabulous. But do we have the room for it?" I thought of our rare books room upstairs. *Crowded* might be the applicable word.

"He's considering giving it to us, Lucy." Bertie came back into the main room. "That's the problem. Other institutions are being considered."

Charlene let out a long breath. "Competition is going to be deadly. Figuratively speaking."

"Something happened last night you might need to know about." I filled them in on the incident at Owens'.

Bertie groaned. "If someone had told me that one of our board members would threaten to derail the deal, I would have guessed Diane and Curtis right off the bat. Blast them."

"They were arguing over some business deal gone wrong, at least from Curtis's point of view. Jay threatened to take Curtis to court, and Curtis threatened to . . . uh . . . kill him."

Another groan.

"That might not be a problem, Bertie," Charlene said. "We can subtly let Jay know that although Curtis and Diane are on our board, they aren't exactly popular around here. The enemy-of-my-enemy situation."

"I'll be in my office. I feel the need for a few sun salutations." Bertie walked away.

"I hate to be the one to point this out, Charlene," I said, "but we're stuffed to the gills here as it is. Without putting a large part of our collection into storage, I can't see where we can put

Jay Ruddle's. Surely, Bertie's not thinking of closing the children's library?" A jolt of fear ran through me: there was space, pending a lot of renovations, on the fourth floor. Space that was currently my beloved Lighthouse Aerie.

"Not a problem," Charlene said. "The gift comes with enough money to build a dedicated home for the collection. A separate building, climate controlled, perfect conditions; an office for the curator; and desk space for visiting academics who might want to consult the papers."

"Wow!" was all I could say.

"Wow, indeed. I was up most of the night putting a proposal together of how we can best use the collection, and Bertie's been reading up on our competition. Blacklock College in Elizabeth City seems like it's our strongest rival. Fortunately for us, Jay never went to college, so he doesn't have an alma mater; and his only grandchild studied English lit at Berkeley, which he doesn't consider a worthy place to house the history of the East Coast. He's coming back this afternoon to talk about it further."

"Why's he doing this now? Getting rid of his collection, I mean. He seems like a healthy man, although I'd guess he's in his eighties."

Charlene shrugged. "He told Bertie that Greg Summers, who's the curator, is leaving for a new post in December. Bertie assumed Jay doesn't want the responsibility of it anymore."

"Charlene!" Bertie bellowed. "I've finished calming down! Get in here."

"Desk's all yours," Charlene said to me. "Needless to say, I'll be tied up all morning."

* * *

Theodore came in around eleven. He asked me if I was well. I said I was. He settled into a chair near the magazine rack and picked up a stack of reading material. He flipped idly through it for a few minutes and then got up and moved the chair so it was facing the circulation desk rather than away from it. I didn't have to wonder for long why he'd done such a thing: soon the door opened and he jumped to attention. He didn't care about facing me and the desk, I realized, but the door.

It was a patron with a stack of books to return, and Theodore returned to his copy of *Sports Illustrated*. I'd never known him to have an interest in sports before, nor in sitting by himself in the library. Then again, he was turning pages without paying much attention to what was on them. Today, he'd abandoned his English-country-gentleman persona and was dressed in chinos and an oatmeal sweater over a button-down shirt. He'd combed his hair and abandoned the plain glass spectacles he thought made him look older and more serious.

"Everything okay, Theodore?" I called.

"Perfectly fine, thank you, Lucy," he replied. "Oh, I won't be able to make book club tonight. I have an appointment with a family that inherited a set of Mickey Spillane they don't know what to do with. I'm the only collector they've approached—so far—so I'm confident of getting them for an excellent price."

"We'll miss you," I said. "Did you read the book?"

"No, I didn't." He shifted uncomfortably in his seat. "I . . . uh . . . that is, I can't abide ghost stories."

"*Sleepy Hollow* isn't really a ghost story. Two men are competing for the affections of the rich man's daughter, and his rival frightens poor hapless Ichabod Crane right out of town by pretending to be the Headless Horseman. And as for *Bracebridge Hall*, it's just a bunch of people telling each other spooky stories. Are you okay, Teddy?"

He'd turned very pale and wrapped his arms tightly around himself despite the warmth of the room.

"Ghosts," he whispered. "How I hate them. Oh, I know they don't exist, Lucy." He laughed without mirth. "But the idea of them is something I don't even want to contemplate. When I was a child, I . . ." He swallowed heavily. "I thought I saw one, in my room. A ghost materializing out of the toy box. I was frightened and ran to my mother crying. My father thought it was so very funny, and for several weeks after that, he'd make moaning noises outside my door, and one night he came in with a sheet over his head, waving his arms and wailing. That was the most terrifying night of my life."

"That's terrible!" I said. "What a mean thing to do."

"For the rest of my childhood, Halloween was a nightmare, but these days, it seems to be more about dressing up like superheroes or princesses than ghosts, so I'm okay with it."

"You've never seemed to mind Louise Jane and her stories."

"I don't like them, but I can accept hearing them because it's Louise Jane telling them, and I've known her since we were kids. I can't say I'm entirely comfortable with that ship over there and the condition of the sailors, but it's just a toy. None of them are likely to start waving their arms around and moaning, are they?" He fingered the pages of his magazine nervously. "You won't tell anyone about this, will you, Lucy?"

"Your secret is safe with me," I said.

He returned to his magazine. At noon, I called Bertie's office and told her I was going into town—did she want anything? She asked me to get sandwiches for her and Charlene. I left Ronald to take over the desk and the phone. I ran a few errands in Nags Head and picked up our lunches at Josie's bakery.

When I got back, Theodore was still ensconced next to the magazine rack. He'd finished with back issues of *Sports Illustrated* and had gone on to *Coastal Living*. Charles was keeping him company, curled up on the floor under the chair.

"No sign of our guests?" I said to Ronald.

"You mean the Ruddles? No. Bertie's in her office and Charlene has gone back upstairs." He lowered his voice. "What's up with Teddy? He's sitting there, not reading a magazine, and practically leaping out of his skin every time the door opens."

"I've no idea." At that very moment, the door did open, and all was made clear.

Theodore jumped up so fast, the chair almost fell over, barely missing Charles, who leapt to his own feet with a startled hiss. The magazine fluttered to the floor. Theodore's color changed from white to pink, to red, back to white, and then straight to red again.

"Good afternoon." Jay Ruddle said to me.

"Hi," Julia said to Theodore.

Greg said nothing.

I introduced Ronald and then said, "Go in, please. Bertie's in her office. She's asked Charlene Clayton, our academic and reference librarian, to join you. I'll give her a call." I headed for the phone. I needn't have bothered, as I could see the tips of Charlene's bright red sneakers on the stairs, but I made the call anyway. I spoke into an unanswered phone while Jay headed for the hall. Julia and Greg didn't go with him.

Theodore smiled shyly at Julia. "May I say, you look quite lovely this afternoon."

She blushed and ducked her head. I thought she looked efficient and professional in a plain skirt and crisply ironed blouse, but *lovely* wasn't the word I'd have chosen. Charles wandered over, and Julia bent to give him a scratch behind the ears.

"Would you like a tour of the library, Julia?" Theodore said. "It's a unique setting, situated as it is here in the lighthouse. The lighthouse itself was first built in 1872 to replace one that had been destroyed during the War Between the States."

"That would be nice," Julia said. "Greg, do you want to come with us?"

"Why not?" he said.

Theodore looked as though he could give the assistant a great many reasons why not, but off they went, Charles leading the way. "Our children's library on the second floor has won state awards for initiatives in programming." The desk phone rang, and I left Theodore to act as tour guide.

They must have climbed all the way to the top, because when they got back, Theodore and Julia's faces were flushed, and they were breathing heavily. Greg looked like he'd been resting comfortably in an armchair. Julia carried a happy Charles. "Thank you," she said. "That was interesting."

"Sure was." Greg smothered a yawn.

Julia smiled at Theodore. Theodore smiled at Julia. Charles purred.

"I love that model ship," Julia said. "It's a genuine work of art. The detail is amazing. All those little sailors and everything."

"It's beautiful," Theodore agreed. He was not looking at the ship.

"My father likes his history pristine and completely accurate, but I disagree. Surely, sometimes, we can have fun with it."

"We can have fun, as you put it, with made-up stories, Julia," Greg said. "But never, never with history. If you allow inaccuracies to go unchallenged, they grow and spread, and before long truth and fiction blur into one."

"Nonsense," she said. I got the feeling this was well-traveled ground. "History needs to be brought alive. Not just a recitation of facts and figures and the deeds of famous men, but the story of people. And as the story of most people was never captured, we have to recreate it as best we can."

Greg turned to me. "Julia and I have agreed to disagree."

Her color rose. "Because you'll never admit that I'm right."

Theodore said, "I've said to Lucy many times, history needs to be personalized, haven't I, Lucy?"

"Uh . . . sure." As far as I was aware, Teddy had not the slightest interest in historical fiction. "The ship is for our Halloween exhibit," I explained, "as you've probably guessed by all the other stuff we have around." I waved my hand at the gravestones and giant spiders. "At our book club tonight, we're discussing Washington Irving's *The Legend of Sleepy Hollow* and *Bracebridge Hall* to get us in the mood."

"Oh, you have a book club!" Julia's eyes shone. "I adore book clubs, but I don't have much of a chance to get to one. Can I come? I haven't read Washington Irving in years, but I remember loving him. *Sleepy Hollow* is such a delight. What time's the meeting?"

"Seven," I said. "When the library closes."

"That would be perfect! We have no plans tonight, do we, Greg?"

He shook his handsome head. "Jay's having dinner with one of his old buddies. I'm sure you can bow out of that."

"Marvelous." She clapped her hands in delight. "I hope I can come, Lucy. That's all right, isn't it?"

"Guests are always welcome," Theodore said.

I nodded in agreement. I liked our book club very much and always looked forward to the meetings and the discussion. But even I didn't think it something to get too excited about.

"I myself am a member of this book club," Theodore said. "I'll enjoy discussing Mr. Irving with you."

"I thought you had—" I said.

"A simple business meeting. It hasn't even been confirmed yet. No problem putting it off. I've a wonderful idea. Why don't I collect you for the meeting, Julia? I can drop you off again after. Where are you staying?"

"We're at the Ocean Side Hotel," she replied.

"Washington Irving, eh?" Greg said. "I read him in college. No need to put yourself out, buddy. I'll bring Julia and stay for the meeting myself."

Theodore's smile froze on his face. "How nice," he said through gritted teeth.

* * *

I was returning to the desk after helping a lady find a book for her granddaughter ("It has an apple on the cover"), when Jay came out of Bertie's office, carrying a stack of papers, followed by Bertie and Charlene. Greg was leaning against a shelf, reading *Paris 1919* by Margaret MacMillan, and Theodore was telling Julia everything there is to know about collecting rare books. She actually looked interested.

"That was most informative, thank you," Jay said. "Nice meeting you, Ms. Clayton. I'll be in touch." He headed for the door. Julia and Greg said quick goodbyes and hurried after him. Theodore hurried after them.

"How'd it go?" I asked when the door had closed behind our visitors.

Bertie let out a breath. Charlene punched the air with her fist.

"I won't say it's in the bag," Bertie said.

"But darn close," Charlene added.

"He was highly impressed with the proposal Charlene put together. He wants to go over it with Greg, his advisor."

"Greg's coming to book club tonight," I said. "He and Julia. She expressed an interest, so I invited them. Is that okay?"

"Great!" Charlene said. "Let them know the library is a community center as well as a serious place for the study of books."

"Don't talk about the donation, Lucy," Bertie said. "We don't want to look like the invitation is part of a hard sell." She went back to her office, the slightest of springs in her step.

"Speaking of book club," I said. "I had an idea. I checked the weather earlier, and it's going to be a clear night with a nearly full moon. Let's set up outside. We're talking about ghost stories. It'll be perfect."

"You aren't afraid of scaring anyone?" Charlene said. "Suppose Mrs. Peterson brings her kids?"

"No one likes horror movies more than teenagers. But that's not likely to be a problem. Washington Irving's stores aren't exactly frightening. If anything, they're charming in their innocence and simplicity." I shoved aside a feeling of guilt as I remembered Teddy and his confession. He'd invited himself tonight, and I hoped the presence of Julia would more than make up for silly ghost stories.

"True," she said. "Sounds like fun. What are you going to do for light? It's dark outside after seven. Except when the lighthouse light comes on, and you can't read by that."

"Flashlights? I have one in my car and another one upstairs. Bertie keeps a couple in the office in case of a power failure."

"I have one you can borrow."

"I'll pop into town and see what I can get cheap. A handful of those key chain ones should do."

* * *

The Bodie Island Lighthouse Library Classic Novel Reading Club didn't usually get together on Fridays, but this was a special pre-Halloween meeting. Louise Jane had proposed it, saying it would help her get in the mood for her talks on Saturday and Wednesday. She'd also suggested that, to honor the approaching holiday, we dress in costume, and club members eagerly agreed. We'd decided to keep our costumes to the theme of our club—classic literature.

Not surprisingly, the first to arrive this evening was Theodore Kowalski. I was laying napkins and plastic glasses on the refreshments table when he strolled up. "Are we meeting outside?"

"I thought it would add an extra touch to the Halloween atmosphere. I hope you don't mind. Where's your costume? We were supposed to dress up." I eyed Theodore's stiff black jeans and black turtleneck. Not only not a costume, but not a Harris Tweed thread in sight.

"I considered it but decided I have no desire to be childish. This is a serious book club we have here. Besides, we didn't mention costumes to Julia. I wouldn't want her to feel out of place. You're not trying to be Elizabeth Bennett or Jane Eyre, I hope. Not in that hat—it's far too ornate."

"I'm Lady Bracknell."

"Lady Bracknell? Really, Lucy. Lady Bracknell is not a character from a novel, but a play."

"Gee, Teddy, lighten up. I tried, didn't I?" When I was in town earlier, scooping up flashlights, I'd popped into a costume jewelry store and bought a pair of earrings about the size and shape of chandeliers—not to mention the weight. I'd gathered up my hair and plopped my elaborate Victorian-era hat on top of it. I completed the costume with a floor-length skirt I sometimes used as a beach wrap, and a long, fringed shawl. Nothing award winning, but it would do for tonight and for Halloween day itself, when the staff were planning to wear costumes.

"You look very . . . literary, Lucy," Theodore said.

"Literary Lucy, that's me. Turn around; you've got a tag still attached to your collar." I pulled the offending item off. A price tag. I hid a grin. Those jeans were so new, they creaked when he walked.

Lights broke through the row of tall pine trees lining the long access road to the lighthouse as book club members began to arrive.

Josie, costumed as a scullery maid from Dickens, always provided some delicious treats from her bakery, and today she'd outdone herself with cookies decorated to look like pumpkins and ghosts, and dark chocolate brownies topped with eyeball candies. The library provided pitchers of lemonade and tea. As well as stackable plastic chairs, Charlene and I had dragged a table out of the library to use as the refreshment station.

Steph came up the walkway, holding hands with Butch Greenblatt. "Hey, we're sitting outside?" Butch said. "Great idea. It's a perfect night for it."

Butch and Steph were dressed in early-twentieth-century men's suits with string ties and bowler hats. Butch had a Hitler-type mustache stuck to his upper lip and strands of long, stringy black hair protruding from his hat.

"You look great," I said, giving them both hugs of greeting. "But I can't guess who you are."

"Stan Laurel and Oliver Hardy," Steph said. "The size difference was one of their gags."

"That's hardly literary," I said in protest.

"It was her idea." Butch spotted the refreshment table and left his beloved to explain.

"We're going to another party tomorrow. The theme is historical couples. I didn't want to make two costumes. It was hard enough to get the big lug into that one."

I laughed. "You look great."

And they did. The costumes were perfect for them because their differences extended to more than size. Butch is a police officer, a rugged, good-looking man at six foot five and two hundred pounds. He loves nothing more than heading out for a morning's fishing, time spent alone on the beach or in the marsh, or playing pickup basketball. Steph is a defense lawyer with a reputation as a hard-hitter, who tips the scales at hundred pounds after a big meal. She loves opera and the symphony and European art films. They are the most opposite people I have ever met. They're head over heels in love, but I suspect conversation on their dates can get a bit tense sometimes.

She found a seat, and Butch brought over a handful of cookies and glasses of lemonade. They scooted their two chairs closer together and sat at the edge of the circle, holding hands and smiling at each other. Butch, who was the younger brother of Josie's fiancé, Jake, and I had flirted when I first arrived to live and work at the library, and we'd casually dated. This situation could have been awkward, but I was nothing but happy that my two friends had found each other.

Others began to arrive, and we exclaimed over each other's costumes. CeeCee Watson was Wilkie Collins, dressed in black trousers, a checked vest, a black jacket far too large for her, necktie, and bowler hat. Grace came as Sherlock Holmes, with a cape, deerstalker hat, and pipe, and a couple of the women wore long dresses with shawls or capes. Mrs. Peterson, quick to complain that her daughters all had other things to do on a Friday night than keep their mother company, presented a puzzle.

"Who are you?" I asked.

"You have to guess," she said. Usually Mrs. Peterson dresses like the affluent Southern matron she wants to be. Tonight she was all in orange. Orange pants, orange sweater, orange stockings, even a knitted orange cap, and streaks of orange makeup on her cheeks and beneath her eyes.

"I have no idea," I said, mentally racing through everything I knew about classic works of literature.

"Give up?" Was that a twinkle in her eye? I looked closer. Why, yes, it was. In all the time I had known Mrs. Peterson, one of the library's staunchest patrons, I'd never seen the slightest hint of humor or fun in her.

"I do," I said.

"Anyone else want to try?"

"I can't guess who you are, Mrs. Peterson," Butch said, "But you look great. Like Halloween itself."

"That's it," Josie shouted. "You're the Great Pumpkin!"

Mrs. Peterson laughed. I hadn't known she could do that.

"From *Peanuts*," I said, "the cartoon strip. Definitely an American classic."

"It was Phoebe's idea," Mrs. Peterson said, referring to one of her five daughters. "I do believe one of those orange cookies will accent my outfit suitably."

Theodore hadn't taken a seat, but paced up and down the walkway, constantly checking his watch. I could sympathize with how he was feeling, because I was equally edgy. I also glanced at my watch. Ten minutes after seven. Most of the club members had arrived. Chairs were filling and refreshments had been decimated. I'd have to call the meeting to order soon.

Theodore and I both jumped, trying not to, as a car turned

into the parking area. We let out matching sighs of disappointment as we recognized Louise Jane's rusty van.

Louise Jane stepped out of her car. Everyone sucked in a breath as she walked toward us. Although *walked* isn't quite the right word. More like *floated*. She was dressed in a long oyster-colored satin gown with layers of petticoats beneath, a lacy neckline, and multilayered sleeves. The front of the dress touched her toes, and the back trailed behind her. Yards of white beads were wrapped around her neck, and an enormous gray wig was perched on her head. A veil fell over her face and cascaded around her head and shoulders. The light breeze lifted the edges of lace. I glanced at my book club. Butch was frozen with a brownie halfway to his mouth. Grace and Josie's eyes almost popped out of their heads, and CeeCee's mouth was a round O. Even Theodore had stopped his pacing to stand stock-still.

Louise Jane didn't smile, and she said not a word. She simply drifted, very slowly, down the path toward the lights cast by our group. As she got closer, I could see that the lace hung in tattered shreds; the figure of a mouse was buried in the depths of the wig; and the edges of the sleeves, the hem of the dress, and the long train were thick with dirt.

She stopped at the edge of the circle of chairs.

"Wow!" Butch said.

"Miss Havisham," I said.

"A living ghost," she replied, her voice deep and unearthly.

The Bodie Island Lighthouse Library Classic Novel Book Club broke into applause. Beneath the veil, Louise Jane allowed herself a small smile.

"Are you going to wear that tomorrow when you give your talk?" Josie asked.

"I'm undecided. My lecture is about legends of the Outer Banks, shipwrecks, happenings at the lighthouse. I know of no abandoned brides."

"Make one up then, why don't you?" Grace said. "Maybe there was an innocent young woman on one of those ships that got wrecked. She was heading for a new life in the Carolinas to be married to the man she loved. He'd gone on ahead to get a home ready for her. But she drowned, dreaming of her wedding that was not to be."

Louise Jane looked horrified. "I do not make things up!"

"Embellish then," Grace said. "Now, are we going to talk about the book or not? I've always loved *Sleepy Hollow*."

"I liked it too," Butch said. "But I sure didn't like that *Bracebridge Hall*. What a lot of nothing. I have to confess I didn't get more than a few pages in." Our main club selection tonight was Irving's most famous story, *The Legend of Sleepy Hollow*, but because that story is very short, I'd also suggested the much longer *Bracebridge Hall* for those interested in further reading. I'd forgotten just how long and how dense *Bracebridge* is.

"You didn't get to when they tell the story of the Flying Dutchman?" Louise Jane said. "That's the best part."

"I guess I gave up long before that," he said. "Does he keep calling the young woman 'the fair Julia' the whole way though?"

"Every time," I said.

Butch shook his head.

Theodore had finally taken a seat, but at the sound of a car coming down the drive, he leapt to his feet with enough force to knock the chair to the ground. My heart began to pound. It settled back into place with a disappointed thud when I recognized the bulk of a Cadillac Escalade rather than the sleek lines of Connor's BMW.

Connor McNeil had said he'd try to make it. I knew he was busy. I knew he had a lot of things on his plate. I knew we were just a little book club. Still, I was disappointed.

Theodore, however, was not disappointed. He ran down the path and soon came back with his arm linked through Julia's. Greg walked on her other side, not touching, but keeping proprietarily close.

Butch got to his feet.

"Oh," Julia gasped. "You didn't tell us you were wearing costumes!"

"As the invitation was at the last minute," Theodore said, "I assumed you wouldn't have the time or materials to dress up."

She gave him a smile. "You're so thoughtful."

He beamed.

I made the introductions. I said our guests' first names only and that they'd visited the lighthouse earlier. I didn't say why they'd been in our library.

Theodore guided Julia to the refreshment table, and Greg followed.

Once Julia had a glass of tea and a napkin with a cookie and brownie, Theodore hustled her over to two empty chairs. She took one seat, and he dropped into the other. He edged his chair ever so slightly toward her.

Unfortunately for the love-struck Teddy, he'd given Julia the seat on the outside of the circle. He sat between Julia and the Great Pumpkin, aka Mrs. Peterson, but no one was on Julia's other side. Greg picked up a chair, carried it across the circle, and put it down beside her.

"If we're all settled at last," Louise Jane huffed, "*Sleepy Hollow* is a classic American ghost story. Isn't that right, Lucy, honey? Although we can debate whether or not it's a real tale of the supernatural—"

"No stories of the supernatural are true," Butch said firmly.

"Quite right," Teddy said.

"I beg to differ." Louise Jane said. "I myself have seen . . ."

Her voice drifted into the distance as I tuned out. Another car was approaching. I held my breath until I recognized Connor's BMW.

I left Teddy, Louise Jane, and Butch squabbling over the existence of ghosts and walked down the path.

Connor greeted me with a deep kiss. "I'm sorry I'm late, Lucy. I got tied up at work and then wanted to go home and get out of my suit because you'd asked us to come in costume."

"You needn't have worried about that." I straightened my hat, which had been knocked aside by the kiss. "I'm just glad you're here."

He put his arm around me, and we started walking up the path toward the lighthouse. Flashlights broke the dark shadows of the historic old building, showing the people gathered in a circle on the lawn. "Don't tell me we're sitting outside," he said.

I stepped back and studied Connor's costume. "Sorry," I said with a laugh.

He wore beige shorts and a dirty white T-shirt, with

flop-flops on his feet and a straw hat with a raggedy brim on his head. The shorts were torn and the shirt, full of holes.

"Robinson Crusoe, I presume," I said.

"This is no tropical island. I'm going to freeze out here."

"Come and show the others your costume," I said, "and then you can have my shawl. I don't need it."

He pulled me close. "Never mind the shawl. You can keep me warm, Lucy."

"Are you two going to stand there all night?" Butch bellowed. "Connor, I need someone to explain to Louise Jane here the significance of the smashed pumpkin found in the road at the end of *Sleepy Hollow*."

Chapter Four

The moment my eyes opened on Saturday morning, I leapt out of bed and pulled back the drapes. I live on the fourth floor of the lighthouse, and my single window looks east, above the marshes, across the highway, over the wide stretch of beach, and out to sea. The sun was a huge orange orb touching the calm smooth waters of the ocean. Not a cloud was to be seen. For once, the weather reports had been accurate.

Charles jumped off the bed and wandered into the kitchen area. My apartment's not very big—being in a lighthouse—but I adore it. It's small and perfect, with curved whitewashed walls decorated with paintings of the Outer Banks. The color scheme is white, yellow, and sage green, giving the place a bright cheerful feeling. As I do first thing every morning, I filled Charles's bowl. "It's going to be a busy day today."

He picked delicately at the food and didn't say anything.

"You, however," I said, "are not going to enjoy it." He was a library cat, accustomed to people coming and going all day. He never tried to escape, but I'd decided that with the numbers of people we were expecting today, he'd have to be confined to the utility closet. I trusted Charles, but I didn't trust some children not to decide they'd like to take him home.

He lifted his head and gave me a disapproving look. He was already mad at me, I guessed, at having to miss book club last night because it was outdoors. Charles loves book club.

"Sorry," I said. "It's for your own good."

He stalked off, bushy tail held high.

"Sorry," I said again, wondering, not for the first time, why I was apologizing to a cat.

I got ready for work with a warm, happy glow. Book club last night had been a lot of fun. We had a great discussion about the work of Washington Irving, and we laughed at the antics of poor Ichabod Crane, frightened away from the pursuit of the wealthy heiress by a ghostly legend and a man on a horse with a pumpkin on his head. No one minded when Louise Jane went off at length on the story of the famous ghost ship *The Flying Dutchman*. The atmosphere had been perfect: Louise Jane in her wig and tattered, flowing gown, the light of the 1000-watt lamp overhead flashing in its regular 2.5 seconds on, 2.5 seconds off pattern while we huddled in a circle with our small flashlights and told frightening tales of the undead.

If Theodore occasionally shifted uncomfortably in his seat or appeared to be trying to tune the conversation out, I was the only one who noticed. Me and perhaps Greg, who kept one eye on his potential rival.

When book club ended and everyone drifted away into the night, the evening got even better. Connor came into the lighthouse, and we sat in the library for a long time, sipping our glasses of wine in the soft light from the alcove, chatting and catching up on each other's news, me in my chandelier earrings and beach wrap, and Connor in shorts, T-shirt, and straw hat. When he got up to leave, he kissed me long and hard and said, "Only a few more days until this election is over and life can get back to normal. Can you wait that long, Lucy?"

I'd kissed him in reply.

* * *

By one o'clock on Saturday, people were beginning to arrive for Louise Jane's lecture. Today she'd be telling stories and legends of the Outer Banks suitable for children and families.

Our original plan had been that this would be a small talk. Louise Jane would stand at the front of the room and speak to a handful of interested patrons. We'd lay out rows of chairs with a podium in front and provide a few light refreshments. But we soon came to realize the afternoon was threatening to be more popular than we'd expected. People had been calling the library all week to confirm the time, and my daily check of our website analytics showed a large uptick in visitors, most of them focusing on the events page. Louise Jane reported that there was "enormous interest" in her lecture in the community. Our library, she said, was not going to be nearly big enough. She wanted us to rent a hall.

That we couldn't do without charging for admittance.

Midweek, we checked the weather forecast and decided to risk moving it outside. The weather could be variable on the coast, and things changed fast, but if more people showed up than we could accommodate inside, we'd have to turn people away, and we always hated doing that.

Saturday morning we dragged chairs out of the storage shed onto the front lawn and laid them out in semicircular rows facing the podium. Inside the library we never worried much about sound, but once we'd decided to have the event outdoors, we realized acoustics would be a problem. Ronald called a friend who worked as a sound engineer, and he agreed to do us a favor and supply a microphone and amplifiers.

As these things do, our little event began to grow. The local independent bookstore called to ask if they could sell books at the event, and Bertie agreed (for a share of the profits as a donation to the library). They'd arrived before noon and set up a booth selling children's books and Outer Banks history and legends. A makeup artist friend of Charlene would do face painting, and at some point a local jewelry maker arrived with a selection of goods, a folding table, an awning, and a cash box. The national political parties brought tents, material, and volunteers, but we were saved from the mayoral candidates campaigning. Doug Whiteside was a vocal opponent of the Lighthouse Library, and it would have been pretty nervy, even for Doug, to solicit votes from our patrons on our own grounds.

"I'm worried we're not going to have enough chairs." I stood at the window, watching the steady stream of early arrivals. "It's already filling up out there, and we have almost an hour still to go. This might have been a mistake. In the building, we can control the numbers."

"It'll all work out fine," Bertie said.

"Somehow," Charlene said, "it always does."

"Nothing we can do about it," Ronald said. "Hopefully,

some folks will bring blankets and not mind sitting on the grass."

Ronald and Nan, his wife, had been in theater in New York City in their youth. I sometimes thought they must have brought an entire wardrobe department with them when they moved. The children's Halloween party had been held this morning, and Ronald had dressed for it as a sea captain. His thigh-length, high-collared blue jacket had a double row of gold buttons down the front, and gold epaulettes with tassels on the shoulders. He wore black pants tucked into high boots and a big tricornered hat. Fake whiskers were stuck to his jawline.

"You look marvelous, by the way," I said.

He grinned at me. "Thanks. Nan's coming to give us a hand soon. With all the activity going on outside, we don't want to lose sight of a child."

I glanced out the window again. "Good heavens, is that a clown I see?" A brightly costumed figure with giant shoes and a wild pink and lime-green wig wandered the grounds, twisting balloons into fabulous shapes for excited children.

"My friend Rosemarie McGovern," Ronald said. "Nan asked her. Hope that's okay, Bertie?"

"The more, the merrier," Bertie said.

We didn't want to close the library in the middle of a Saturday afternoon, so it had been arranged that Charlene would staff the circulation desk and assist patrons who weren't interested in the talk. Bertie would introduce Louise Jane, and Ronald would keep an eye on the children. My job was to keep things outside running smoothly.

"Have you heard anything more from Jay Ruddle?" I asked Bertie.

"No, but it is the weekend. I don't suppose anything was mentioned at your book club last night?"

"The subject didn't come up. Julia seemed to enjoy herself. She participated eagerly in the discussion—she's very well read—and Greg sat there looking totally bored." I didn't mention that Theodore leapt in to agree with every word Julia said and cut Greg off when he did try to speak. "Butch called her 'the fair Julia,' and she seemed amused at that."

"I'll worry about Jay Ruddle and his collection tomorrow," Bertie said. "Now, let's get out there and make this another Lighthouse Library success. Lucy, is the mayor coming to open the festivities?"

"Last I heard, he intended to."

"Good," she said. "Everyone in the audience needs to be reminded he needs their vote."

"He won't campaign," I said. "Not at a library function."

"I know that, and good for him. His presence should be enough."

Charlene took the desk, and the rest of us went outside.

It was a lovely day for an outdoor event. A handful of small, fluffy white clouds drifted lazily across the blue sky. The temperature was in the mid-seventies, perfect for people sitting out in the open.

I was watching the clown form a swan out of a balloon for an excited child, when Bertie slipped up beside me. "Drat! I was hoping they'd forget to come."

I turned to see Diane Uppiton and Curtis Gardner walking up the path.

"Diane insisted on being the official representative of the library today," Bertie said.

"Why not Mrs. Fitzgerald?" I asked, referring to the board chair.

"She's in Raleigh for the weekend, visiting her daughter."

Diane had obviously vacated the beauty parlor only moments earlier and was dressed to the nines in a pink suit with gold jewelry. She saw us watching and waved. I waved back. Curtis wore a suit and tie. He did not wave. They picked their way across the lawn toward the small section of chairs in the front row marked as reserved. The minute they sat down, they pulled out their smartphones and began typing.

As the expected audience grew and the venue expanded outside, almost by themselves formalities began to fall into place. Not only would an official welcome from the library board be extended, but the mayor himself had been invited as an honored guest.

More cars were arriving, and people either found seats on the lawn or wandered around, checking out the booths. Some of the earliest arrivals, those eager for a good seat, pulled thermoses and packets of sandwiches out of beach bags. More than a few produced books and settled back to read.

"I wonder if next year we might want to do more," Bertie said. "We didn't advertise except among our own patrons, and look at the turnout. Perhaps we could invite a local author or a guest lecturer from a university."

"Louise Jane won't like that," I said. "Half the people in the audience are probably her relatives."

"Don't you worry, Lucy. I know better than to shove Louise Jane off center stage. She'll appreciate a warm-up act or two."

"Ms. James?" A couple stood in front of us. He was tall and exceedingly thin, with slicked-back black hair and a full dark mustache. She was short and chubby, with coke-bottle-bottom glasses and gray hair tied in a bun. Her expression indicated that her shoes pinched. He peered down his long nose at us.

Bertie smiled. "I am she. Welcome. Are you here for the lecture? We'll be starting in about fifteen minutes."

"We thought we'd drop by and see what all the fuss is about." He glanced up at the lighthouse tower. "This is your library? It's rather . . . small isn't it?"

"It's bigger inside than it appears from the outside," I said, rushing to defend my beloved library. "Sort of like the Tardis or Hermione Granger's beaded handbag."

"The what?"

"Never mind," I mumbled.

"I get the reference," the woman said. "Still, small is small. You're close to the ocean, and this building is old. It must get exceedingly damp."

"Everything in the Outer Banks is close to the ocean," I said. "That's why we love it here."

"You might," the man said, "but damp is not good for old documents."

A lightbulb went off over my head. "Even Blacklock College isn't far from the coast."

Bertie's eyes opened wide.

"Fortunately, we have adequate space to incorporate the most up-to-date methods of climate control," the woman said.

"Fortunately for us, we have a highly qualified librarian well acquainted with the preservation of documents far older than

52

anything to do with North Carolina." Bertie was referring to Charlene, who'd spent several years working in the hallowed halls and bookshelves of the Bodleian Library in England. She'd quit the job she loved and came home to Nags Head when her mother fell ill and needed care. No one had said so, but I thought it likely the Lighthouse Library was on the short list for the Ruddle collection because Charlene would be the curator. "You know my name," Bertie said. "May I have yours?"

"I'm Norman Hoskins and this is Elizabeth McArthur."

Bertie introduced me, and we all shook hands. Elizabeth's grip was firm, but Norman's felt like the last piece of cod in the fishmonger's display case at the end of a long, hot day.

"You're welcome to have a look inside," Bertie said. "We're a public library, and we'll be open all day." A group of children—a pirate, Batman, and something all in black—ran inside. "As you can see. But the rare books room will be closed while the lecture is in progress."

"Perhaps later," Elizabeth said. "As long as we're here, I'm interested in what this *amateur* lecturer has to say. Most of the seats are taken, Norman—we should get ours."

They nodded politely, although a bit formally for a sunny day in the Outer Banks, and left us.

"The competition," Bertie said. "I'm not impressed. I've remembered something I have to do. I'll be in my office." I assumed she was rushing off to check out Norman Hoskins's and Elizabeth McArthur's bios.

Chapter Five

I wandered into the crowd, smiling and greeting library regulars. Louise Jane's tales of the history and legends of the Outer Banks made her popular, and the depths of her family's roots ensured she was related to about half of the permanent population.

Grace and Stephanie had found seats toward the front, and Theodore was standing at the end of their row, chatting to them. When they spotted me, they gave me enthusiastic waves and thumbs-up. My aunt Ellen had joined a group of library volunteers who would be helping with the after-presentation refreshments.

We definitely should have brought in more chairs. A couple of parents nudged their children to give up their seats.

Theodore left Grace and Steph and wandered over. "Impressive turnout." He spoke to me but kept one eye on the driveway.

"Aunt Ellen sent one of her friends into town for a rush on the supermarket to buy more cookies and drink mix. Plus a whole lot more plastic cups and napkins. We've brought out all the office chairs that will move. We'll be starting in a few minutes. You'd better find a seat—not many left."

Teddy was in his early thirties and perfectly capable of sitting on the ground. But somehow he never seemed like a ground-sitting sort to me.

"I can stand," he said. A moment later, an Escalade pulled into the lot, and his entire face lit up. "She's here!"

Three people emerged from the car. Theodore's face fell. "That . . . assistant . . . tagged along."

"Perhaps you can nab two chairs together. Leaving no place for Greg."

"Excellent idea!" He hurried to meet the fair Julia and stumbled through a greeting. She smiled shyly at him. A ray of sunlight flashed on a small diamond at the center of the thin gold necklace around her throat. Jay Ruddle detached himself from his party and approached me.

"Good afternoon, Ms. Richardson. You've got a nice day for it."

"And a nice crowd," I said. "There's far more people here than we were expecting."

"Adds to the festive atmosphere."

"You should have been here the day we decorated the outside of the lighthouse to advertise the forthcoming election."

He studied the building. "Decorations?"

"They soon started to look wind-blown and tattered, so we had them taken down. They'd served their purpose."

Over Jay's shoulder, I saw Curtis Gardner get to his feet, his face set in a deep frown. Diane stuffed her phone into her purse and plucked at his sleeve. Two rows back, Norman Hoskins nudged Elizabeth McArthur and pointed toward us. Her already thin lips formed a tight line.

"I don't see Ms. James," Jay asked. "Is she around?"

"She'll be out in a minute to start the program."

"I'm not interested in listening to a bunch of fables about ghost ships and wandering spirits, but Julia thought it would be interesting. I don't know why; she's never expressed any interest in supernatural rubbish before."

Could it be that Julia returned Theodore's admiration? I couldn't help but glance toward them. He was showing her to a seat in the center of a back row. Teddy dropped into the next chair, the only one vacant. He couldn't hide a triumphant smile as Greg was left standing on the edges.

"I thought I'd bring her and take the opportunity to examine your map collection," Jay said.

I was about to tell him that the rare books room was closed this afternoon. But I decided this man could be trusted to handle the precious things properly. Not to mention that Bertie would have my head if I turned him away. "I'll unlock the room for you."

We reached the front door as Bertie was coming out. "Oh. Jay. I didn't expect to see you today. Not that it isn't a pleasure, of course. We're somewhat busy, I'm afraid."

"Not a problem. I like to see libraries well used."

"Mr. Ruddle wants to spend some time in the rare books room," I said.

"Let me take you up," Bertie said. "Charlene's on the circulation desk at the moment, but it will be quiet when the lecture starts, so I'm sure she can help you find anything you need."

"Thank you. I don't want to disturb anyone's work."

They went inside. I checked my watch. Almost two. All the chairs had been taken, and the crowd overflow leaned against the lighthouse walls, stood behind the rows of chairs, or sat on the lawn. The mood was festive as people browsed the booths, munched on their sandwiches, shared thermoses of tea (or perhaps something stronger), and chatted to their neighbors. Children ran through the long grasses of the marsh, threw balls to one another, or squirmed in their seats. A line had formed at the face-painting table.

I was beginning to wonder if Louise Jane was going to be late, when I saw her making her way down the path, grinning from ear to ear at the size of the crowd. Today, she was dressed in an eighteenth-century ordinary seaman's outfit, the clothes ripped and torn. Black makeup created deep circles under her eyes and accented her sharp cheekbones, and she had a dirty rag with spots of red paint dotted on it wrapped around her head.

I hurried to greet her. "You look like one of the sailors on that model ship."

"That," she said, "is not a coincidence, Lucy, honey. Quite the crowd."

"Nice costume," I said.

"I decided last night not to wear the Miss Havisham getup. Despite what some people might think, I do not make my stories up. I believe in total historical accuracy. Where's the ship?"

"What ship?"

"The *Rebecca MacPherson*. I want it near me to illustrate my talk. Let's get it. You can carry the table. Set it up beside the podium."

"You think that's a good idea?"

"Of course it's a good idea. It's my idea, isn't it?"

I shrugged. "Whatever." The wind was picking up, bringing the strong scent of salt off the ocean.

Louise Jane and I set the table and the model ship next to the podium. The tiny sails fluttered in the wind. A few people left their seats to give it a closer look.

"I sent my biography to Bertie earlier," Louise Jane said. "Where is she? She's going to introduce me, isn't she? I can't just go up there and start talking."

"Yes, Louise Jane. It's all organized."

"I would hope so. What's the time?"

I glanced at my watch. "Three minutes to two. Nervous?"

She gave me a withering look.

"Too bad you don't have a book to sell, Louise Jane." Aunt Ellen had wandered over to join us. "The bookstore is here, and you have a ready-made audience."

Louise Jane's eyes lit up. "What a great idea! I can call it *Supernatural Legends of the Outer Banks*. My grandmother and great-grandmother know all the real stories. The ones too terrifying, *too real* to put in the tourist books. Like the *Rebecca MacPherson* or Frances, known as the Lady who lives in your apartment, Lucy."

"She does not." But, as usual, I protested in vain.

Bertie joined us. "Jay's happily settled in the map collection. I might have dropped hints that we'd love to have a roomier space for our rare books, but funds are limited. Ready, Louise Jane?"

"Need you ask?"

"Is Connor coming, Lucy?" Ellen asked.

"Last night he said he was. Maybe he got delayed." I glanced toward the crowded parking lot. "That looks like him arriving now."

"Then we can begin. I have a short bio of Louise Jane here somewhere," Bertie said. Papers fluttered in the breeze. "Not that Louise Jane needs much of an introduction to anyone from the Outer Banks. Lucy, you go up and get everyone's attention."

Feeling hugely self-conscious, I approached the podium and tapped the microphone. No one paid me any mind. "Attention, please. Can I have your attention." My tinny voice rang out over the marsh. A flock of Canada geese took flight.

Ronald's friend in charge of the sound equipment gave me a thumbs-up. The front row shifted slightly as Connor arrived, nodding and greeting people and shaking hands. He sat down and mouthed, "Sorry." He then puckered his lips into a kiss. I felt flames leap through my face. I glanced over the crowd to give myself a second to compose myself. Grace and Steph waved.

I tapped the microphone again, and eventually the buzz of conversation began to die down. People took their seats, and children were reined in. Smiling faces looked up at me. "Thank you," I said. "Please welcome Bertie James, the director of the Bodie Island Lighthouse Library and your host for this afternoon."

I stepped down to polite applause as Bertie took the podium.

Bertie finished her words of welcome, invited everyone to partake of refreshments on the lawn after the program, and—reluctantly I thought—called on Diane to say a few words on behalf of the library board.

Bertie stepped back about half an inch as Diane took the podium. Diane was in the midst of regaling those assembled with memories of her late, lamented (not by her, as we all knew) husband, Jonathan, who'd been the chair of the board, when Bertie yanked the microphone aside. "Thank you so much, Diane. Now, it's my pleasure to introduce our mayor, Connor McNeil."

Connor simply thanked everyone for coming, thanked the library for hosting the event, said he was looking forward to what our guest had to say, and wished everyone a safe and happy Halloween. He then sat down.

Short and to the point. What everyone loves in a politician. *Me, most of all.*

Louise Jane took her place, cleared her throat, and began to talk. She was a born storyteller, and her deep voice was soon rolling over the marshes. Perhaps, I thought, the idea of her putting her stories into a book wasn't a bad one. It should do well. Tourists loved to buy books about local history, and it might make her happy enough to stop plotting to get rid of me. Louise Jane had never liked me, thinking—incorrectly—that I'd stolen her job at the library, but I tried hard to get along with her. I sometimes thought her shell was cracking, but then she'd turn on me and make another well-placed jab. She particularly delighted in relating stories of the supposed haunting of the lighthouse in general and my apartment in particular, hoping to frighten me right out of North Carolina and back to Boston, where I'm from.

"It's said that the crew of the great ship cursed their cold-hearted captain, and for their treason, the curse was turned upon them when . . ."

Despite my skepticism, as she talked I felt myself falling under her spell.

The stories for this afternoon were kept child and family friendly, suitable for a sunny afternoon as well as the audience. Louise Jane had plenty of darker stories, truly frightening ones. She'd bring those out on Halloween evening, when she was scheduled to give an adult lecture at the library.

I stood behind Louise Jane and off to one side, looking over the crowd and into the marsh surrounding the lighthouse. It's a popular place for bird-watchers, nature enthusiasts, and walkers. A boardwalk crosses a section of the marsh, leading to a small dock on the calm waters of Roanoke Sound. No one was out there at the moment. Earlier I'd seen a group of hikers dropping onto the lawn to listen to Louise Jane.

It was a bright sunny day in the Outer Banks, the sun hot on my shoulders. As I watched, at the edges of the marsh, a fog began to roll in. My first thought was to be glad Louise Jane's program was only speaking, and it wouldn't matter if visibility was restricted. That might even add to the atmosphere. But once it arrived, the fog settled into place and didn't come any closer. Tendrils of mist waved and shifted, and gradually a vague shape began to form. A horse, a tall sleek white horse. It tossed its mane and pawed the ground, the long tail sweeping the mist behind it. It lifted his head and stared directly at me.

It was incredibly beautiful and totally mesmerizing. Louise

Jane's voice fell away, and all the people between us faded into insignificance as I gazed into the deep, liquid brown eyes.

I blinked at a burst of applause and glanced toward Louise Jane, expecting her to draw everyone's attention to the horse, but she didn't seem to have noticed it. "Men who go down to the sea in ships, more than anyone else, know to fear the power of the unworldly. The *Rebecca MacPherson* . . ."

I looked toward the marsh again. The mist was moving, thinning, dissipating, the yellow ball of the sun reemerging. The horse was gone.

"Time to get to work," said a voice at my elbow.

I jumped. "What!"

"Heavens, girl!" Aunt Ellen said. "You were a thousand miles away. I didn't think Louise Jane's story was that interesting. You asked us to help with the refreshments."

Two of the women from the Friends of the Library group stood with her.

"Oh, right. The refreshments. Yes. Thanks."

I led the way into the library. Everything we needed had earlier been laid out in the staff break room. Jugs of tea and lemonade were in the fridge, and cookies were stacked on trays on the table. We hadn't asked Josie to cater today, but instead we bought packages of baked goods from the supermarket in an attempt to keep costs down.

The sound of a broken-hearted creature came from the utility closet. "Good heavens," a volunteer said. "Has one of Louise Jane's ghosts gotten trapped inside?"

"That's Charles, the library cat," I said. "He's trying to get your sympathy."

"It's working," she replied.

"Everyone seems to be enjoying the talk." Aunt Ellen picked up a tray laden with cookies.

"Louise Jane is an Outer Banks treasure," one of her friends said. "Her understanding of the old stories comes from her grandma and her mama before her. That's the sort of knowledge you can't find in books."

"She's talking again on Halloween night," the second woman said. "Are you planning to come?"

"Heavens no! Some of the stories her great-grandmama told would scare the life out of you." She shuddered. "I only came today because I knew children were going to be here."

"I'll carry out glasses and napkins," I said, "if you can bring the drinks and the cookies, please." Charlene got up from the circulation desk and followed me outside, saying no one would be in the library while food was being served. Bertie called to Ronald, asking him to stand by the door, to keep an eye on the place while everyone was outside.

A plastic orange cloth had earlier been placed over a folding table, held down by four rocks, and we laid out the spread as Louise Jane wrapped up. "Thank you." She bowed deeply.

Applause rang out over the grounds, scaring birds out of trees. And the rush for the refreshments was on. Aunt Ellen and her friends poured drinks while I stood behind the table, telling the pushier of the kids, "One cookie at a time, please." Bertie and Charlene moved through the crowd, accepting compliments on the day. The clown twisted balloons into fabulous shapes, and the bookstore and jewelry booths were doing a brisk trade, although everyone pointedly ignored the political party tents.

Louise Jane remained beside the podium and her model ship, talking to a group of admirers.

Diane Uppiton was trying to push herself into a circle of women chatting on the lawn, but Curtis Gardner had disappeared. The people from Blacklock College stood apart, clutching glasses of tea and muttering darkly to each other. Connor casually worked the crowd, shaking hands and slapping backs. He'd wanted to keep this event nonofficial, so Dorothy, his campaign manager, wasn't with him. Everyone here knew Connor was a strong supporter of the library, whereas Doug Whiteside wanted to see us shut down and the lighthouse and marsh turned into a "revenue-generating" attraction.

"Excellent day, simply excellent," Theodore said to me. "Two glasses of tea, please." Aunt Ellen handed the drinks to him, and he thanked her. He then stood on the outskirts of the pack clustered around the refreshments table, holding a plastic glass in each hand and looking around as if searching for something. Or someone. I didn't see either Julia or Greg.

"Are any of these treats gluten-free?" a woman asked me. "I'm on a strict diet."

"I don't think so." I said. "Sorry."

"Oh, well. I suppose one won't hurt." She snapped up a chocolate-chip cookie, considered it, and then took a lemon cream also.

Gradually people began to disperse. The pitchers were empty, and all that remained of the cookies were a handful of crumbs. Final purchases were made, children corralled, goodbyes said, hugs and kisses exchanged. A steady line of cars drove down the pine tree–lined road heading to the highway.

I helped Aunt Ellen and her group clear up the crumpled napkins and empty glasses, and then the friends departed. The bookstore, the jeweler, the clown, and the face painter packed up their goods and thanked Bertie for letting them participate. Ronald, Charlene, and I began stacking chairs, and Grace and Steph pitched in to help.

Theodore had located Julia, and they sat together, their knees almost touching, while Greg loomed over them like an eighteenth-century chaperone.

"Up you get," I said. "We're putting the chairs away."

Julia smiled at me. She wore a scooped-neck blouse, and I noticed that the necklace she'd had on earlier was missing. "That was so interesting. Your library is fabulous. Not only the setting, but the sense of community you have and the obvious love you all have for it. Everyone I spoke to says it's an absolute treasure. I'm going to insist Granddad give you his collection."

"Thank you."

"Don't get people's hopes up, Julia," Greg said. "Your grandfather and I will make that decision based on what's best for the artifacts, not community sprit or the quality of the lemonade."

"Surely they're one and the same," she said.

"Quite right," Teddy said.

"Speaking of Granddad," Julia said, "he must be enjoying your maps, but I'm ready to go."

"Why don't I give you a lift back to your hotel, Julia?" Theodore said quickly. "No need to bother Mr. Ruddle."

"Thanks, buddy," Greg said, "but that won't be necessary. Jay loses track of time when he gets caught up in old documents. He'll be ready to go."

Theodore's face fell.

"It's kind of you to offer," Julia said.

Theodore's face recovered.

"I have to get back to work," I said. "I'll tell him you're waiting."

A few people had come into the library after their snack and were browsing the shelves. Ronald and Nan had helped Louise Jane bring the model ship back inside, and she was carefully checking the placement of every sailor and sail.

"Good job, Louise Jane," I said.

"Thank you, Lucy. It's awful kind of you to say so after all the opposition you and Bertie put in my way regarding this event."

"I didn't . . ." I said. Never mind. There was never any point in arguing.

The blue velvet rope we strung across the back stairs when the rare books room was closed was nowhere to be seen. I cursed under my breath. Some child fooling around, no doubt. Fortunately, this staircase only went up one level. I hoped the miscreant hadn't disturbed Mr. Ruddle. I climbed the spiral iron staircase to the landing. The door to the book room was closed. I tapped lightly before pushing it open.

"Sorry to interrupt, Mr. Ruddle, but the event's over, and your granddaughter's ready to leave."

Our rare books room resembles a library of old. Whereas the rest of the library is a modern place with warm light, comfortable seating, bright colors, and no stern librarians putting their fingers to their thin lips and scolding, "Shush," this room is a place for reading and contemplation. There's no window at this level, so no danger of sunlight touching the papers. The yellow bulb in the ceiling casts a weak light that barely reaches the curved, whitewashed walls or the corners of the aged wooden bookshelves. A red leather chair that squeaks when you sit in it and a gorgeous antique secretary occupy the center of the small room. The secretary is made of aged oak polished to a brilliant shine, with a high back dotted with pigeonholes and multiple drawers.

It's the perfect environment in which to read old manuscripts or examine historic maps and sailing charts. I love a modern library, these days as much a community center as a place to store books, but there's something magic about a true old-fashioned library that speaks to me of centuries of learning, the sharing of knowledge, and the reach of civilization.

If we were lucky enough to get the Ruddle collection, I'd argue for it to be kept in a room such as this. Someplace Wilkie Collins, Washington Irving, or Edgar Allan Poe would feel at home in.

Although if those gentlemen did pop in for a visit, we'd forbid them their cigars and glasses of whiskey.

Jay Ruddle sat in the leather chair, an old map spread out across the secretary and a couple more stacked beside him. His head rested on the document.

I coughed. "Mr. Ruddle?"

He didn't move.

I was conscious of my heart beating in my chest. My hands suddenly felt clammy. I crossed the room in two quick steps. "Mr. Ruddle?"

I touched his shoulder. He didn't stir. I lifted his hand.

Chapter Six

I pulled my phone out of my pocket. Cell reception in these thick stone walls is irregular at best, and I couldn't get a signal. I ran downstairs and headed for the front door. Startled patrons watched me pass. I threw the door open.

Only a handful of people remained on the lawn. Theodore, Julia, and Greg faced the marsh. Theodore's arm was raised as he pointed something out. Bertie had walked with Connor to the parking lot, where they stood by his car chatting. I didn't want to run and get them. I had to go back to the rare books room before anyone wondered what was going on and went to investigate. I texted Bertie: *Code Blue. It's Jay.* Then I sent a message to Connor: *Come to the lighthouse. Urgent!*

To my great relief, I saw Connor check his phone. He said something to Bertie, and she pulled hers out.

Ronald climbed the steps to stand next to me. "What's going on, Lucy? What's wrong? You're as pale as one of Louise Jane's ghosts."

I kept my voice low. "Jay. Inside. Dead."

He didn't bother to ask, "Are you sure?" Instead he pulled out his own phone. "Have you called 911?"

"Not yet. Bertie first."

"I'll do it."

Connor arrived at a run, Bertie following. Heads turned to watch them pass.

"Upstairs," I said. "I think . . . he's dead. Ronald called 911."

Patrons' heads popped out from between the stacks, and they murmured to one another.

"What happened?" I whispered to Ronald. "I thought you were watching the door."

"I saw the Manikan twins heading off toward the marsh. I don't know why their mom brought them, but she did. Couldn't get a babysitter maybe, as she had the baby with her too. As usual, she wasn't paying much attention to the boys, so I figured I had to chase after them and drag them back. Then, well, you know how it is, Lucy: one parent wanted to chat, and Mrs. Peterson cornered me with this great idea for an advanced reading program for Primrose, and—"

"Not your fault," I said.

He glanced at the ceiling. I couldn't keep my eyes from following. "I should have been here."

"You're going to have to say something to the people still here, Bertie," I said to her. The sound of sirens was approaching.

"I'll talk to the people outside." Connor kept his voice low. "I'll tell them a guest has taken ill, and hope they'll leave without asking any awkward questions."

"Like that's going to happen," Ronald muttered.

Bertie straightened her shoulders and spoke in her best

stern-librarian voice. "Everyone, can I have your attention, please. A visitor has taken ill in the upstairs room. If you don't mind, I'd like you all to leave. The authorities will need room to work. Thank you so much. Don't worry about checking out your book, Mrs. North. We know you're good to return it."

I whispered in Bertie's ear. "I don't think they should leave. The police will want to question them."

"The police?" She forgot to keep her voice down and the word 'police' spread throughout the room. Noticeably, a rush for the exit did not begin.

The door burst open. Paramedics came in, pushing a stretcher.

"Follow me," I said. "Up the back stairs."

I led the way and then stood outside the room with my back pressed up against the wall. I could hear the paramedics talking to each other. They did not sound as though they were in a big hurry.

Butch Greenblatt ran up the stairs, his equipment belt jangling. "Lucy, what's going on?"

I jerked my head toward the rare books room. "He's in there."

"Wait here."

I stood in the doorway and watched him speak to the medics. The woman handed Butch the blue velvet rope and gestured to Jay's neck. They'd turned him over and unbuttoned his shirt.

"Gone," one of the medics said.

Butch spoke into the radio on his shoulder.

I swallowed and went back into the hallway.

Butch joined me a moment later. "Do you know that guy?"

"His name's Jay Ruddle. He wanted to examine our map

collection, so we let him work here while our presentation was going on outside. I came up to tell him it was time to leave and . . . found him. Have you called a detective?"

"Yes. Looks like we need one."

I nodded. "I agree. This wasn't natural causes."

"No!" Julia darted past us and ran into the room. "No!" She threw herself on top of Jay. Before I could move, Theodore had wrapped his arms around her and was lifting her to her feet. "Come away," he said, his voice calm and soothing. "Don't look, don't look. Lucy?"

"Take her downstairs and into the break room," I said. "I'll get help."

Julia pushed Theodore away. Greg moved to take her arm, and she swatted at him. "You're wrong, Lucy. No one would harm him deliberately. My grandfather's the nicest, kindest man in the world." She burst into tears.

"Julia's right," Greg said. "Mr. Ruddle is in excellent health, but the man is eighty-two years old."

"Why don't you wait downstairs?" Butch said. "Someone will want to talk to you."

"Theodore, you know where the break room is," I said. "Put the kettle on."

"Excellent idea. A cup of hot tea would hit the spot."

Theodore took Julia's arm, but she pulled away. "He's not dead. I don't believe you! Greg, tell them he's napping. He does that sometimes, falls asleep at the oddest moments."

The medics stood in the doorway watching. "I'm sorry," one of them said.

"Come with me, please, Julia," Greg said. "You don't need tea—you need to lie down. Officer, we'll be at our hotel. We're staying at the Ocean Side."

"No one goes anywhere until the detective says so," Butch said.

Greg looked as though he was about to argue. Theodore gave the other man a quick glance and then also assumed an argumentative face. Butch stepped forward, and Greg and Teddy deflated. Julia swayed between them.

"Lucy?" Butch said.

"Come with me," I said. "We'll find you someplace comfortable to wait."

I started down the stairs. Julia followed, and Greg and Theodore brought up the rear, jostling for position on the narrow staircase.

I considered showing Julia to Bertie's office so she could have some privacy, but I knew (unfortunately, from experience) Detective Watson would want to use it to interview witnesses. The break room would have to do.

Bertie, Charlene, and Connor clustered at the bottom of the stairs.

"What's going on?" Bertie said.

"Julia needs to sit down," I said. "Detective Watson's been called."

Bertie gave Charlene a nod.

"Come on, honey," Charlene said. "We'll wait in the staff break room. I'll put the coffee pot on, and we might even have a box of cookies in the back of the cupboard. There's an old CD player in there somewhere. I'm sure I can find some music to keep us entertained." She led the way. Greg and Theodore followed, Julia between them.

"How are you?" Connor asked.

"I'm fine, Connor, truly," I said. "I hate to say it, but I'm getting used to this." A soft murmur of conversation came from the main room. "What's happening? Are many people still here?"

"A few are talking to Louise Jane."

We walked slowly down the hallway together and through the library. From the broom closet, Charles howled to be released.

The *Rebecca MacPherson* was back in its place, and a handful of people clustered around admiring it and asking Louise Jane where she'd found it.

"I have a campaign stop I can't get out of," Connor said. "Tea at a seniors' residence."

I smiled at him. "And as we all know, seniors are reliable voters."

"Exactly. I'll call you when I'm done." He laid his lips on my forehead. And then he left, leaving a lovely warm spot in the center of my head. He opened the door to find Detective Sam Watson and a uniformed officer about to come in.

"Going somewhere, Mr. Mayor?" Watson's picture could be used to illustrate the word *cop* in a dictionary, with his square jaw, crew cut, and piercing gray eyes.

"I have an appointment, Sam," Connor said. "I don't know anything about what went on here, but I can pop into the station later and make a statement if you need me to."

"The caller tells me this looks like a suspicious death."

"Butch Greenblatt's upstairs. He seems to think so."

Watson looked past Connor into the library. His eyebrows rose when he saw me watching, and he let out a sigh. "CeeCee told me she was coming to some function here. How many people do you think you had, Lucy?"

"Seventy-five, maybe a hundred? Far more than we were originally expecting."

He groaned. "You can leave, Connor. We'll talk later."

Connor left, and Watson looked around the room. Interested faces stared openly back. "All you folks give your names to Officer Franklin here and be on your way. I'll contact you later for a statement." The policewoman moved into the room, pulling a notebook out of her pants pocket. A circle quickly gathered around her, eager to help. Anyone who didn't care for police attention would have slipped away long ago.

"Lucy, who else is in the building?" Detective Watson asked.

"Ronald's in the children's library. Bertie and Charlene are in the staff room with Julia and Greg."

"Who are they?"

I explained. "Oh, and Theodore Kowalski."

"All the usual suspects," Watson muttered.

The door opened once again, and people carrying heavy equipment bags came in. "Be right with you," Watson said. "I'm going to have a quick look at the scene, and then I want to find out what's been going on here. I'll talk to you first, Lucy. Don't leave."

"I don't intend to."

The paramedics came down the stairs. They did not have Jay with them. I couldn't help glancing at the ceiling as they left.

One by one the last of the patrons filed out. The police-woman put her notebook away and then went to join Detective Watson.

Ronald came down the stairs and dropped into a chair. He'd taken his sea captain's hat off. His jaunty costume didn't suit the mood that had fallen over the library. The Halloween decorations were no longer fun—simply cheap and tacky, and seriously out of place. "Any idea what happened, Lucy?"

"No. But I'm sure it has nothing whatsoever to do with us."

"Except for him dying in the library."

"Except for that. This time I am absolutely not going to get involved."

Watson beckoned to me from the hallway, and I went to join him. "We'll use Bertie's office," he said.

"Can I get Charles? He's sounding very distressed. I promise, I'll keep him with me."

Watson gave me a look as though I'd asked if our cat could play with all the nice forensics equipment his people had brought. "No."

"Okay," I mumbled.

The feline in question howled as we passed the door to the broom closet. I tried to close my ears. The sound of a woman crying and low voices came from the staff break room.

Once in the library director's office, I sat in the visitor's chair, and Watson took Bertie's seat. I focused my eyes on the poster behind the desk. A woman doing a downward dog on the beach as the rising sun outlined her in shades of orange. I took deep, calming breaths. In and out. In and out. I lifted my hands to my chest and lowered them again. Up and down. Up and down.

"Are you okay, Lucy?" Watson said.

"Just trying to center myself."

"You look centered to me," he said dryly. "Okay. CeeCee told me about this shindig here today. Louise Jane doing something for Halloween."

"That's right. Mr. Ruddle brought his granddaughter, Julia, but he wasn't interested in Louise Jane's lecture, and he asked if he could look through our map collection."

"Jay Ruddle. I've heard of him. I don't mean in my professional capacity—just as a man lots of people know. I wasn't aware he'd come back to the Outer Banks. Was he a regular patron here?"

"I'd never met him until the other day. He still lives in New York City." I explained about the collection and Jay's search for a new home for it.

"You say you found him. Take as much time as you need, and tell me about that."

I swallowed and began. I told Watson about showing Jay to the rare books room and leaving him there. And how, when the program was finished and Julia ready to leave, as I was coming into the library anyway, I offered to tell her grandfather it was time.

"Were you alone when you found him?"

"Yes, and I ran downstairs to get Bertie and Connor and call 911."

"Did anyone other than emergency personal go into the room after you?"

"Julia and Greg. And Theodore."

"Tell me about them."

"Greg works for Jay as the curator of his collection, and Julia is Jay's granddaughter. I'd never met either of them, or Jay either, until they came into the library on Thursday to talk to Bertie about possibly giving the collection to us."

"What does this collection consist of?"

"Historical documents, including maps and ships logs, from the earliest days of exploration along this coast."

"How much is it worth?"

"I can't say. I haven't been involved in the discussions. Bertie and Charlene are handling it. Considering that he has an employee whose job is to manage it, probably a lot."

"What's Teddy's interest? I thought he collected mid-twentieth-century detective and spy fiction."

"Serious collectors will collect anything that might prove of value later down the road. But in this case, I suspect he's more interested in the fair Julia than in old maps."

" 'The fair Julia'? Why do you call her that?"

"Just a line from a book."

Watson's penetrating gray eyes studied me. I shifted uncomfortably in the hard chair.

Surely he wasn't considering that I had a reason to want Jay Ruddle dead?

"So this man was alone in the library. For how long, until you found him?"

"Probably an hour and a half."

"Alone in a locked lighthouse," he murmured.

"Uh. No. Not exactly."

"Not exactly? I hope you're not referring to that cat if you mean someone else was in here. Who?"

"He was alone, but the lighthouse wasn't locked. The library wasn't even closed. The main event was happening outside, but we were open as normal. Some of our patrons weren't interested in Louise Jane's talk. Charlene was on the circulation desk while the rest of us were outside, but . . ."

"But?"

"When the refreshments were served, she came outside."

"Leaving the library unattended?"

"Uh . . . yes. Ronald was supposed to keep an eye out, but he got distracted by some wayward children."

"So seventy-five to a hundred people could walk in and wander upstairs unnoticed?"

"Even before that, I'm afraid. When we're on the desk, we're not exactly chained to it. We can go to the restroom, get a glass of water, help a patron find a book, shelve stray books—even work on the computer. We don't always know who's in the building at any given time."

"Your security is a thing of wonder."

"We're a public library. Not a bank or a jewelry store. The rare books room is always locked when it's not in use." And my apartment, of course. But Watson knew that from past . . . inquiries.

"Tell me about this Greg and the fair Julia. Where were they at the time in question?"

I thought. I thought hard. I couldn't place anyone with any degree of certainty. The lawn was packed, people coming and going all the time. Even when Louise Jane was speaking, the people standing shifted position, chased children, or greeted their friends. Things were even more confusing when the refreshments came out and the vendors and entertainers went back to business. "Theodore Kowalski seems somewhat enamored of

Julia. He stuck to her like white on rice, as they say." I stopped talking.

"You've thought of something."

Theodore had fetched lemonade for himself and Julia. When he'd taken the drinks to her, he couldn't find her. I remembered his blank expression as he searched the crowds, plastic glasses in hand. "I'm sorry, but I can't say for sure if they were together all the time. Easy to get separated."

About the only person I could be positive hadn't killed Jay Ruddle was Louise Jane. She'd talked to me from when she'd first arrived until she went to the podium, where she'd been in plain view of a hundred people. After her lecture, friends gathered around to compliment her and ask questions. She was still with people when I came downstairs after finding Jay.

"Most of the folks who'd been at this talk had left by the time I arrived," Watson said. "It's going to be a nightmare gathering all the names. Give Officer Franklin a list of everyone you can remember."

"I will."

"I'd like to talk to the fair Julia next. She's in the break room?"

"You can't keep calling her that," I said.

"I suppose you're right."

I led the way down the hall and opened the door. Theodore, Julia, and Greg were seated at the table. Charlene had stayed to keep them company. Theodore and Greg sat straighter, and Julia looked at me through red eyes. She blew her nose into a tattered tissue. I didn't introduce anyone, knowing Watson liked to do things his way.

"Good afternoon. I'm Detective Watson. Can you tell me who you are please?"

"This is Julia Ruddle," Greg said, "Mr. Jay Ruddle's granddaughter. I'm Greg Summers, Mr. Ruddle's curator."

"I am Theodore Kowalski, rare book collector and close friend of Julia."

"I know that, Teddy, thanks," Watson said.

"Just stating it for the record."

"What's a curator do?" Watson asked.

"I manage Mr. Ruddle's collection of rare and valuable artifacts and documents. All that is surely irrelevant at the moment. You seem to be under the impression foul play was involved here. Have you caught the person responsible?"

"Give me time," Watson said. "Ms. Ruddle, I'd like to speak to you in private, please."

Greg's chair clattered as he pushed it back. "I'll accompany Julia."

Theodore leapt to his feet.

"I said, 'in private,'" Watson said. "You'll get your turn. Wait here. Both of you."

I followed the detective and Julia out and closed the door behind me. "Won't be too much longer," I shouted to the broom closet as I cowardly ran past. I averted my eyes from the people coming and going on the back staircase, ran though the library, and burst out the front door into the welcome fresh air and sunshine.

An officer was guarding the door, logging everyone who came in or out into his notebook.

Chapter Seven

Watson remained ensconced in Bertie's office with Julia for a long time. Next he spoke to Greg and then gave them permission to leave. I gave her a hug and told her to call me if she needed anything. Teddy was still hanging around and offered to drive Julia back to her hotel.

"Thanks, buddy," Greg said, laying a protective hand on Julia's arm, "but we came in a car."

"Perhaps we'll run into each other again, Theodore," Julia said.

His face lit up. "I certainly hope so."

They left. Theodore stood on the front steps, watching her walk down the path.

"Time you were going too," I said.

"Do you like Julia?" he asked me.

"Yes, I do. She seems very nice."

"I think so too. It's a shame about her grandfather. She was obviously extremely fond of him. I hope this doesn't mean she'll be going home to New York anytime soon." He walked away.

Watson decided that as the murder had happened in the room off the back staircase, he wouldn't need to secure the entire building. Instead, yellow police tape was strung across the stairs, and we were told to keep out until further notice.

The library, however, was closed for the rest of the day. The last of the lingering patrons were told to leave. Eventually, only the library employees and Louise Jane remained.

Watson gave her a look and opened his mouth to tell her to leave, but she spoke first. "Halloween is fast approaching, Detective. The night before All Saints Day. It's a well-known fact that the spirits are on the move this week."

"Not in my jurisdiction they aren't," Watson said.

"Why don't I give the room a quick going-over for you?"

"My people can do that," he said.

"Not in the way I mean. If I don't sense something, my grandmother would be willing to come down. She's powerfully attuned to the spirit world."

"If you go up there, Louise Jane," he said, "with or without your grandmother, you'll be investigating the spirits in cell block C. And I can tell you, they come from the corner liquor store, not from beyond the grave."

She huffed. "I'm only trying to help."

"Duly noted," he said. "Make sure Officer Franklin has your contact information. And then get out of here."

After giving their statements, Ronald, Charlene, and Bertie were told they could go home. As the library director, Bertie insisted on staying.

A van arrived from the coroner's office, and Jay was taken away. Bertie and I stood close together, watching silently.

Bertie gave me a hug. "Are you going to be okay here tonight by yourself, honey?"

Two forensic officers lumbered past with their equipment.

"I will. There's nowhere I feel safer," I said. And that was the truth.

"Don't let Louise Jane's stories get to you."

"They don't," I said. "I've never felt anything the slightest bit supernatural here." An image of the shadowy horse I'd seen on the marsh flashed through my mind. I pushed it aside. "Louise Jane would say that's because I don't have much of an imagination. I'd say it's because I'm a practical Yankee from a long line of practical Yankees on my father's side."

"As was Ichabod Crane," she said with a smile.

"True enough. But poor Ichabod was a fool for love."

"As we should all be at least once in our lives," she said, and I caught a trace of sadness in her voice. "Good night, dear."

"Good night, Bertie."

At last I was able to free Charles, and I carried the furious, squirming ball of tan and white fur up the one hundred steps to my Lighthouse Aerie.

I fed the cat and then got into a warm pair of flannel pajamas. By the time I'd brushed my teeth and washed my face, Charles was curled into a contented ball in the center of the bed. I hadn't had dinner (nor lunch, come to think of it), and it wasn't even fully dark out, but I needed to be snuggled up, warm and comfy. I checked the voicemail on my landline phone, hoping for a message from Connor, but found nothing. Thinking that he might have called my cell, forgetting about the spotty reception, I climbed onto the window seat, opened the window, stuck my arm out, and squinted at the little screen. One bar appeared. No messages.

I clambered back down.

I didn't know if I was disappointed or not.

I didn't know what I thought these days.

Connor had been loving and warm and affectionate toward me this afternoon. It had been nice—more than nice—but I was bothered by a sense of unease.

I cared for Connor, a lot. I liked him very much—I might even love him. But was I ready to settle down? To choose him to be *the one*?

I wasn't sure. For almost as long as I could remember, I'd been paired with Richard Eric Lewiston III, the son of my father's law partner. For years, it had been expected that we'd be married one day, and I simply went with the flow. It was only when Ricky finally made the long-awaited formal proposal that I realized I would be falling into a trap if I married him. Not only that, but I didn't love him. He'd become nothing but a habit, someone I was used to having around, the habit nurtured and tended by my mother and Ricky's mother.

And so I'd fled Boston and my job at the Harvard Library, and come to my favorite place on earth, the Outer Banks.

All that had happened a few short months ago.

I suspect Ricky was relieved. He hadn't exactly hurried down to the Outer Banks to persuade me to come home.

I hadn't heard from him at all. Mom tells me he's "giving me space."

Had I fled the habit of Ricky only to fall into the habit of Connor? My feelings for Connor were much different from those I'd had for Ricky, to be sure. But was it enough? Maybe I needed some time to be on my own to sort out what I wanted in life.

If I ask for too much time, will I lose him?

I rubbed my eyes. I'd think about that tomorrow.

I snuggled deep into the covers. Charles crawled onto my chest and purred gently as he drifted off to sleep.

I was awoken by the sun streaming through my east-facing window. I'd slept more than twelve hours and felt much better for it.

I filled Charles's dishes and made myself a big pot of coffee. I sat at the table and opened my iPad to check the news online. As could be expected, Jay Ruddle's death was the number-one topic. Sam Watson was quoted as saying they were treating the death as a homicide and were close to making an arrest. None of us, the library community, were mentioned, and that was a good thing. I intended to have nothing to do with the police investigation. I wasn't even going to think about who might have been responsible. I knew nothing about Jay Ruddle's life or any enemies he might have had, so there was no point in speculating.

The library is closed on Sundays, and today I intended to relax at home in the morning and get caught up on my reading. I'd have a nice, leisurely, early lunch and then drive into town to meet Josie, as arranged, to go canvassing for Connor. Then he and I were planning to have dinner together. A perfectly normal Sunday.

My phone rang, and I answered it, thinking that, whatever the result, Connor needed this election to be over. He had looked tired yesterday.

The Spook in the Stacks

"Lucy!" A man yelled so loudly I blinked and moved the phone away from my ear. "Something terrible has happened."

"Theodore, is that you?"

"You have to help."

"Help with what?"

"It's Julia. My fair Julia. She's been arrested for murder. I'm on my way to the police station. I'll meet you there. Lucy, you have to do something!"

He hung up. I was left staring at the phone in my hand.

Chapter Eight

I had absolutely no idea why Theodore thought I could help Julia. The trek to the police station would be a useless endeavor. Detective Watson was never inclined to let me sit in on his questioning of a suspect, but I would go anyway. I'll admit I was curious as to what they had on Julia, but mostly I figured that, as my friend had called me for help, I'd show up and offer a sympathetic shoulder.

I drove into Nags Head to the police station. I saw a few costumes on the streets, and decorations draped the front of some of the bars and shops, but at the police station you'd never know this was Halloween week.

Probably just as well.

I found Theodore sitting in one of the hard, uncomfortable (as I knew from past experience) plastic chairs in the outer room. He jumped to his feet the moment he saw me. "Lucy, thank heavens you've arrived." He wrapped his arms around me in a hug so ferocious I struggled to breathe. He was dressed in a T-shirt and jeans, not the Harris Tweed that smelled heavily of pipe smoke.

I patted his back feebly. When he finally pulled away, I noticed that we were not alone. Greg Summers watched us through narrow, suspicious eyes.

"Hi," I said.

"Hi," he replied.

"What happened?" I asked Theodore. He dropped into a seat. I took the third chair, the one between him and Greg.

"I have absolutely no idea," Theodore said. "Other than that the police have arrested Julia for the murder."

"It's ridiculous," Greg snapped. "An incompetent, small-town cop jumping to conclusions."

"Why?" I said.

"I don't know," the two men chorused.

"The cops came around to the hotel first thing this morning," Greg said. "We were sitting down to breakfast, when they marched into the dining room and told her to come with them. Poor Julia didn't even understand what was going on at first. The police could have shown some consideration for Julia's embarrassment. Everyone stared at her. Some people even took pictures. I might sue."

I looked at Theodore. "How did you hear about it?"

"I . . . uh . . . just happened to be standing outside the hotel when the police came out with Julia."

"Right. You just happened to be there," Greg said.

I glanced between the two men. Theodore with his thinning hair, pinched face, bad teeth, nervous manners, and brand new clothes. His pants too tight, the T-shirt unfashionably tucked in and secured by a heavy belt. Greg, handsome, smooth, sophisticated in black jeans and a gray golf shirt worn under an open denim shirt with sleeves rolled up. He pushed a lock of casually coiffed hair off his forehead.

"Did they actually say they were arresting her?" I asked. "Give the warning and everything? Or only ask her to come with them?"

"I didn't hear a warning," Greg said.

"Then they've just brought her in for questioning," I said.

Theodore beamed. "See! I told you Lucy would be able to help."

"I can't help! I don't know anything about it."

"You solved those other cases, Lucy," he said.

"I didn't. I just happened to be in the right place at the right time." Or more to the point, the wrong place at the wrong time.

"I have faith in you, Lucy," he said, throwing a satisfied smirk at his rival.

"Well, I don't," Greg replied. "I've called Jay's lawyer and asked him to arrange for someone to represent Julia. I don't want some overworked, underpaid public defender, nor—pardon me, Lucy, but it's time to be blunt—a part-time detective who's also a small-town librarian."

"I'm not—"

"I recommend Stephanie Stanton," Theodore said. "As I told you, she has an excellent reputation."

"So excellent, she lives in Nags Head," Greg replied. "No, I want nothing but the best for Julia."

"Ms. Stanton—" Theodore began.

I lifted my hand. "A moot point. It's unlikely Steph can represent Julia. She was at the library yesterday and could possibly be called as a witness. If it ever comes to trial."

Greg tried not to smirk.

"How long have you worked for Jay?" I asked.

"Three years. It's a good job, pays well, and isn't too demanding. But, well, time to move on. I got a good offer from a museum, and I wanted to take it. Jay interviewed a few other candidates for my job, but he didn't care for any of them, and so he decided to find a new home for the collection."

"Do you think some of those rejected job applicants might have a grudge against him?" I asked.

"I can't see it. He didn't seriously consider any of them."

"Excellent," Teddy said. "Now we're getting somewhere. Write that information down, Lucy."

I was determined not to be pulled into playing detective. Instead of making notes, I said, "Did Julia have much interest in the collection?"

Before Greg could answer, the door to the inner sanctum opened, and Julia and Sam Watson came through. We leapt to our feet. Julia's nose and eyes were red and swollen, her pale face streaked with tears. Watson glanced at the waiting trio and did not smile.

"Ms. Ruddle's free to go," he said, "for the time being. She is not to leave Dare County."

"Detective, why—?" I began.

He turned and walked away.

Theodore grabbed one of Julia's arms, and Greg the other. She gave them each a sad smile. "Thank you for waiting. Let's get out of here."

Neither of Julia's two escorts appeared to be ready to release her arm, so they had to turn themselves sideways to squeeze through the door, three people in a row. I brought up the rear.

"I have my car," Theodore said. "Allow me to take you to the hotel, Julia. Greg can follow us."

"Not a problem, buddy—I'll take her. Come on, Julia."

Teddy's smile required considerable effort.

"At the moment, I need a cup of coffee and to eat the breakfast I didn't get," Julia said. "Do you know any nice places, Theodore? I don't want to go back to the hotel—not with all those people staring at me."

"Josie's Cozy Bakery does an excellent casual breakfast," he said.

"Thanks for the tip," Greg said. "See you later, buddy."

"Why don't I drive us over?" Theodore said. "You'll never find it on your own."

"I have a GPS," Greg said.

"Please join us, Theodore," Julia said. "If you have the time, that is?"

He nodded like an enthusiastic puppy.

"It was kind of you to come down to the station to give me moral support," Julia said. "I'll come in your car, and Greg can follow. Lucy, would you like to join us?"

"Excellent idea," Theodore said. "She's a private detective."

"I'm nothing of the sort!"

"I thought she was a librarian," Julia said.

"I *am* a librarian."

"That's settled then," Theodore said.

"Are you sure you want us all with you, Julia?" I said. "You might need some alone time to process everything."

"Alone time. I'm afraid of alone time. My grandfather and I were close. I slept well last night. My subconscious hasn't yet absorbed what's happened." She took a deep breath and glanced back toward the police station. "That detective isn't helping."

A cruiser pulled out of the parking lot under full lights and sirens. The hot sun shone on our heads, but the strong wind off the ocean was sharp with the threat of winter soon to come.

"Why don't you come in my car, Lucy?" Theodore said. "I can drop you back here later."

"Okay."

"In that case," Greg said, "I'll go with you too."

"Not necessary," Theodore said. "Josie's is less than a mile away."

"I thought you said I'd need a map to get there."

"Store fronts can be confusing."

"Then I'll need your help to find it, won't I?" Greg said.

The men engaged in a surreptitious shoving match to see who'd open the front passenger door for Julia. Greg won, but as Theodore was the owner and driver of the car, he didn't take his loss too badly. He ran around to the driver's seat while Greg and I squeezed into the back of the 1998 Neon.

"Toss all that stuff on the floor," Theodore said.

I swept aside soda cans, fast food wrappers, and empty potato chip packages. I picked a book off my seat. *Kiss Me Deadly* by Mickey Spillane. It was in excellent condition. I checked the inside pages. A first edition. "This must be a valuable book. You shouldn't leave it in the car."

Theodore glanced over his shoulder. "Oh, there it is. I've been looking everywhere for that book, and Lucy found it. See what I mean about her being a detective?"

The old car started with series of jolts and jerks, and we

rolled out of the police station parking lot. The tourist season was mostly over, and traffic through town was light on a Sunday morning. Although that didn't prevent Teddy from almost rear-ending a SUV that had slowed to allow the car ahead to make a turn, or running a light and nearly colliding with a big sedan packed with mom, dad, grandparents, and kids, heading home after church. I clung to my seat belt with one hand and Mickey Spillane with the other, in fear for my life. I glanced at Greg. His handsome face was looking somewhat seasick.

Julia stared out the window and said nothing.

"How long do you plan to stay in the Outer Banks?" I asked.

"No longer than I have to." Greg flinched as Theodore changed lanes, pulling in behind a motorbike, leaving inches to spare. I might have flinched myself. "That detective told us not to leave Dare County. Another reason I want Julia to get a lawyer ASAP. She needs to be able to go home. There are a lot of arrangements to be made."

"Home is in New York State?"

"Yes. Jay has—had an apartment in Manhattan and a vacation place near Sag Harbor."

"What about Jay's children? Is he married?"

"Widowed a long time ago and never remarried. His only son was killed in a car crash when Julia was three. She was his only child. Jay raised her."

"I'm sorry to hear that. Is Julia's mother still alive? Have you notified her of Jay's death?"

"She's out of the picture." Greg lowered his voice. "I don't know the whole story, but it seems as though she's never been in it."

"Happy to be of service," Theodore shouted as he pulled into the parking lot of the strip mall that houses Josie's Cozy Bakery. Greg and I collided in the middle of the back seat.

We screeched to a halt. One at a time, I released my fingers from the death grip they had on my seat belt.

"Breakfast is my treat," Julia said. "As you've been kind enough to hire a private detective, I'd like to talk things over with her."

"What private? Oh, you mean me? I'm not—" But I was speaking to an empty car. I tossed the book aside and jumped out.

It was ten to ten, and the café was mostly empty. Breakfast diners had left, and the lunch crowd was still to arrive. Like everywhere in the Outer Banks, business was slowing as the tourist season came to an end.

Theodore led the way to a table for four in a quiet corner. He and Greg took the chairs on either side of Julia, leaving the one directly facing her for me. I didn't sit down. "They don't have table service here," I said. "You have to go to the counter to order."

"Coffee for me, thanks," Julia said. "And a muffin or something."

"Same," Greg said.

"I'll have the breakfast sandwich with sausage, if they're still serving," Theodore said. "And coffee."

I went to the counter and placed the order.

"Heard you had some trouble at the lighthouse yesterday," Alison said as she punched buttons on the cash register.

"To put it mildly. Is Josie in?"

"Taken the day off."

"Oh, right. I'm supposed to be canvassing with her this afternoon."

"You can tell Connor he's got my vote."

"I will." Alison gave me four empty mugs and put the muffins on plates. I handed over the money. "Thanks," I said. So much for this being Julia's treat.

I delivered the muffins and then poured coffee from the self-serve dispenser. I ran back and forth to the table, asking who wanted cream or sugar. I could have used some help here—never mind help in paying—but Julia and Greg were sort of like guests, and Teddy wasn't going to give up his seat in case Greg managed to somehow spirit the fair Julia away when he wasn't looking.

At last everyone was served, and I was able to sit down. "First, let me make it clear that I am not a private detective. I am not a detective of any sort. I am a librarian, and proud to be a librarian. I'm here because Theodore is my friend and he asked me to come."

"I understand." Julia smiled at Theodore, and he preened.

Alison brought the breakfast sandwich. "Who's having this?"

Theodore lifted his hand, and she put it in front of him. When she was out of earshot, Greg said, "No point in beating about the bush here. Why'd that hick cop haul you down to the station, Julia?"

"Don't underestimate Sam Watson," I said. "He's no fool."

"Whatever," Greg said.

"I'm serious," I said. "He was with the NYPD in homicide for many years."

"Whatever," Greg repeated.

"If you don't want to discuss the matter," Theodore said, "don't feel you have to." He picked up the sandwich with his left hand and took a bite.

"It's okay," Julia said. "I've done nothing wrong." She studied the depths of her mug. No one spoke for a long time. "It seems," she said at last, "Granddad was holding something of mine when he died."

"So?" Theodore said.

"What was it?" Greg said.

"My necklace." Instinctively she put her hand to her bare throat.

"How'd it get there?" Greg said.

"Who told Detective Watson it belonged to you?" Theodore put the sandwich back on its plate.

"Anyone at all might have mentioned it," she said. "It was my necklace."

"I remember," I said. "A thin gold chain with a small diamond." Julia had been wearing it when she arrived yesterday afternoon, and I'd noticed it was gone when everyone was enjoying refreshments after Louise Jane's talk. I'd next seen the necklace when I found Jay's body. It had been dark in the windowless room, full of shadows, but the light from the desk lamp had caught a flash of gold between his fingers. Watson hadn't asked me about it, and I was glad I hadn't been the one to tell him. Maybe he hadn't seen it yet when he questioned me.

A tear leaked out of Julia's right eye. "It broke. I was fingering it, and the chain snapped. He grabbed it out of my hand and said I had to pay attention. Those were the last words my grandfather ever said to me." She wrapped both hands around her cup, as if seeking warmth. "I can be clumsy sometimes."

"Easy enough to explain." Theodore stuffed a piece of his sandwich into his mouth. "Detective Watson didn't need to make such a fuss of it. I've had a brilliant idea. As you're staying here longer than planned, would you like to tour the Wright Brothers historic site this afternoon? It's fascinating. I haven't been in years."

"We're not here as tourists, buddy," Greg said.

"I don't believe I invited you."

"I'll remind you that Julia's grandfather has died."

"All the more reason to get her mind off her tragic loss. A nice outing would be precisely what the doctor ordered."

I ignored the men's bickering as I tried to recall the sequence of events yesterday afternoon. "Julia, you were wearing the gold chain when you arrived at the library. You and your grandfather went your separate ways. If it ended up in his hand, it's natural enough for Detective Watson to want to know how it got there."

She ducked her head, and a lock of black hair fell over her eyes. "I . . . I went inside the library. After we found our seats." She glanced at the two men. "I told you I was going to the restroom. I didn't. I went upstairs to talk to Grandfather. I didn't agree with giving away the collection. I wanted to keep it in the family. I wanted to learn to take care of it myself. I loved my grandfather very, very much, but he had some old-fashioned opinions on the roles of women. My degree is in English literature."

"Then we have something in common," I said.

"So we do. Grandfather thought that a suitable field of study for a woman, but he absolutely refused to consider letting me take responsibility for the collection."

"You never told me you wanted that," Greg said.

"Why would I? You're as bad as Grandfather, the way you always brush off any interest I try to show in it."

"I didn't—"

"I'm sure you're more than capable of being in charge," Theodore said.

"I don't much care what you think, buddy," Greg said.

"I don't believe I was speaking to you."

I lifted one hand. "Leave that for now. What happened yesterday?"

"I went upstairs," Julia said. "He was studying a map when I came in, and he said that its excellent condition proved that the Lighthouse Library knew how to care for old papers. He told me he'd made his decision. He would be giving his full collection, and the funds to care for it, to you, Lucy. To the Bodie Island Lighthouse Library. Ironically, much of his decision was because Charlene's credentials had impressed him, as well as her previous work at the Bodleian. He didn't think I, his granddaughter, capable of assuming the responsibility, but it was Charlene's profession, so somehow he'd overlook that she's also a woman."

I didn't feel as joyful at the news as I would have yesterday. Jay Ruddle had made no formal offer to the library, and we couldn't stake our claim on a casual comment. Not that we'd want to get into a fight over his estate, in any event.

"I asked him to reconsider," Julia said. "To let me run it. He called me a . . . foolish girl and told me his mind was made up. That's when he ripped my necklace out of my hand and yelled at me. I left. For heaven's sake, I didn't kill my grandfather. The collection isn't that important to me. I told Detective Watson. I don't think he believed me."

Chapter Nine

Julia burst into tears. Her cup crashed to the ground, spraying coffee and shards of white porcelain across the floor. She leapt to her feet. "I didn't do it! I didn't. I need to get out of here. I need time to think. I'll walk back to the hotel."

She fled. Greg and Theodore shoved their chairs back.

"Let her be," I said sharply. "Julia needs to be alone. She has a lot to process. A walk will do her good, and it's not far to the Ocean Side. It must be tough enough to have her grandfather die, never mind that the last words they exchanged were angry ones."

The two men stared at the bakery door for a long time, and then they slowly settled down. They perched on the edge of their chairs, looking much like Charles when he was getting ready to pounce. The muffins and breakfast sandwich lay on the table, abandoned.

"Goodness," Theodore said.

"No wonder the police had questions," Greg said.

"It's preposterous," Theodore said.

"Ridiculous to think Julia would kill her grandfather," Greg agreed. "They were devoted to each other. More like father and daughter."

"They'll find the real killer shortly, and Julia will be in the clear."

"Very soon."

I wasn't so sure. That Julia went into the library, argued with Jay, and a short time later he was found dead, looked mighty bad.

"I need a ride back to the police station for my car," I said. "Teddy, let's go. Greg?"

"Might as well," he said.

"What about our expedition to the Wright Brothers Memorial?" Theodore asked. "Do you think Julia still wants to go, Lucy?"

"Leave it for a while," I said.

The drive back to the police station was no less perilous than the one to Josie's bakery. From the front passenger seat, I had an even better view of close calls and narrow escapes. Greg leapt out of the Neon before it had come to a full stop. He did not bother to say goodbye.

We watched Greg get into the Escalade and drive away. "Take some advice from a woman," I said to Theodore. "Don't hover. Give Julia some space. If she doesn't want to go for an outing, don't push it."

"I don't like that man. That curator. He's up to no good."

"Teddy, you can't say that."

"He's only interested in Julia for her money."

"What makes you think she has money? Just because her grandfather was wealthy . . ."

"I suspect she'll inherit, don't you? She's his only living relative, and he must have been worth quite a bit."

I leaned back in my seat. Unwittingly Teddy had voiced a good reason for Julia to have murdered Jay Ruddle. She seemed quiet and unassuming. She seemed to have been fond of her grandfather. Was it possible all that was nothing but a pretense? Did she want control, not only of the collection but the rest of his money as well? Had she had been prepared to wait until the inheritance came to her over the course of time, but the announcement of his intention to give away his historical documents inspired her to act?

I thought about Julia the first time I met her. I remembered the tenderness she had toward her grandfather, the obvious love between them.

I didn't believe Julia killed Jay Ruddle.

I glanced at my friend's unattractive, innocent, love-struck face.

If I could do anything to help Julia—and Teddy—I would.

* * *

When I got back to the lighthouse, I was pleased to see that no police cars or forensic vans remained in the parking lot. They must have finished whatever they needed to do.

The library was dark and quiet. I switched on every light as I passed. I normally love the library, any library, when it's empty. The peace, the solitude, knowing that I'm surrounded by centuries of great literature, the breadth of history, the evolution of human thought. But today it seemed, dare I say it, almost sinister. The room was not precisely as I'd left it—the printer sat on the wrong side of the desk, the wingback chair was pushed against the mystery fiction shelves—but neat and tidy. No evidence remained to show that a murder had been committed not far from this room and that police officers had been tramping all over everything. A gravestone lay on the circulation desk, reminding me that next week was Halloween. The holiday decorations were still in place, but rather than fun, they were moody and menacing, as was the *Rebecca MacPherson* with its grinning skeletons, tattered sails, and shattered hull.

Get a grip, I said to myself. Charles had not appeared to greet me. I rattled my keys and called out.

"Meow." The big Himalayan strolled into the room, his tail high, his ears up, his gait swaggering. If he could talk, he would have said, "And where have you been, young lady?"

I laughed. Simply having Charles in the library made the shadows recede and the aura of menace disappear. He jumped onto the shelf beside me, and I gave him a hearty pat.

What were we going to do about Halloween? It didn't seem at all proper to continue with a celebration of the spooky and the undead, no matter how tasteful (and isn't that an oxymoron), in light of what had recently happened here. But Ronald hated to disappoint the children, and he'd been creating a big buildup to Wednesday's events. Not to mention the adults also looking forward to their party.

I went upstairs, and Charles ran nimbly ahead. I stood at the window of my Lighthouse Aerie for a long time, looking out over the marsh, across the highway, to the beach and the ocean beyond. Clouds were building in the southeast. Poor Theodore, who wanted nothing more than to be regarded as a respected book collector and literary scholar, and instead, with his Harris Tweet suits, plain glass spectacles, lingering aura of cigar smoke, and fake English accent, was little more than a joke. This week, I'd seen another side of Theodore: the smile on his face when he looked at Julia, the way the light lit up behind his eyes when she spoke. His gentle kindness to her and his deep concern at her fate.

Julia seemed like a good match for him. She was as quiet and serious as he.

And then there was Greg. Hard to imagine what attracted the handsome, sophisticated Greg to a woman like Julia. Other than her grandfather's money, that is.

Which, now that Jay was gone, would probably soon be Julia's money.

Was it possible Greg killed Jay, expecting Julia to inherit?

That seemed pretty far-fetched. They weren't married, didn't even seem to be a couple. Was he romantically interested in her, or did he simply not want Theodore to be? How voluntary was Greg's leaving Jay's employ anyway? Maybe, unlike what we'd been told, he was being pushed out. Did he want to keep the job and believed that if Julia was the owner, she'd let him stay on?

I gave my head a shake. I was letting my imagination run away with me, looking for reasons for Greg's guilt because I was on Teddy's side in the wooing of the fair Julia.

Still, the fact remained that Jay had been murdered. If not

Greg, who else might have wanted to see the end of Jay Ruddle?

As much as I might not want to think about what had happened here yesterday, the thought of the fair Julia and her two suitors brought it all back. Why did this keep happening to me? Why did I keep finding myself dragged into murder investigations?

I dropped into a chair and ran everything that had happened yesterday through my head.

The people from Blacklock College had been at Louise Jane's lecture. Had they found out that Jay'd made his decision, and he was giving his collection to us? Had they decided they needed to kill him before he made the announcement? Did they have reason to believe that Julia, Jay's heir, would favor them? Again, it seemed far-fetched to kill someone over a collection of old papers, but some collectors, academic or otherwise, could be total fanatics. A business client of my father had paid almost two hundred thousand dollars for a copy of *Beeton's Christmas Annual* from December of 1887, which contained the first Sherlock Holmes story. The man wasn't rich: to raise the money he had to mortgage his house, sell his wife's car (without her knowledge), and take his son out of college.

He kept the magazine, but lost his wife, custody of his younger child, and eventually his home when he couldn't make the new mortgage payments.

Who else had been at the library at the time in question? Aside from a hundred or so history lovers?

Curtis Gardner.

I'd been present at an altercation between Jay and Curtis at

Owens' restaurant the other night. Clearly there was bad blood between the men. Bad blood on Curtis's part anyway—Jay had made no attempt to talk to Curtis. Diane and Curtis had sat in the front row for the lecture, but they'd mingled with the guests over refreshments. It would have been easy enough for Curtis to slip away unnoticed.

Easy enough for Curtis to slip away.

Easy enough for anyone to slip away. We didn't have guards watching the guests or logging people in and out of the library.

It was entirely possible Jay's enemy had nothing at all to do with the library community. He or she might have snuck onto the grounds under pretext of being part of the crowd and then slipped into the library during the program. Anyone who knew Jay and his interests would assume he'd be in the rare books room. Did that mean our killer knew the layout of the library? Not necessarily. Jay might have told that person where he'd be spending the afternoon and how to get to the rare books room via the back stairs.

I poured myself a glass of milk, made a peanut butter and banana sandwich on white bread (a childhood favorite from summers at the beach), and settled back at my small kitchen table. Holding my lunch, I opened my iPad, accessed Google, and typed one-handed. I wasn't getting involved—I was just interested.

I had no trouble coming up with information on Jay Ruddle. He was a well-known man in North Carolina, with business interests throughout North America. I learned that Jay had been born in Nags Head, where his father had owned a furniture store. Mr. Ruddle Sr.'s store had featured high-quality items, many of them made by North Carolina family businesses. On the premature death of his father, Jay took control and quickly expanded throughout the state and eventually across the country. His business model was vastly different from his father's. Jay's model appeared to be to offer the lowest possible prices, drive nearby stores out of business by undercutting them, and then, when the competition had closed, raise his own prices. His stores aimed at the lower end of the scale, and his furniture was described in one business magazine as "shoddy but cheap."

Jay's only son died a number of years ago, leaving him without an heir to take over the business. Two years ago he sold his entire furniture empire to a big-box chain, and the day he turned eighty he retired to devote his attention to his "extensive collection of historical documents." As part of the deal his stores kept his name, and he got a seat on the board of the big-box chain and was rumored to still be active behind the scenes at Ruddle Furniture.

I found lots of information on Jay in the business press and some articles on his historical collection, but nothing you might call gossip. His wife had died when the couple was in their fifties, and Jay had never remarried. He didn't seem to spend his time dining or golfing with politicians or dating actresses half his age.

His business practices would have made him a few enemies over the years, but I had trouble imagining that he'd agree to meet any of his rivals in the rare books room of our library. Had someone seen him going into the library and followed?

Someone like Curtis Gardner? Curtis's father had established a chain of stores catering to the tourist trade throughout the Outer Banks. Today, the Gardner business empire was nothing more than a handful of shops selling made-in-China tourist trinkets and inexpensive beach accessories. Rumor was, so I had heard, that Gardner Beach Wear was in financial difficulties. Everyone knew the red Corvette Curtis drove had been purchased (with unseemly haste) by Diane Uppiton out of what she'd inherited on her husband's death.

I leaned back with a groan. This was useless. Almost anyone could have snuck into the library unnoticed and slipped out again to mingle with the crowd. Julia had. She'd told her friends she had to go to the restroom, and instead had gone to the rare books room, where she argued with her grandfather, leaving her thin gold chain clutched in his fingers.

I had to admit, things looked bad for Julia. I couldn't bear to think what it would do to Theodore if she was charged, never mind convicted and sentenced.

I shut my iPad. I was not going to get involved. Not this time.

Still, it might not hurt to ask a few questions.

I checked my watch. Almost time to meet Josie, but enough time to make a few calls first.

"What's up, Lucy?" Butch Greenblatt asked.

"Nothing much," I said. "Your people are finished here, and I'm at home. If you're working, I can call back."

"Nope. Enjoying a day off. If your eyesight is really good, you might be able to see us. Steph's waving."

I leapt to my feet and reached for the powerful binoculars I keep on the shelf by the window. I love to watch the seafaring world go by, and from up here I can see a long way. The wind was high and the sea rough, but several people were on the beach, walking or fishing. Two tiny figures looked to be jumping up and down and waving their arms. I laughed. "I see you!" I waved back.

"What's up?" Butch said.

"Thursday night there was a minor altercation at Owens' between Curtis Gardner and Jay Ruddle. Nothing came of it, and Curtis left peacefully. But I was wondering if there were other similar incidents involving Jay Ruddle."

"Why do you want to know?"

I took a breath. "Jay made enemies over his years in business. Then he came back to the Outer Banks. I'm just wondering."

"Don't get involved in the murder investigation, Lucy."

"I didn't say I was doing that."

"You don't have to. Oh, all right. You won't let this go until I give in, so I might as well give in so Steph and I can continue our walk. Watson's been doing some checking into the man's past, and you're right that Ruddle wasn't popular around here. He ruined a lot of family businesses, made himself a ton of money, and then upped and left. But most of that happened a long time ago. A very long time ago."

"People, Bankers in particular, have long memories." Bankers was the affectionate name used for people born in the Outer Banks. "Thanks, Butch."

"Have a nice walk." I hung up and then made another call.

"Theodore Kowalski speaking,"

"Hi, it's Lucy."

"Lucy! What have you learned?"

"Calm down. I haven't learned anything."

"Oh."

"I do, however, have an idea of a way you can help."

"Anything!"

"Jay Ruddle is a Banker, born and raised. He got his start in business in Nags Head, running his father's furniture store."

"That's common knowledge, Lucy."

"It wasn't common knowledge to me, and that's why I'm calling you. Bankers have long memories, or so I've been told. Jay made some enemies in his climb up the ladder of success."

"So?" he said.

"So, I'm wondering if one of those enemies saw the chance for revenge. And took it."

"You want me to investigate? Good thinking, Lucy. I'd be happy to help."

"Try not to be too obvious," I said, thinking that was unlikely to happen. "Ask around a little bit. Listen in to what people are saying about Jay's death. Think back to yesterday afternoon. Did you see anyone who was an old rival of Jay's at the library?"

"My mother might remember Jay Ruddle," Theodore said. "I'll start with her."

"Great. Where are you now?"

"I'm . . . uh . . . at the Ocean Side Hotel. In the . . . uh . . . parking lot."

"Teddy! Don't hover. Women don't like that. Too much attention can cross the line into creepy."

"I'm here to ask Julia if she's ready to go to the Wright Brothers Memorial."

"You asked her. The offer is out there. Leave her to answer in her own time."

"If you say so, Lucy. How will she let me know when she's ready to go?"

"She'll call you or send a text."

"But she doesn't have my number."

I rolled my eyes. Charles yawned. Poor Theodore. Like Ichabod Crane, a fool for love. And equally hapless. "I'll handle that," I said. "But only if you promise me you'll go home and stop hovering over her."

"I knew I could count on you, Lucy. You're very wise in these matters. I promise. I have some detecting to do, don't I?"

"That you do," I said.

We hung up and I, reluctantly, called the Ocean Side Hotel. I was hoping to get the voicemail for Julia's room, but she answered.

"Hi, it's Lucy here," I said. "I'm calling to check that you got back to the hotel okay. You were pretty upset when you left the bakery earlier."

"I'm fine, Lucy. It's kind of you to think of me."

"Why don't you take my phone number?" I said. "If you need anything you can give me a call."

"Thanks. I'll do that."

I gave it to her and then I said, oh so very casually, "I have to be back at work tomorrow, but if you need anything during business hours, Theodore Kowalski would be happy to help. Why don't I give you his number too?"

"Okay," she said. I rattled it off, and we said goodbye.

Oh great. Now I'm not only a detective but also a matchmaker.

I next called my aunt Ellen. My mother and her sister were Outer Banks natives, the daughters of a long line of fisherman and fish plant workers. My mom fled the coast and the small-town life the moment she could, but Aunt Ellen had remained. My best childhood memories are of summer vacations with Aunt Ellen and Uncle Amos and a pack of sun-kissed, sand-encrusted cousins. I said much the same to my aunt as I had to Theodore: think over yesterday afternoon and if anyone in particular might have wanted to see Jay Ruddle dead.

"I won't say he was a popular man around here, honey," she said. "Not among some of the old-timers, at any rate. But life goes on, and we all have other things to worry about. Jay wasn't the first, and is definitely not the last, to deliberately run local families out of business. Not many of them left any more. I heard last week that Leon Badenberg sold his family's hotel to a big chain, and his old mama is mighty angry. So angry, they say he's been told he's not welcome at her house for Thanksgiving dinner. Anything Jay Ruddle might have done is likely long forgotten."

I thought of Curtis Gardner. "Maybe not entirely. Jay only gave up total control of his business two years ago. If he made enemies when he was starting out, it's likely he continued that pattern. I'm just asking you to keep your ears and eyes open."

"I can do that, honey."

* * *

I would have loved to spend the rest of the day relaxing over my book in the comfortable window seat in my apartment while Charles snoozed on the bed, but I'd made an appointment for the afternoon and I had to keep it.

I changed out of jeans into my more respectable librarian "uniform" of black skirt with pantyhose, blue button-down shirt, and pumps with one-inch heels. As rain was still threatening, I tossed a folding umbrella into my tote bag, told Charles to guard the lighthouse, headed back out, and drove into town toward Connor's campaign office.

With only a few days remaining until the election, the place was hopping: volunteers staffed phones and folded brochures, and canvassers dashed in and out. As I arrived, Nancy, the volunteer coordinator, put down the phone with a puff of a breath. She saw me and gave me a wave. Her phone rang, and she shrugged at me and answered while pointing toward a pile of brochures stacked on a table by the door.

I scooped them up. They'd been tied into a bundle secured by an elastic band with a sheet of paper tucked underneath, containing a map with a list of street addresses.

The door opened and Josie came in. "Don't you look the proper politician's wife," she said to me with a laugh.

I felt myself blushing. "I didn't intend to." I eyed her outfit— denim capris, red T-shirt, black jacket cropped at the waist. "Do you think I overdressed? This is what I wore Tuesday evening when I hit the streets with Connor."

Nancy put down the phone. "You're perfectly fine, Lucy. Sunday afternoon's a mite less formal, but together you two remind folks that Connor has a variety of supporters."

Josie laughed. "In dress sense, if not exactly demographic. Particularly as Lucy and I are first cousins."

"Good thing some of us have other groups covered then."

An elderly black man glanced up from the printer. "Are you two first cousins going to chew the fat all day or get out there?"

Josie saluted. "We're on it, Eugene."

"Is Connor in?" I asked. The door to the back room was closed.

"He's having an early lunch at a seniors' home, a late lunch at another seniors' residence, afternoon tea at a third, and then attending a pre-dinner wine and cheese reception at a service club," Nancy said. "Once all this is over, poor man won't be able to move for a month. He told Dorothy to keep his dinner hour clear."

I hid a smile. Dinner would be with me.

Josie read my mind, as she usually did, and gave me a wink.

We headed out, brochures in hand.

Josie and I had been assigned an area of nice houses on large treed lots at a point where the peninsula thickens enough that the usual Outer Banks yards of sand dunes, beach grass, and sea oats are replaced by grass and trees: live oaks, hickories, and beech. Many of the homes back onto the network of canals that cut through the thin strip of land between the open ocean and the calm waters of Roanoke Sound. I parked my car beneath a grove of pines, and my cousin and I set about door knocking.

The threatened rain held off, the sun came out to play, and we enjoyed the afternoon. We handed out brochures, chatted about policy and Connor's vision for the future of Nags Head, and otherwise made polite conversation. Most people, we were pleased to see, assured us that Connor had their vote, and those who were supporting Doug Whiteside were polite about it. We usually found someone at home, it being a Sunday afternoon with rain in the forecast, but if they weren't, we put a brochure in the mailbox with a handwritten note saying, "Sorry to miss you!"

One woman, after hearing our pitch, asked me when Connor and I were getting married. She'd seen a picture of us together in the paper. "Young people these days," she told me, "are waiting too long to tie the knot." She eyed me. "Children are for the young."

"I totally agree," Josie said. "Once the election is over and Connor's comfortably settled back into office, he can give some thought to his personal life. It would be too bad if he had to rebuild his dental practice first. A lot of work's involved in that."

The woman took our information, and we left.

"Another vote in the bag," Josie said.

"You don't think it was somewhat underhanded to suggest that he needs to win so he can get married?"

"Whatever works," she said.

We turned onto the sidewalk. Two little girls sped toward us on tricycles, horns beeping and colorful steamers flying from their handlebars. Their mothers walked behind them, takeout coffee cups in hand. "Good luck, Lucy!" one of them called to me as they passed. "Any friend of the library has our vote."

I gave them a thumbs-up and said, "Thanks." I turned to my cousin. "Speaking of getting married, any news on that front?"

"On the part of anyone other than my dad's mother and aunts, no. The season's slowing down, but we're still busy at the bakery, and I want to help out with the election whenever I can."

"Thus you are here today with me, on your day off, rather

than having tea with your mother and planning your wedding."

"Exactly. There's plenty of time. Jake and I want a small, casual, family wedding. The reception's going to be canapés at the restaurant, so that's a whole lot of details settled right there. Mom and I will send out a few invitations in early November, and you and I will go dress shopping one day. What else is there to do?"

"Put like that, it does sound pretty straightforward. What's happening with your grandmother?"

Josie groaned. "My dad's from Louisiana."

"I know that. Can't mistake that old-fashioned Southern charm."

"They're an old plantation family fallen on hard times after the War of Northern Aggression, according to his mother."

"Meaning?"

"Meaning, she doesn't think a small, casual, family affair is at all suitable for her only granddaughter."

"Good thing she doesn't live near here then," I said.

"Good thing. But her tentacles reach far and deep."

We stopped chatting and put on our friendliest smiles as we turned up the next walkway. No one was at home, so Josie slipped campaign literature under the door. From inside the house, a dog barked at us.

"What do you hear in the café?" I asked Josie as we continued on our way. "About the election, I mean."

"Not a lot," she said, "I don't serve the customers, but my staff know Connor and I are friends, so they keep me posted. It's not going to be a cakewalk, Lucy. Doug Whiteside has his supporters."

I snorted.

"For plenty of reasons, but mostly because they think he'll be better for attracting new business and development."

Another snort.

I would never forgive the odious Doug for taking advantage of the death of his estranged sister Karen to promote his political agenda and to attack the Lighthouse Library at the same time.

As if we'd had a premonition, the issue of Doug came up at the next house we visited.

The door was opened by a middle-aged man neatly dressed in golf shirt and chinos. The sound of Mozart drifted through the air behind him, and something delicious was roasting in the oven.

"Lucy," he said. "Good afternoon. Nice to see you."

Library patron. Two preteen boys. Twins. I struggled for his name. He thrust out his hand. "Brian Covington."

I shook and introduced Josie.

"From the bakery," he said. "Best muffins in town."

"Thanks," she said.

"My mother's Glenda Covington."

"Oh, yes," Josie said. "She's good friends with my mom."

"And a stalwart of the Friends of the Library volunteer committee," I added.

He read the campaign buttons fastened to our shirts. "Connor's got the vote in this house—don't you worry. I left OBX for a few years, couldn't get back fast enough. Doug Whiteside might have some not-bad ideas about development, but he'll move too far and too fast. Once changed, things can't be put back."

Josie and I nodded enthusiastically.

"Sorry to hear about the death of Jay Ruddle," Brian went on. "I wasn't there, but Mom was helping serve refreshments after the lecture. I can't imagine Doug'll be too pleased."

"Why do you say that?" I said. "No one was pleased at the man's death."

"Sorry," he said. "I phrased that badly. Although, according to my mother, some folks will be dancing a jig at the news of his passing. I meant Doug was counting on Jay's support to influence some of his friends in Raleigh."

"Meaning?" Josie asked.

"Meaning, Doug hasn't got any important political contacts. No friends in high places to help him get the rougher parts of his agenda through. That's assuming he wins, of course." He winked at me. "If I was even inclined to consider voting for Doug, my mother would disown me if there's the slightest chance it might benefit Jay Ruddle in any way."

This was news to me. I had no idea Jay had any intention of getting himself involved in Nags Head politics. He didn't even live here anymore. Was he looking for something to do with his time and energy? He'd sold his business interests and was giving away his historical collection. A man needs to keep busy in retirement. Was Jay planning to work for Doug if we were unlucky enough to see him installed as mayor? How effective could Jay have been? As Brian had reminded us, Jay had a bad reputation with some old-timers.

How much influence did the old families have on local politics these days anyway?

I had absolutely no idea. I'd had no involvement in politics until I met Connor, and I was only working on his campaign because . . . well, because it was for Connor and because he was a huge supporter of the library. Did it matter if Jay was not popular with the established Outer Banks families? Younger people and newcomers wouldn't care if he'd undercut his competition fifty years ago.

Maybe Jay wasn't going to get involved. Not publically anyway. Might he have wanted to pull strings from behind the scenes?

"I haven't heard anything like this," Josie said to Brian. "How do you know?"

"I keep my ears to the ground," he said with a smile. Men always smiled at Josie. "I have to. My wife and my mother are both powerful forces in the birding and wetlands preservation communities, and I own a construction company. We build houses. I have a foot firmly in both camps. Sometimes, that's not a safe place to be."

We laughed, and Josie said, "Thanks for your time."

Another smile. "Always a pleasure."

"Next time you're in the bakery, ask for me. Muffin's on the house."

"I'll do that," he said.

We walked away. The moment the door shut behind us, I said to Josie, "Now we're bribing voters? Isn't that illegal? Even if the currency of exchange is one muffin."

"Brian's a good guy, or so my mom says. He tries to balance

his construction business with our delicate beach and dune environment. Not easy sometimes."

"Do you think Connor knows about that? About Jay and Doug, I mean?"

"I have no idea. But he'll want to. For no other reason than to have a heads-up in case someone attempts to imply that Connor wanted Jay dead to foil Doug's ambitions."

I sputtered. "That would be ridiculous. If what Brian said is true, Jay was going to advise Doug if he became mayor. He wasn't involved in the campaign."

"He might have made a hefty donation," Josie said.

"So? Even if he did, that's no reason to kill the man now."

"Rumors don't have to make sense, Lucy. Sometimes the less sense they make, the faster they spread. Give him a call."

"Give who a call?"

"Connor."

"He's busy with all that eating and tea drinking and being friendly."

"True. Dorothy will be minding his phone."

I made the call. As Josie guessed, Connor's campaign manager answered. "I'm sorry, Lucy," she said, "but Connor can't talk to you at the moment."

"It's not a personal call," I said. I told her what we'd heard.

As always her voice gave nothing away. "Thank you, Lucy. I'll give His Honor the message. How are things on the street today?"

"Generally going well," I said. Our stack of brochures was almost finished, and most of the houses on our list had been ticked off.

"Glad to hear it." She hung up.

Josie and I finished our assignment and headed back to the campaign office to report in.

* * *

I'd enjoyed my afternoon of door knocking and canvassing, and as an added bonus it had completely taken my mind off Julia Ruddle and her troubles. As I let myself into the lighthouse, I began thinking about it again, and I wondered if there had been any new developments. I hoped Theodore had taken my advice and was waiting patiently for Julia to call him—or not.

Unlikely. Patience was not one of Teddy's strong suits.

I stood in front of my small closet, deciding what to wear for dinner with Connor tonight. We might dine alfresco, which meant comfortable and relaxed attire, but the evening was likely to be cool. A flowery, summery dress with a jacket would do the trick, I decided. I pulled out the dress and held it up against me for inspection. "What do you think?" I asked Charles.

He jumped off the bed and went to the kitchen to see if he'd forgotten to eat any of his dinner.

"I'll take that as a yes," I said.

I'd left my phone on the windowsill to pick up any incoming calls. It buzzed to tell me I had a text.

Connor: *Sorry, dinner's off. Police chief has called press conference for seven.*

I stabbed at the buttons to reply: *OK.*

Connor: *Quick drink at the LH after?*

LH, I knew, meant "Lighthouse." Without taking time to think, I replied: *Sorry. Bushed.*

I took a deep breath. Why, oh, why had I done that? All he wanted was a quiet drink and a chance to kick back and relax after what would surely be a stressful press conference, on top of a day of being at his most charming. Whether he wanted to be charming or not.

Connor: *Another time then. Night.*

The reply was short and brusque. His hurt feelings almost came through the phone. I cursed myself. I liked Connor. I wanted to be with him.

I was a darned fool. I considered texting back. Something like: *Sounds like a great idea!* And finish it off with a line of little Xs.

I didn't. Somehow, that would make things even worse.

When it came to other people's love lives, I might be, as Teddy had said, wise. When it came to my own, I was quite the failure.

Chapter Ten

M onday morning, I pulled back the drapes to reveal a wall of thick gray fog. When the great first-order Fresnel lens high above me flashed, it did little to break the gloom. Tendrils of mist, as insubstantial as the fingers of a ghost, drifted around the solid walls of the lighthouse. As I peered out, a patch of fog separated, and far below, at the edges of the marsh, something moved. It wasn't a morning for bird-watchers or nature lovers, so I grabbed my binoculars. At first, all I could see was shades of gray. I searched where the marsh should be, but found nothing. I was about to put the glasses down, when the fog shifted once again.

And, to my shock, I saw a horse.

I couldn't tell if the animal itself was gray or if a blanket of fog covered its coat, but it was tall and slim and powerful. Muscles rippled beneath the smooth, glistening coat. I could see no rider, nor anything to hold a person on. No saddle, stirrups, or bridle. The strong, sleek neck turned; the big head lifted; and I swear the animal looked straight at me through liquid brown eyes. As I watched, tendrils of fog closed in again, and the horse slowly disappeared back into the mist.

I stood at the window for a long time, searching, but the only thing I saw was the glow of headlight beams as Bertie's car turned into the parking lot, and I realized I would be late for work if I stood here much longer.

I fed Charles, who'd had no reaction to what I'd seen (thought I'd seen?), and put on a pot of coffee to brew while I showered and dressed. When I next went to the window, the air was clearing as the rising sun burned the mist away. I could see no horses, fog draped or otherwise. I shook my head.

The book I'd been reading lay on my night table. *Bracebridge Hall*, which I hadn't finished in time for book club last week. *Bracebridge Hall* is not a novel as we know it, with a linear plot leading to a climax and conclusion. Instead, it's a series of character sketches about a group of people gathered at an English country house, visiting and telling stories. Many of the stories they tell are traditional, to do with tales of the supernatural. Noises in the marsh. The Wild Huntsman. A ghostly horse. A storm ship.

Must have been a combination of the book, the remnants of a dream, my mind clouded by the fog, and the approach of Halloween.

I poured my coffee into a travel mug and shoved a granola bar into my pocket, and Charles and I went downstairs to work.

Bertie stood at the window, looking out. She turned at the sound of footsteps on the iron stairs and gave me a smile. "Good morning."

"Morning. What are you looking at out there?"

"We have company. And not of the good sort, I fear."

"What sort of company?" Charles leapt onto the windowsill, and I peered over Bertie's shoulder. At first, I thought she meant the horse's rider was about to knock on the library doors, but that wasn't it at all. Four cars and one satellite van bearing the logo of a TV station had arrived, and people—some of whom carried large cameras—were poking around the grounds. Of the fog, only a light cover remained, rolling rapidly away over the wet ground of the marsh.

"Other than those people, whoever they are, you didn't see anything . . . unusual when you arrived, did you?" I asked my boss.

"Unusual? In what way?"

I was reluctant to tell her what I'd seen. Or thought I'd seen. "Anything out of the norm."

"I couldn't see much at all, normal or not. The fog was particularly thick. I have to say, for a moment it put me in mind of Sherlock Holmes and Doctor Watson dashing across the cobblestones of London. It's breaking up now, and the forecast is for a nice day." She changed the subject as we watched some of the new arrivals snapping pictures of the lighthouse and the grounds, while the others poked around, presumably searching for signs of murder and mayhem. "Did you watch the press conference last night?"

"I don't have a TV," I said, "but the local station put some of it on Twitter, and I followed that. It was picked up by the cable news networks."

"A considerable number of outside journalists came to hear what the police had to say. Interest seems to be growing. Jay's death is becoming more than a local story. I wouldn't have thought Jay Ruddle was worth that much attention, but he was rich, and these days rich equals celebrity I suppose. I came in early, in an attempt to avoid anyone hoping for a statement from me. Good thing I did, as the pack is assembling. I don't have to tell you, Lucy, that no comment is the only statement any of us will make."

"Goes without saying. How did the press conference go?"

"Fine, I thought. Sam Watson and the chief handled themselves well, as they usually do. Sam said nothing of consequence, without appearing to be holding anything back. Connor came on at the end to remind people that Nags Head is a safe place for residents and visitors alike."

"Was anything said about the election?"

"No. Doug Whiteside tried to get a word in edgewise when the formal press conference ended, but the outside reporters weren't interested in anything he had to say."

"I bet he had a few things to say privately."

"No doubt," Bertie said.

"At least Doug and Bill Hill, his campaign manager, are in the clear this time. I didn't see them here on Saturday, and if they had been, Doug doesn't exactly make himself unobtrusive."

"That he doesn't. Here's Ronald. He's about to be ambushed."

We watched as our children's librarian pulled up and parked his car. He got out, looking highly surprised as a cluster of eager reporters gathered around him. Cameras were produced, pictures snapped, and questions shouted. I could only hope the accompanying newspaper copy would explain that the photos had been taken during Halloween week. Ronald had worn his pirate costume. He hefted his stuffed parrot in one hand, his leather briefcase in the other, and made his way through the crowd to the lighthouse.

I opened the door for him, in he dashed, and I slammed it against the babble of shouted voices.

"What on earth was that all about?" he said.

"We are," Bertie said drily, "in the news."

"Are we going to open as usual?" I asked. It was five minutes to nine.

"Yes," she said. "A stern 'no comment' will be given to every question. Photographs will be permitted—I don't see how we can stop it—but fortunately there's nothing to take pictures of. Ronald, put the ropes with the private sign across both sets of stairs."

"The police have taken away one of them," I reminded her. No need to also remind her it had been used as a murder weapon.

"I can find something to replace it," Ronald said.

"Access to the upper levels will be restricted today," Bertie said. "We can't keep an eye on the ladies and gentlemen of the press if they're wandering all over the place willy-nilly. What time do the children's programs begin?"

"The preschool story time is at eleven," Ronald said. "Then nothing until after school, when we have the first-grade Halloween party."

"Hopefully, we can get rid of the press before then. If any children are on the premises, we will absolutely forbid photographs. Except by parents and others we know personally. Your instructions for today are to be totally boring."

"At the Lighthouse Library?" I said with a weak laugh. "That won't be easy."

"The press have short attention spans. If nothing happens, and I certainly hope nothing does, they'll be gone before long."

"What about Halloween itself?" I said. "Are we going ahead with the plans? Louise Jane is giving a talk at the party for the younger teens at five, and then another for adults who don't have a party to go to or children to take trick-or-treating."

"Wild horses wouldn't keep Louise Jane away." Bertie rubbed at her eyes. "Certainly not a little murder."

"I wouldn't be surprised," Ronald said, "if she alerts the press herself."

"I considered canceling all our Halloween events," Bertie said. "It does seem tasteless in light of what happened here on Saturday. But then I decided it's best to carry on as normal. Our patrons expect the unexpected at the Lighthouse Library."

I eyed Ronald the Pirate. "That's certainly true."

"And we never want to disappoint the children. I'll stay out here with Lucy this morning as long as the press are here. Ronald, you are free to escape to the children's library."

"Happy to." He fastened his parrot to a clip on his shoulder; growled, "Argh, matey!"; and made a dash for the stairs. He disappeared after putting the rope in place.

The hands of the big clock over the circulation desk reached nine, and I unlocked the door. I was almost knocked off my feet as the press flooded in. Bertie stood by the entrance, her arms crossed tightly over her chest and a no-nonsense scowl on her face. I was pelted with questions—Had I met Mr. Ruddle? Had

I seen anyone acting suspicious? Where exactly had he died?—to which I merely shook my head and tried to look like the village idiot. Pictures were taken, but as the police had never said exactly where the man was found, or even how he had died, no one made a beeline for the rare books room.

Not being at all wary of journalists or bad press, Charles jumped onto the returns shelf, where he sat preening and posing for pictures. "Oooh," a woman cooed, "what an adorable cat." She scratched his favorite spot behind his ears, and he purred happily. The traitor.

When one enterprising woman—all short, tight skirt, heavy makeup, and long, flowing blond locks—tried to bypass the private sign on the stairs, Bertie cleared her throat and thrust out her arm. The woman retreated rapidly and said, "We're done here, Jerry," to a man with an enormous camera on his shoulder. They left, and the rest of the pack soon followed. Only Charles was disappointed to see them leave.

By nine thirty, the library was once again just a library.

"If they come back," Bertie said, "let me know." She headed toward her office. Charles jumped off the shelf and went upstairs to see what Ronald was doing.

I peered outside. Most of the reporters' cars were driving away, although the blond woman was standing at the edge of the marsh, talking into a microphone while Jerry filmed her. No doubt they were collecting background color. And it was colorful. All traces of the morning's fog had gone, and the big yellow sun was rising in a soft blue sky. As I watched, a flock of Canada geese flew overhead in the classic V formation, calling loudly to stragglers to keep up.

Of gray horses, there remained not a trace.

Of course not, I told myself. I'd been dreaming while awake.

* * *

I'd lain in bed last night for a long time, wide-awake, my mind churning. I'd gone over—and over and over—every detail of the moments surrounding Jay Ruddle's death, thinking about Connor and wondering why I was being such a coward in the face of romance; and, it would seem, rehashing stories of headless horsemen and ghostly horses. In the midst of all that, I finally decided I could do nothing more about investigating Jay's death. Sam Watson wouldn't thank me for my help, and it had been highly presumptuous of Teddy to tell his new friends I was some sort of hotshot private detective. I wanted to believe in Julia's innocence—for Theodore and because I liked her—but I had to admit to myself that some people could be deceiving. *"Who knows what evil lurks in the hearts of men?"* If something in his Outer Banks background had caused Jay's death, my friends would find it and hand that information over to the police.

With that thought, I finally drifted off to sleep with the contented Charles at my side.

Shortly after noon, all my good intentions fled when Norman Hoskins and Elizabeth McArthur from Blacklock College walked through the door. Parents and caregivers were collecting children after story time, and the library was packed with pirates and princesses, ghosts and gracious ladies, *Star Wars* characters and Ninja warriors, and a good number of other costumed characters I didn't recognize.

Bertie had come out of her office to exclaim, in either delight or fear (as appropriate), over the children's costumes. The children had run upstairs, laughing and chattering, and the parents settled down to find books for themselves or have a good gossip while waiting. Charles hadn't reappeared, and I knew he'd stay upstairs for a while. Charles enjoyed preschool story time as much as any of the children.

I was pleased the events of Saturday hadn't ruined everyone's mood for the holiday. It's mighty difficult to put a preschooler off Halloween.

Elizabeth cringed as a child dressed as a scientist in large glasses, frizzy wig, and white lab coat darted past her, and Norman forced his face into a smile. "Good afternoon. Is Ms. James in?"

"I think so," I said.

"We'd like a few minutes of her time," Norman said.

Ronald had come down to say goodbye to the kids. He wiggled his eyebrows at me, and the parrot on his shoulder bounced. Charles leapt onto the returns shelf beside the desk and eyed our visitors.

"I'll see if she's free," I said.

Charles arched his back and hissed.

"A . . . cat," Elizabeth said.

"Most unsanitary," Norman added. "You don't let that creature anywhere near the historical documents, I trust."

I didn't reply. Charles hissed again.

Bertie came out of her office and nodded politely to the visitors. "Can I help you?" The three of them stood stiffly, arms at their sides and backs straight. Three fake smiles were locked firmly in place.

"Perhaps we can help each other." Norman looked around. The library was full of patrons, parents selecting books, and kids laughing and playing. "Can we talk in private?"

"Certainly," Bertie said. "Ronald, will you take the desk, please? Lucy, you can join us."

I didn't ask why she wanted me there. As a witness, no doubt. Bertie politely stepped back to allow them to precede her down the hall. I mouthed, "Coffee?" and she shook her head. Uninvited, Charles followed us.

Elizabeth and Norman took the visitors' chairs in the library director's office. I stood next to the wall. Charles took a seat on a high shelf, from where he could glare malevolently down upon our visitors. He was normally a very friendly animal. But sometimes he almost seemed to have an instinct for people.

Bertie sat at the chair behind her desk and said, "How can I help you?"

"Let's get straight to the point, Ms. James," Elizabeth said. "We want the Ruddle collection."

Bertie's right eyebrow rose. "That is straight to the point. I don't see why you're telling me. I don't have it. You don't have it. You are aware Mr. Ruddle passed away on Saturday?"

"We are. He died right here. In your library."

"Very careless of you," Norman said.

Bertie fought down an angry retort. "Which is why I have to ask what brings you here."

"Mr. Ruddle had narrowed his options down to us at Blacklock College and to you at this . . . library. In light of his death, we're assuming his only heir, who we understand to be his granddaughter, will continue with his plans."

"She might. She might have ideas of her own." Bertie threw me a glance. I shook my head. I hadn't told her that it was possible, likely even, that Julia would want to keep the collection.

"Why don't we wait until we hear from Ms. Ruddle," Bertie said.

"Wills can take a long time to sort out," Norman said, "although as Mr. Ruddle has only one blood relative, we assume that will not be the case here. And then we'll have another round of inspections and negotiations over the collection. All of which is simply delaying the inevitable. We would like you to withdraw yourself from the running."

High above our heads, Charles's tail swished back and forth. Back and forth.

"Why on earth would I do that?" Bertie said. "But first, let me say this conversation is in extremely poor taste. The man died two days ago. His granddaughter is grieving."

Norman straightened his tie. "His granddaughter is about to be charged with the murder."

Bertie gasped. Her eyes flew to me. I gave my head another shake.

"And as your library is implicated—"

"Preposterous."

"—we're prepared to offer you a tidy sum to thank you for your trouble," Elizabeth said.

"If Julia Ruddle is charged," I said, "then won't any will leaving his estate to her be null and void?"

"Not necessarily," Elizabeth said. "As she is his only living relative, the bulk of his estate will go to her even in the absence of a will or concerns over the cause of his death. We believe

Ms. Ruddle will be happy to have the collection taken off her hands. It was her grandfather's last wish, after all."

"I still don't see why you're talking to me about this," Bertie said, "and not to Ms. Ruddle."

"We're asking you to take your . . . library out of the running, Ms. James. We'll pay you for your inconvenience, and the path for Ms. Ruddle will be clear."

"You're making a lot of assumptions," Bertie said.

Norman straightened his tie. "Always best to be ahead of the game. We all know Blacklock College is the natural home for the Ruddle collection. Our North Carolina History Department is without equal, and we don't"—he glanced toward the shelf—"allow felines anywhere near valuable artifacts. Will a thousand dollars do it?"

Bertie laughed.

"We're authorized to go to two thousand," Elizabeth said. "And not a penny more. All we ask is a simple phone call from you to Ms. Ruddle, telling her you've decided you can't assume the responsibly of the collection."

Bertie got to her feet. "This conversation is over."

I opened the door for our visitors.

"Can we trust that you'll think about it?" Norman said.

"You can trust that I think that's about the rudest offer I've ever had," Bertie said. "Good day."

They stood up. Charles braced himself to leap off the shelf. I braced myself to intercept flying claws. Norman headed for the door, but Elizabeth leaned over Bertie's desk. "The man died here, in your little public library. And today you have people in costume running through the place. I saw a woman give a child a candy, of all things! He grabbed it with his sticky fingers. Never mind a cat wandering at will. The Lighthouse Library is no home for something as valuable as the Ruddle collection. I made you a generous offer, Ms. James. I withdraw it, but I can assure you that I'll see your entire rare books collection removed, if I have to. Imagine, a library in a lighthouse! You have no idea how to care for historic and priceless documents. A man died in here, for goodness sake."

"And that wasn't the first time either," Norman said.

"Get out." Rage flashed behind Bertie's eyes. She was a part-time yoga instructor, into careful breathing, relaxation, and thoughtful contemplation. The picture behind her desk was intended to spread an aura of peace and goodwill throughout the room. Today, it failed to have the desired effect.

"We'll find our way out," Elizabeth said. She looked straight into my eyes as she passed. "Norman, can you remind me what happened to the Jane Austin first editions when they were on loan here?"

"Stolen," he said with a sad shake of his head.

"They were all recovered," I said. "In perfect condition."

"You were most fortunate," Elizabeth said. "That time."

Chapter Eleven

I thought steam might rise from the top of Bertie's head.

But it didn't, and she and I, accompanied by Charles, followed the couple from Blacklock College to the front door. Not from any desire on our part to be polite, but to ensure they left the premises without pocketing any goods or peeking into corners in search of incriminating evidence.

"Was that weird, or what?" I said, as we watched their car disappear between the tall pines. I rubbed the top of Charles's head. *Good cat!* He'd refrained from sinking his claws into our visitors. That would have been satisfying to see, but we didn't need a lawsuit.

"It was weird, all right," Bertie said. "Subtlety is not their middle name. Today's Charlene's day off, and Ronald has a children's program later. Tomorrow, you and I are going to Blacklock College."

"Why?"

"I can't truly say. To dig up the dirt maybe. If there is any dirt to dig. Those two are academics; maybe they aren't aware of how offensive they've been."

"They know," I said.

"I was trying to give them the benefit of the doubt. I want to find out what, if anything, is going on at that college."

We went back to work. Ronald took his lunch break, and I set about tidying the library after the hordes of children and parents had passed through. When everything was once again (temporarily) to my satisfaction and no one needed my help, I went outside to check my phone. Cell phone signals have trouble penetrating the thick stone walls of the library. Sometimes they get through, and sometimes they don't. I haven't yet determined what's the deciding factor—other than the more important the call, the less likely it is to work.

The minute I stepped outside into the warm fresh air, my phone beeped. Julia had left a message on my voicemail, asking me to call her back.

I did so, and she answered on the first ring.

"Hope you don't mind," she said, her voice low and hesitant, "but you did say I could ask you if I needed anything."

"I'm happy to help."

"Will you have dinner with us tonight?"

"Dinner?"

"If you don't have plans, that is."

"No, I don't have plans." I'd gone outside to check my phone, sort of hoping while at the same time sort of not hoping to hear from Connor.

"Great. I'm sick of this hotel. Do you know a nice restaurant? Dinner's on me."

"Jake's Seafood Bar is good, and not too far."

"I'll make a reservation for seven o'clock. Is that too early?"

"No, seven is fine. Will anyone else be joining us?"

"Greg, of course."

Of course.

"I asked your friend Theodore also," Julia said. "He's so sweet. He said he'd be delighted."

I bet he was.

"And . . . uh . . ."

"Yes?" I asked.

"My mother." Julia gave a laugh that came out more like a strangled choke. "I need all the backup I can get. Gotta run. See you at seven." She hung up.

I stared at the phone. Julia needed people around her when she met with her mother? That didn't sound good.

As long as I had phone in hand, I sent Connor a text.

Sorry bout last night. I heard press conf went well.

I waited for a response, but nothing came.

I told myself I wasn't too disappointed, and went back to work.

* * *

I must have checked my phone about twenty times that afternoon. Eventually a message came. Not a text, but a voicemail.

"Hey, Lucy," Connor said. "I can't talk for long. It's been a crazy day so far, and likely to get even crazier. I'd like to make up for missing last night, but tonight I have a retired fishermen's dinner group to meet. You don't want to come, believe me. All that bunch are going to expect me to do is listen to their stories about how great everything was in the old days. I keep telling myself, not much longer and all this will be over."

His voice, I thought, sounded beyond tired.

"How about an early breakfast tomorrow? The forecast looks clear. I'll pick you up, and we can go to the beach and watch the sun rise. I'll bring a picnic."

I felt myself smiling. What a good idea.

"I'll be on the hop all day. I'm only able to make this call because Dorothy thinks I needed to use the men's room, and she can't follow me in there. The advantage of a female campaign manager. Send me a text, yea or nay." Long pause. "Oh, and thanks for the tip about Doug and Jay Ruddle. I hadn't heard that they had any relationship at all. Dorothy's looking into it." He paused and then said very quickly, "Do you know that I love you?" The message clicked off.

I sucked in a breath. He'd used the L word. It was the first time it had been spoken between us.

My heart pounded. Whether with fear or exultation, I didn't know.

* * *

Louise Jane came in as the last patron was leaving and I was about to lock the door. "Oh, good, you're still here."

"It's closing time," I said. "I have an appointment in town." I had learned not long after my arrival not to beat about the bush with Louise Jane.

"Won't be long." Louise Jane had learned not long after my arrival not to pay attention to anything I said. "I wanted to check on *Rebecca*. You are taking care of her, aren't you, Lucy?"

"Of course we are," I said. "It's a marvelous piece of work."

"It's much more than that." She studied the model ship. "Why's the captain on the lower deck?"

"I don't know."

She picked up the little figure. "He should be on the quarterdeck. Along with George."

"George?"

"The cat." She arranged the figures the way she wanted them. Charles jumped up to have a look. He hissed at George.

"That's not really his name," I said.

"It is," Louise Jane said. "It's a matter of historical record. Captain Clark mentioned the cat in his letters home. He named the cat after the king. George II at the time."

"Wasn't that a bit *lèse-majesté*?"

"There's a reason Captain Clark and his ship and crew—and cat—have never found rest. Insulting the king was the least of their transgressions." She changed the subject so abruptly, I almost fell off the train of conversation. "I hear you're investigating the death of Jay Ruddle."

"I am not. And where did you hear that?"

"Martha Kowalski and Ellen O'Malley have been asking questions about Jay's past of people who remember him. My grandmother, prominent among them. I assume you put them up to it."

"Is Martha Kowalski Teddy's mom?"

"Yes."

"I might have suggested it was something to look into. I hear Jay made enemies back in the day."

Louise Jane sniffed. "That's an understatement. To hear my grandmother talk, he was the devil incarnate."

"Was she here on Saturday for your lecture?"

"No, and that's just as well. Or she'd be on the suspect list."

"What did he do to her?"

"Nothing. But Grandmama is awful loyal to the Outer Banks, no one more so. Jay Ruddle destroyed the livelihoods of many local families and then, worst sin of all, he upped and moved to New York City. I wonder . . ." Her voice trailed off.

Despite myself I had to ask. "Wonder what?"

"If it wasn't *someone* who wanted Jay dead, but *something*."

"You mean . . ."

"Not only the living are proud Bankers, Lucy. Jay was alone in the lighthouse on the second level when he died. As far as I know, the lighthouse isn't haunted by anyone who died in the last fifty years, but it is possible."

"It isn't haunted by anyone, Louise Jane."

"So you keep saying, Lucy, dear." She turned to look at me. Her eyes were dark and her face serious. I sometimes wondered if Louise Jane believed all the stories she told me, or was just having fun teasing me (and trying to chase me away). Being the storyteller gave her a lot of cachet in the community. As proved by the turnout for her Saturday lecture. But right now, standing here in the empty library, I felt a chill run up my spine. Charles had disappeared.

"It is something to consider," she said slowly. "There might be spirits at work here who've been forgotten. Such as the woman who died back in the 1990s."

"Bertie says that story isn't true."

"Which proves my point. She's been forgotten." Louise Jane picked up the little captain and studied him. "I wonder what stories you can tell, my friend. What do you see when the lights are out and silence descends? Even if no one lingers in the lighthouse who knew Jay, personally or by reputation, when they were living, some of the old ones might have sensed he was not a friend of the Outer Banks."

"I am not going to debate what old ones that might be," I said. "But Jay was a friend of the Outer Banks. He was going to give his historical collection to the library. Along with adequate funds to build and maintain a home for it."

"That's it!" She slapped her forehead.

"That's what?"

"The reason he died. His bequest would have made considerable changes to the library. The old ones wouldn't stand for that. They don't like change."

"Wow! That's totally believable, Louise Jane. You'd better take that theory to Detective Watson immediately."

"Your skepticism does you credit, Lucy, but someday it's going to trip you up. And I'll be watching." She returned the skeletal captain to his quarterdeck and left the library.

Chapter Twelve

Jake's Seafood Bar is rapidly becoming one of the hottest restaurants on the Outer Banks. The down-home North Carolina cooking can't be beat, and neither can the view. Set far back from the Croatan Highway, the restaurant overlooks the calm waters of Roanoke Sound and the twinkling lights of Roanoke Island beyond.

"Your party's here, Lucy," the hostess said to me as I arrived. "Follow me, please."

We walked through the dining room, past the fishing motif decorations, and kept going. We were heading outside, and I was pleased about that. Not many outdoor evenings remained, and I wanted to take advantage of every one. Jake's is a casual place, so I hadn't gone to much trouble to dress up, and wore jeans and a loose, comfortable blouse topped with a colorful scarf. In hopes of sitting outside, I'd pulled on thick socks and sneakers and carried a heavy sweater.

The patio was about half full, as could be expected at this time of year. Candles nestled in hurricane lamps shone on every table, and round white globe lamps hung from posts and the roof of the bar. The sun had set, and the lights from buildings on Roanoke Island and boats in the Sound twinkled in the clear air. The fourth-order lens of the Roanoke Marshes Lighthouse, a modern reproduction, flashed in the distance.

Julia, Theodore, and Greg were seated at a table for six next to the railing. Five places had been set for dinner.

Julia waved when she saw me crossing the deck. Theodore politely rose to his feet, and after a moment's hesitation Greg followed. Unexpectedly, Theodore greeted me with a fierce hug. He was not usually the hugging type.

All was explained when he mumbled in my ear. "I've learned something extremely important for our investigation. We can't talk here."

He released me, and I slipped into the chair next to him. "Isn't it a gorgeous evening?" I said.

Julia had taken the seat at the head of the table, with Theodore and Greg on either side of her. "Lovely," she said. "I was telling Greg earlier that I might think about buying a vacation property in the Outer Banks."

Theodore's face lit with such a glow, it put the Roanoke Marshes Lighthouse to shame. "That would be marvelous!"

"Early days yet," said Greg, the wet blanket. "Can we first sort out our more immediate problems?"

"I hope I can still plan ahead," Julia said. Her face was wrapped in shadow, dragging down her cheekbones and adding to the dark circles under her eyes. She wore a pair of brown corduroy slacks with a navy-blue blouse and brown sweater, causing her to disappear further into the shadows.

"Of course you can," Theodore said. "I'd be delighted to help you tour properties. I know many of the best locations."

"I'm sure you do," Greg said.

"Can I get you anything to drink, Lucy?" the waiter asked.

I looked around the table. A martini glass sat in front of Greg: clear liquid, two olives on a cocktail stick. Theodore had a mug of beer; and Julia, wine. "A glass of Sauvignon Blanc, please."

"We don't have to talk about it, if you don't want to," I said, "but did you hear from the police today?"

Greg grunted, and Julia dipped her head. "Detective Watson came to the hotel around five. All the same questions about all the things I've already told him."

"He's fishing," Greg said. "He's got nothing, and he's trying to pin the killing on Julia to cover up for his own incompetence."

"Please don't say that," she said. "That can't be true."

"It's routine for them to keep asking the same questions," I said. And I know of which I speak. I too have been a suspect in a murder inquiry. It isn't fun.

"He won't be doing any more random digging," Greg said. "I told Watson, Julia has nothing more to say to him until her lawyer arrives. And that will be first thing tomorrow morning."

"Don't you worry, Julia," Theodore said. "Lucy's investigating possible leads. She has recently learned of something that might prove to be highly significant." He couldn't help throwing a smirk across the table at Greg.

"What's that, Lucy?" Julia asked.

"She can't talk about it yet," Theodore said. "It's still too early to go public."

Greg threw back his martini, and I didn't bother to say I'd learned nothing of the kind. Julia turned to Theodore with a grateful smile.

I leaned back to allow the waiter to put my drink in front of me. "Are you still wanting to wait for the rest of your party to arrive?" he asked.

Julia sighed. "Yes, please. Promptness is not one of my mother's virtues, I'm sorry to say . . ." Her voice trailed off. "That's what I remember anyway."

A kitchen helper placed a heaping platter of hush puppies in the center of the table. "I told Jake you were here, Lucy," the waiter said, "and he sent these out with his compliments."

"Mmm," I said. "My favorite. Thanks."

Julia eyed the lumps of fried dough suspiciously. "What are they?"

"Hush puppies," I said. "If you move to the Outer Banks, even as a summer resident, you'll be eating them all the time. I can't get enough of them. And Jake's are just about the best around." I picked up one of the hot, delicious balls of crispy batter with my fingers and dunked it into the small bowl of spicy dipping sauce provided. I bit half of it off and chewed. Pure Southern bliss.

Julia took one and nibbled tentatively. "They are good."

"Definitely not recommended for anyone on a diet." I popped the second half into my mouth.

Greg tasted one. He tried not to look as though he was enjoying it too much.

Theodore dug in with enthusiasm and was soon licking dipping sauce off his fingers.

"When do you start your new job, Greg?" I asked, simply trying to make polite conversation.

"New job? Oh, my new job. That's on hold for the time being. I have to see Julia through this. It wouldn't be fair for me to leave her in the lurch."

"That's thoughtful of your *new employer*," Theodore said. "They're not usually so accommodating." He turned to me and his right eyelid twitched. *Was that supposed to be a wink?* His voice had taken on a strange tone.

"I don't think my employment situation is any of your concern, buddy," Greg said.

"I'm only expressing polite interest. You must be lucky with this *new employer*."

Another attempt at a wink.

"Are you implying something?" Greg asked.

Julia looked from one man to the other as though they were playing tennis.

"Not at all," Theodore said. "If it's inconvenient for you to delay the start of your new job, I'm more than happy to step in. I'm self-employed; my time is my own. You wouldn't want to lose this opportunity, would you? If you gave up the position of Mr. Ruddle's curator, this new job must be an excellent one."

"I can decide for myself, thanks anyway, buddy. Right now, Julia's welfare has to be my primary concern."

"That's so nice of you." The fair Julia turned her smile on Greg and placed her hand on his. Teddy stared at their joined hands as though trying to summon a death ray.

"Detective Watson told Julia not to leave Dare County," Theodore said. "Did he tell you the same, Greg?"

Greg opened his mouth to reply, and judging by the look on his face, it wouldn't have been polite, but he was interrupted by the waiter asking if we wanted more drinks. Because I was driving, I asked for an iced tea, but the others ordered another round.

"Perhaps we shouldn't wait much longer. It's not good to drink on an empty stomach," said Theodore, who'd finished off the hush puppies single-handedly.

Julia glanced at her watch. "I told Anna dinner was at six thirty, assuming she'd be half an hour late. It's almost seven thirty."

"Is Anna your mother?" I asked. "You call her by her first name?"

"We're not close. To put it mildly. I hope she'll recognize me."

"Recognize you? When was the last time you were together?" That was absolutely none of my business, but how could I not ask?

Julia shrugged. "I'm not entirely sure. I remember that she missed my college graduation. She was touring in Europe, I think. Or that might have been the time she was in rehab."

Theodore and I exchanged a look.

I wouldn't say my mom and I were close, but I'd last seen her over the summer when she hurried down to the Outer Banks with the intention of dragging me back to Boston to marry the man the family expected me to.

Obviously, her plan had not worked (as I was still here), but we kept in touch via email and a weekly phone call. I'd last heard from her the day before yesterday, when she'd told me she was excited about Josie's announcement and was hoping she and I could go shopping together for suitable winter wedding wear.

Shopping, for my mother, if not for me, was a bonding experience.

"That might be her now," Julia said, and we all turned.

The hostess was coming onto the deck, carrying menus. A man and a woman walked behind her. Or rather, the man walked. The woman swept.

She wore a black wool cape fastened with fire-engine-red frogs. As she moved, the cape swirled around her long legs, and the scarlet satin lining flashed. Curly black hair tumbled around her shoulders. Long silver earrings hung from her ears, and a necklace of beaten silver rings flashed at her throat. Her dress was pure white and very tight, the décolletage deep and the hemline short. Four-inch high heels tapped across the deck, and I feared for the old wooden planks.

"My mother," Julia mumbled. She stood up.

Anna gathered Julia into her arms. "My darling. *Moya dorogaya.* My baby. Don't worry about a thing. Mama is here." Her accent was deep. Eastern European, I guessed. Maybe Russian. Theodore, Greg, and I had also risen to our feet. We stared. Theodore and Greg's mouths hung open, and I'm pretty sure mine did also.

"Hi," the man said. "I'm Dave. Dave White. Anna's husband." Dave had a Midwestern accent, short gray hair, and a goatee streaked black and sliver. He was in his mid to late fifties, about the same as Anna. Whereas she looked like she was on her way to opening night at the Met, he was casually dressed in jeans and a checked shirt.

Theodore, Greg, and I closed our mouths.

"Sorry we're late," Dave said, "but Anna couldn't find the

necklace she wanted to wear. You'd think she'd be used to living out of a suitcase, wouldn't you." He turned to the hovering waiter. "Thanks, pal. I'll have a bottle of Bud. An old-fashioned for the lady."

Anna and Julia broke apart, Julia looking somewhat stunned.

"You brought friends. How charming." Anna beamed at Theodore and Greg. She extended her hand, first to Greg and then to Theodore. Her fingernails were cut short, but freshly manicured and painted the same color as the lining of her cape.

Her smile faded as she turned to me. "Hello." Her eyes were the same shade of light blue as Julia's.

"Hi," I said. "I'm Lucy. Pleased to meet you."

"I'm sure you are." She looked at the table. "Only five places set? Tell the waiter to bring another setting, Lucy."

That puts me in my place.

Anna fluffed her cape and took the chair at the foot of the table, opposite Julia. Dave sat next to Greg, across from me, and we all resumed our seats. Greg took a long glug of his martini.

"So," Anna said, "Jay Ruddle kicked the bucket at last."

Greg spat out a mouthful of martini.

"Isn't that a bit harsh?" Julia said.

"Is that not a saying you Americans use?"

"Yes, but . . ."

Anna turned to me. "I believe in speaking my mind at all times, Lucy. I hope you'll agree that honestly is always the best way, particularly among friends."

"Uh . . . ," I said.

"I see I am among friends. Jay Ruddle might have told lies about me to my beloved late husband, forced us apart, stolen the affection of my only daughter, ruthlessly driven me from her life, and spread hurtful rumors about me to those who laughingly call me their peers, but we will talk about all that no longer." The waiter placed her drink in front of her. "Excellent. Thank you so much, young man."

"Are you ready to order?" he asked.

"Certainly not," Anna said. "I have only just arrived. I will inform you when I am ready to order." She took a long sip of her drink. "Jay Ruddle has gone to what my grandmother would have called . . ." She finished the sentence in a language I didn't understand.

"What does that mean?" Theodore asked Dave.

"Haven't a clue. The only Russian I speak is what's called pillow talk." He laughed and lifted his beer bottle in a salute. "Cheers!"

"You and Grandfather had your differences," Julia said. "He would have interpreted his actions a different way. I hope you're not here to gloat."

"Gloat! Certainly not. I am here to provide you with comfort and to help you through the grieving process." Anna almost gritted her teeth. "I know you and Jay were . . . uh . . . fond of each other."

"I loved my grandfather a great deal."

"And so you should. Regardless of all his faults—"

"Anna," Julia warned.

"—he loved you."

"Thank you." Julia relaxed fractionally.

"Although he loved no one else, and few loved him. It would

appear that at the end of his days, there was someone who didn't love him at all."

"What do you mean by that?" Julia asked, her voice rising.

"Someone killed him, didn't they? Those were not the actions of a friend." Anna sipped her drink. "Although sometimes they can be that of a lover."

"Do you know something about Jay's death?" Greg said.

"Me? I know nothing that is not common knowledge. We were stuck at the airport in Atlanta for a ridiculous amount of time. Something about a storm in the Midwest. Aren't they always having storms in the Midwest? Why the airlines haven't allowed for that by now, I do not understand. The news was playing on the TV in the bar in which we took shelter. Tell these nice people what we saw, David. I am far too upset to repeat it."

He put down his beer. "The news report said your grandfather had been murdered, Julia. And it also reported that, I'm sorry to say, you're a person of interest in the police investigation."

"Gross exaggeration," Theodore said.

"If they don't withdraw that insinuation, we'll sue them for all they're worth," Greg said.

"Imagine, my own daughter on the TV," Anna said. "Like a common criminal. Next time, Julia, try to fix your hair before the cameras arrive."

"I'll remember that," Julia said.

"Do you have a lawyer?" Dave asked.

"The firm arranged one," Greg answered. "He's arriving tomorrow."

"I hope he is the best," Anna said. "Never mind the expense."

"Easy to say when you're not paying his fee." Julia opened her menu. "I'm starving. You might have arrived late, Anna, but we've been here for ages, and I'm going to order."

*   *   *

Dinner passed without further incident. Anna did most of the talking. And she talked mostly about Anna. She had been in Europe, I understood, touring. I attempted to ask what she was touring as (it had to do with something musical I guessed), but I soon came to realize that I was expected to know that.

Dave and Greg talked to each other about sports. They both seemed to be fans of the New York Islanders and were looking forward to the upcoming hockey season. Theodore, who was no sports fan, attempted to participate in the men's conversation but was soon left far behind.

Julia stirred her food around on her plate and said little.

At last the waiter brought the bill. He hesitated for a moment, unsure of whom to give it to. Dave jerked his head in Julia's direction.

"Where are you staying, my darling?" Anna asked.

"The Ocean Side Hotel." Julia picked up the bill. Theodore reached for his wallet, but she said, "Dinner's my treat. You've all been so kind, it's the least I can do to say thank you."

"Such a lovely establishment," Anna said. "Much nicer than the unpleasant place David found for us." She named a run-down hotel that wasn't much above the level of a motel on the interstate. Anna turned to her husband. "It is too late tonight, but we will move there tomorrow."

"You don't have to," Julia said.

Anna waved a hand. "I only wish to be close to you, *moya dorogaya*, should you need anything. Paying hotels is so tedious. David, be sure they put our charges on Jay's bill." She pushed her chair back and rose to her feet in a sleek red, white, and black wave. "This has been such a pleasure. We will meet tomorrow for breakfast at the Ocean Side at 9:30. David, be sure and set the alarm."

"Will do."

"It is so tedious trying to adapt to time changes." She rounded the table and enveloped Julia in a hug. When they broke away, she smiled at Greg. "You needn't change your room arrangements to accommodate Julia's mother."

He looked baffled. "Why would I do that?"

Anna laughed lightly. "Modern times, my dear."

"Huh?"

Julia blushed to the roots of her hair. "My sleeping arrangements are none of your business. But if you must know, and in order to avoid further misunderstanding, we're here on business. Greg is . . . was . . . Grandfather's assistant."

"I hope I'm more than that to you, Julia," Greg said.

Anna turned to Theodore. "Surely not you?"

"I'm Julia's friend. Although, I must say, in the short time I've come to know her, I've—"

"Theodore and I are locals," I interrupted. "We live here. Nice meeting you."

Anna pecked Julia on the cheek. She gave Greg a long hug, ignored Theodore, mumbled good night at me, and swept away. Dave followed in her wake like a dinghy attached to the stern of an ocean liner.

Julia let out a long puff of air. "Now you've all met my mother. And I have to have breakfast at ten thirty."

"She said nine thirty," Theodore said.

"Which, if I'm lucky, will be ten thirty," Julia said. "Practically lunch time for me. My grandfather was an early riser, and that's a habit he instilled in me from a young age."

"What does she do?" I asked. "I didn't quite catch it. Something about touring in Europe?"

Julia picked up her bag. "Anna Makarova is a classical violinist."

"Impressive," I said.

"It might have been, once. She's been fired from more orchestras than I can name. Even as classical violinists go, she's too temperamental and unreliable to hold down a job. By touring, I assume she was playing with a third- or fourth-rate orchestra in some former Soviet backwater."

"How long have she and Dave been married?" Greg asked.

"I have absolutely no idea. Never heard of him before. Her last husband's name was Edward. I think it was Edward. Maybe Edgar."

We collected our things and began walking toward the door.

"Still," I said, "Even though you two are not close"—to put it mildly—"it was nice of her to drop whatever she was doing and come here to offer you her support."

"Her support?" Julia said. "As if. She's here because she's hoping for a share of my expected inheritance."

Chapter Thirteen

I n the parking lot of Jake's, Theodore offered to give Julia a ride back to the Ocean Side. Considering that she'd come with Greg, and they were staying at the same hotel, she declined with a light kiss on his cheek. He stood next to his car, under the bright lights, waving until their car had merged into traffic.

"Okay," I said. "Spill."

"Spill what? I never for one moment thought she and Greg were . . . uh . . . rooming together. Still it was nice to have it confirmed wasn't it? Isn't Anna charming? Can't beat those old-world manners, can you?"

Charming wasn't the word I'd use, but I let that go. "You said you had something to tell me privately. I assume it's to do with Greg."

"Oh, right. Meeting Julia's mother drove that completely from my mind." He gave me a big grin: the cat that found the cream bowl unattended. "Greg Summers didn't voluntarily leave Jay's employ. He was fired. He might not even have another job to go to."

"What makes you think that?"

He tapped the side of his nose. "You asked me to do some digging, Lucy. And so I did. The world of collecting is a small one. I don't specialize in historical documents, but I know plenty of fellows, and some women, who do. I send business their way, and if they hear of an item that might be of interest to me, they—"

"Yes, yes. Get to the point, please."

"I'm simply explaining how these things work, Lucy. I mentioned on some of the collecting list servs that I'd been offered a bound collection of captain's logs from an eighteenth-century trading vessel and wondered who might be interested in bidding on it, and I got some queries. I asked about the Ruddle collection, and that's where it got interesting." He paused, waiting for me to reply.

I did so. "And?"

"And that began an entirely different thread. Jay Ruddle, so I was told, no longer wanted the responsibility for his collection, nor did he want it to remain in private hands. He decided, very admirably, I thought, that it should be available to the history-loving public. He was searching for a home for it. His curator, Greg Summers, was assigned to assist in that search and told he'd no longer be needed once the collection had moved."

"That's not being fired," I said. "He was told his job was being made redundant, but he was given plenty of responsibilities in the meantime. He wasn't kicked out onto the curb."

"Greg lied."

"He told a story to save face, more likely."

"Don't you see, Lucy? If Greg didn't leave his position voluntarily in order to take another job, then we have to ask if he had reason to want Jay Ruddle dead. The collection might not be given away after all. Julia now has control of it. Presumably, she'll need a curator. I wonder if she's aware of the real story. Should I tell her, Lucy?"

"Absolutely not. Yes, we're trying to help her with the matter of her grandfather's death, but you don't want her to think you've been poking into her family's affairs. Remember when I said don't hover?"

He nodded.

"That's worse."

He nodded again.

"Good night, Theodore," I said.

"Do you think it's important? What I learned? About Greg, I mean. I told you he couldn't be trusted."

I didn't answer. I said good night again and went to my car. *Did I think it was important?*

Absolutely.

Chapter Fourteen

The driveway to the lighthouse is long and dark, but I'm always cheered by the light over the door and the intermittent flash of the 1000-watt bulb welcoming me home.

I parked my car by the path and got out. I held my keys in my hand and walked slowly, thinking about what Teddy had told me. Greg had jumped to the top of my suspect list. If I had a suspect list. Which I did not.

Sam Watson was always telling me not to interfere in his investigations, but that was proving as impossible in this case as it had the other times. What Detective Watson didn't understand was that I heard things by virtue of *not* being a cop. Watson wouldn't hang around book collector message boards, gathering and spreading gossip, and he wouldn't be invited to dinner to meet Julia's mother. It's possible Julia wouldn't even tell him about the relationship (the non-relationship) she had with her mother, and Watson might not think to ask.

The night air was crisp, cool, and fresh. I took a deep breath. Something in the corner of my eye caught my attention, and

I glanced toward the boardwalk that wandered through the marsh.

I sucked in a breath.

Where I stood, in the shadows of the lighthouse, the air was clear. In the distance, mist, as delicate as gossamer wings, spun through the air, and colored lights—green, blue, and yellow—hovered a foot or so above the ground. There might have been ten of them; there might have been twenty or more. The lights faded almost to nothing and then grew strong again. The mist swirled around them.

No cars other than mine were in the parking lot, and these weren't flashlights at any rate. No hands held the lights, and the glow they cast was soft, almost insubstantial.

I took a step forward. And then another. The lights retreated. Another step. The lights retreated some more. The mist grew stronger as I ventured close, until I was walking through it, and the ground was soft, and I could no longer see where my feet touched the solid earth.

The lights drifted on the mist. The distance between us didn't decrease, even though I was walking toward them.

Another step forward. The lights beckoned to me.

Bracebridge Hall. The story of the marsh candles. Corpse candles, they were sometimes called, or will-o-the-wisps. Luring the innocent to their death.

I gathered every bit of courage I had, and I turned and ran. The bright white light over the front door shone clear and strong and welcoming. The lighthouse lamp came on, and I could see the path laid down in front of me. I stumbled up the steps and reached the door. My hands shook so badly, I could barely get the key into the lock. At last the door opened, and I fell into the library. I slammed the door behind me and stood with my back against it, heart pounding.

Charles strolled out from under the desk. He stretched mightily and then eyed me. His fur lay flat across his back, and his spine wasn't arched. He turned around and headed for the stairs, knowing it was bedtime.

I tiptoed to the window and peered out. The light high above me was in its dormancy period, and I saw nothing but darkness.

Ghostly lights. Will-o'-the-wisps. No such thing.

That silly Washington Irving story was having far too much of an effect on me. "And you are not helping," I said to the cardboard gravestone propped up against the wall next to my feet.

Charles meowed, telling me to hurry up.

And so I did.

* * *

I woke early the next morning with a sense of delightful anticipation.

This was the day of my picnic breakfast with Connor, and I was feeling good about it.

As I'd prepared for bed last night, I'd ordered myself to put the "ghostly lights" out of my mind. Something must have been happening up in the sky last night that threw light into the marsh: a low hanging satellite or maybe military helicopters on maneuvers. Even an alien invasion would be more believable than fairy fire and marsh candles.

My subconscious, inspired by some of the stories I'd been

reading and the approach of Halloween, had simply taken what I'd seen and made me believe those lights were attempting to lure me to my doom.

"Ridiculous," I said to Charles.

I'd taken his meow as agreement and put on the kettle. I made myself a cup of hot tea, sat at the table, pushed aside ghostly stories as well as thoughts of the murder of Jay Ruddle, and tried to sort out my feelings for Connor.

I came to the conclusion that I was spending too much time trying to sort out my feelings for Connor. I liked him, and he liked me. He'd said he loved me, and that had frightened me, but there are many depths and degrees of love. Did I love him in return?

Yes, I did. I thought I did.

Did I love him enough to want to spend the rest of my life with him?

It didn't matter if I did or not. That wasn't on the table. Not yet.

Was I rushing things mentally? Getting ahead of myself?

Yes.

Nothing wrong with dating and getting to know someone slowly.

We had plenty of time. I'd gone to sleep looking forward to sunrise at the beach, good food, and great company.

When I woke, it was still dark, and my thick drapes were drawn against the force of the lighthouse beam. I switched on the bedside lamp and leapt out of bed.

Charles groaned, put one paw over his eyes, and rolled over.

Charles is not a morning cat.

I showered and tied my hair into a high ponytail. I added a touch of pale pink gloss to my lips, but no other makeup was needed for the beach. It would be cool until the sun was fully up, so I dressed in jeans and a thick sweater. At five thirty, I ran down the twisting iron staircase to the bottom level. Round and round I went.

I love the library—any library—at any time of day, but there's something truly magical about a library, any library, empty at night. The books standing silent in their rows, the shelves straight, the chairs waiting. I could almost sense the anticipation in the air as another day approached. Books love to be read. Books need to be read. Otherwise, they crumble to dust, and generations of pleasure, knowledge, and creativity are lost.

"Back soon," I whispered, as though the books could hear me. Sometimes, I thought maybe they did.

I peeked out the window. I told myself I wasn't checking for ghostly horses or flickering candles, but I was glad to see nothing but a star-sprinkled sky. As I watched, a thin line of bright light broke through the trees lining the driveway. The approaching headlights of a modern, practical, down-to-earth, twenty-first-century automobile.

I slipped outside and locked the door behind me as Connor's BMW pulled up. I ran to the car and jumped in.

"Good morning, Lucy," he said. He leaned over, restrained by his seat belt, and gave me a kiss on the lips. I returned it and then fastened my own belt.

"This is such a great idea," I said.

"Not too early?"

"Absolutely not. There are plenty of stars overhead, so that means clear skies. We'll get a good sunrise." My lighthouse window faced east, so I could watch the sun rise over the ocean any time I wanted, but there was something special about doing it with a friend and making an occasion of it. I thought about asking Connor if he'd heard any stories of ghostly horses in the marsh or strange lights, but bit my tongue. It seemed so foolish in the fresh air of a new day.

By the time we made the five-minute journey to the parking lot of Coquina Beach, the sky to the east was lightening. Connor handed me a blanket and then lifted a basket out of the trunk. The blanket was pure wool, thick and heavy, in a pattern of red and green stripes, and the basket was exactly like a picnic basket featured in romantic movies. Square and sturdy, made of wicker, with flip-up handles and a padded gingham lining.

We slipped off our shoes and walked through the dunes and sea grass to emerge on the beach. Gray light caressed the still ocean, but the sun had yet to make its appearance.

A group of joggers ran past, not even sparing us a glance, and further down the beach, fishermen were setting up their poles. Once the runners passed, Connor and I were alone.

I spread the blanket, and Connor put the basket on it. We sat down, and he opened the basket with a flourish and a cry of "Ta-da!" He pulled out cloth napkins and two glass flutes. "Champagne, Madam?"

"For breakfast?" I laughed. "What an indulgence."

"Heavily dosed with orange juice." Out came a mini bottle of sparkling wine. He pulled out the cork, poured a mouthful into each glass, and topped them with orange juice.

"To victory," I said.

"To it being over," he said.

We drank.

He settled back onto the blanket and let out a long breath. He'd dressed casually in chinos and a T-shirt. He looked, I thought, exhausted. He closed his eyes, and I studied his handsome face. New lines had appeared in the delicate skin around his mouth and his eyes. He hadn't shaved yet today, and the dark stubble was thick on his jaw.

"I'm not asleep," he said.

I laughed. Yes, sleepy or not, I did love this man's company. "You must be tired."

"Tired, invigorated. Bored to tears, exhilarated beyond belief. Bursting with enthusiasm and energy, and asleep on my feet. Two minutes from one to the other. A political campaign is like nothing else on earth." He opened his eyes. "It's not for everyone."

"No."

"As much as I'd love to sit here all day, just you and me, I have to get back to pressing the flesh and kissing babies, and you have a job to do. Let's eat."

He sat up, and out of the depths of the basket he brought a checked tablecloth and two sets of plastic dishes. He arranged smoked salmon and pâté and an assortment of cheeses, grapes, and nuts. Next came a baguette and a big bread knife. He sliced thick chunks off the loaf. It was so fresh and warm, I could smell it.

"Is that from Josie's?" I asked.

"I threw myself on your cousin's better nature and convinced her to open early for one special customer. When you've finished your mimosa, I have something else she provided."

He produced a thermos and two plastic mugs. He twisted the top off the thermos and the scent of hot coffee hit me.

"Heaven! Connor McNeil, I think you might be the perfect man."

The corners of his mouth turned up. "My mother would agree with you on a good day, but no one else."

"It's going to be a lovely sunrise," I said. "The sky's completely clear."

We nibbled on cheese and bread, pâté and crackers, sipped coffee, and chatted about nothing of consequence.

A group of women, dressed in form-fitting shirts and black leggings, passed at the waterline, walking fast, backs straight, arms pumping.

"Morning, Mr. Mayor," one of them called.

Connor lifted his hand.

She pulled her phone out of the small pack tied around her waist, lifted it, and took a picture of us. I tried to smile.

"Good luck in the election," one of her friends called. They walked on.

"Am I going to be in the paper tomorrow?" I asked.

"I didn't recognize her, so she's unlikely to be with the media," he said. "Wouldn't hurt, though. Here I am, relaxing, enjoying the best Nags Head has to offer. It's all part of the job, Lucy."

I didn't say it wasn't part of my job. Instead, I sipped my coffee.

"I heard about Josie and Jake getting engaged," Connor said. "About time too."

The women were specks in the distance. No one else was

anywhere nearby. I helped myself to a plump grape, and Connor drank his coffee. I broke off another grape.

"Are you remembering to get your proper number of servings of fruit and vegetables every day?" I asked.

"What?"

"I bet you're not. I bet you're eating nothing but junk food, when you do bother to eat. You need five to seven servings of fruit and vegetables a day. Here's the first one for today." I pressed the grape to his lips.

He grinned at me. He opened his mouth, and I slipped the grape in. His lips closed on my finger. His eyes stared into mine. They didn't look exhausted any more.

His phone rang.

My hand jerked back.

He swore.

He fumbled in his pocket. "That's Dorothy's ring. I told her emergencies only before nine today. So sorry, Lucy." He pushed the button. "What is it?"

I could hear a woman's voice on the other end of the line. Sharp, urgent.

I crawled to my side of the blanket. I curled my feet up and put my arms around my knees.

The great ball of the sun rose over the watery horizon in a fiery blaze of orange and yellow. I watched it rise alone.

"I'm so sorry, Lucy." Connor began gathering up the remains of our feast. "Dorothy got a heads-up from her contact at the local radio station. Doug will be interviewed on the morning show, and he plans to make insinuations about the death of Jay Ruddle."

"What sort of insinuations?"

"About the library. Not a safe place, etcetera, etcetera. Typical Doug rumor-mongering and muck spreading. I need to have a response ready."

He got to his feet and held out his hand. I let him pull me up. He didn't let go. "I am so sorry," he said again. "Can you forgive me?"

I forced out a smile. "You missed the sunrise."

He turned and looked out to sea. The giant orange ball had crested the horizon. "There'll be other sunrises. The election will be over soon. One way or another."

We walked back to the car, carrying the picnic basket between us. I shouldn't be angry at Connor, but I had to be angry at something. Doug Whiteside was the best choice, but if it wasn't Doug running against Connor, it would be someone else. Being mayor meant a lot to Connor. He loved the job, if not the politicking. He was a good mayor. His love of Nags Head and the Outer Banks was always his first priority, unlike some others. In particular, he was a good friend of our library; he believed in the importance of libraries. In these days of budget cuts and the impetus for everything to be revenue generating, that was important.

Doug Whiteside would see us closed down faster than you could say ticket sales.

"The Ruddle collection would have been a big boost to the library," I said to Connor. "It would be hard even for Doug to argue that it should be closed if we'd been given such a prize."

He turned to me with a smile. "You're not thinking Doug killed Jay, I hope. You considered him those other times, and you were wrong."

"I wasn't wrong, as such; I merely had him among my list of possible suspects. No, I'm not thinking that. Neither Doug nor Bill Hill, his campaign manager. Doug might kill to be mayor, but he doesn't really hate the library. It's a means to an end for him. Talking about shutting it makes him sound like he's protecting the interests of the hardworking taxpayer."

"The hardworking taxpayer who doesn't frequent the library and doesn't have children who do or an elderly parent who needs the library community to keep themselves involved."

"Preaching to the choir, Mr. Mayor."

He flicked the fob on his key, put the basket and blanket into the trunk, and we got into the car. We drove the short distance to the lighthouse in silence.

He pulled up to the path and made no move to get out. I unfastened my seat belt.

"Lucy?"

"Yes?"

"On election night, will you come with me to my party? Victory celebration or otherwise, I'd like you to be with me. Officially, I mean."

"I'd be happy to." I said.

I got out of the BMW and waved goodbye as he drove away.

I'd go to the party. After that? I wasn't sure. Regardless of my feelings for Connor—and sitting there, on the beach, in the breaking dawn, drinking mimosas and laughing, I had truly believed I loved him—I didn't think I could handle the life of a politician's wife.

Posing for pictures in what was supposed to be a private moment. Special times interrupted by breaking news.

No.

Thinking about marrying him before he'd even come close to asking me wasn't jumping the gun. If I didn't plan on a future with Connor, it wasn't fair to him—it wasn't fair to me—to let him think that might eventually be a possibility.

Mood thoroughly spoiled, I went upstairs to get ready for work.

*　*　*

Blacklock College is a little over an hour's drive from Nags Head, situated on the Pasquotank River close to Elizabeth City. Bertie and I left at eight. I didn't say anything about my picnic-on-the-beach breakfast to her, but I warned her about Doug's impending radio interview.

She groaned. "Not that again. The man's like a lion with a thorn in his paw over our library."

"More like a rat."

"That too. I'm not going to listen to the show. Someone will be sure to let me know what he has to say about us."

"I met Julia Ruddle's mother yesterday," I said.

"I thought Julia was an orphan. Wasn't she raised by her grandfather?"

"Her father died when she was young, and she was brought up by Jay, yes, but her mother is alive and kicking. They've had little contact over the years."

"That's always sad."

I thought about Jay—successful businessman, stern, proper. And about Anna—none of the above. "She came across as somewhat of a flake. Hard to tell if it's real, though, or an act. She's a concert violinist apparently."

Bertie laughed. "My musician friends say that of all the classical musicians, being a flake is practically a job requirement for a violinist."

"Be that as it may, she says she's here to help Julia through the grieving process. Julia thinks she's here to help her spend her inheritance."

"Whenever I wish I'd win the lottery, I always remember that no one loves me for my money," Bettie said. "And it's better that way."

"I wonder why she stayed away all these years. Was that her idea, or did Jay order her to?"

"Does it matter?"

"If he kept her separated from her daughter, she'd have a powerful reason to hate him."

"Powerful enough to kill him?" Bertie said. "Maybe at one time, but not after all these years, I'd think." She pulled around a van with New York license plates, piled high with kids, dogs, suitcases, and beach paraphernalia.

"True. Unless something changed. I got the feeling Anna has fallen on hard times, and she doesn't like it."

"What makes you say that?"

"She was staying at a cheap hotel. I bet they've never seen anyone dressed quite like her walk through their doors before. She declared, without being invited, that she'd move into the Ocean Side today. She also declared that Jay's account would pay for it. Her husband was quick to see that Julia got the bill for last night's dinner. Anna invited Julia to breakfast at the Ocean Side this morning. I bet that'll end up on Jay's account too."

"Presumptuous of her."

"Very. Still, Anna couldn't have killed Jay. She was in Europe, playing the violin."

"How do you know that?"

"She said so."

Bertie turned her head and looked at me.

"Oh," I said. "That doesn't mean she necessarily was, does it?"

"No, it doesn't."

I stared out the window. We were on the Croatian Highway, passing into the town of Kill Devil Hills. The summer homes and hotels, piers, beaches, and ocean are not much more than a stone's throw away, but you can't tell from here. We were surrounded by strip malls, discount stores, restaurant chain outlets, tourist traps, four lanes of traffic, and acres of paved parking lots. Signs and flags and bouncy characters fluttered in the breeze, all competing to attract our attention. And our dollars.

One shop, the sidewalk around its doors piled with crates stuffed with beach toys, beach chairs and umbrellas, and tacky tourist stuff, featured a huge sign advertising a sale. Everything, it shouted at me, had to go, as the store was closing.

"Look at that," I said to Bertie. "Gardner Beach Wear is having a going-out-of-business sale."

"I've heard things are tough for some of the small businesses these days," she said. "Still, Curtis has six locations, doesn't he? That one might only be moving premises."

"Too much competition, maybe," I said. Less than a quarter

of a mile earlier, on the other side of the highway, we'd passed a Ruddle Furniture store. Among the gazebos, plastic lounge chairs, and picnic tables, they'd also had beach things.

I twisted in my seat and watched the merchandise and signage fade away.

* * *

Blacklock is a small liberal arts college. Built in the 1960s, most of the buildings were constructed in the fashion of the day in the architectural style known as brutal realism. Solid concrete, square corners, and ugliness.

"Not very university-like, is it?" I said as we drove onto the grounds.

"Not for someone who worked at Harvard," Bertie said, meaning me. "But I've heard that their English lit department is top notch."

"In that case," I said, "the ugly buildings don't matter. Do you know where we're going?"

"I did some research on the Internet last night." Once she'd parked the car, she set off toward the main cluster of buildings with a determined step. I hurried to catch up.

A group of young women passed us, all swinging hair, high-pitched voices, laughing faces, short skirts, and long tanned legs. I felt about a hundred years old. We crossed the quad, heading for the liberal arts building. I ducked to avoid a flying football. The sun had fulfilled its promise of the morning, and the day was heating up. Students kicked around a ball, sat on benches reading, or lay under the trees, doing nothing much at all.

Maybe it was exactly like a university, after all.

Some of the windows facing the quad had Halloween decorations in them: spiders and cobwebs, and witches on brooms. A pumpkin adorned the head of a gentleman seated on a bench in a corner of the lawn. He made no move to remove it, which might have been because he and his bench were made out of bronze.

"What's the plan of attack?" I asked Bertie.

"You are assuming we have a plan," she replied. "That would be a misassumption. Last night I found out that this college is struggling. It's in no worse financial shape than many others of its size, but no better either. There's an intense battle going on between one faction, which wants to expand the sports stadium and hire top-ranked coaches to whip the football team into shape, and another that wants improved facilities for the faculty of ancient languages."

"No guesses which side I'm on," I, the non–football fan, said. "What about the North Carolina History Department?"

"That's where things get interesting. The faculty of history is thin. This is very much a school for languages—foreign, dead—and English literature. Most students take history as a general elective or as their minor, if at all. Students majoring in Latin or ancient Greek or medieval English are far more likely to be interested in ancient history than that of North Carolina."

"Meaning the professors of North Carolina history are on thin ice if the college needs to cut back. That's worth knowing, but I doubt anyone is going to air the university's dirty laundry in front of a couple of casual visitors, even if we ask nicely."

"I happen to be acquainted with one of the senior professors here. I didn't call ahead to make an appointment, but I checked his office hours when I was online, and he should be in this morning. In fact, I'm counting on it."

We climbed the steps and shoved open the front door.

A long, dark corridor stretched before us. Doors to either side were closed. A faint buzz came from the room to our left: the monotone murmur of a lecturer in full-on boring mode.

Bertie studied the list of names and office numbers posted on the wall to our right. She found what she was looking for and marched firmly down the hall toward a wide central staircase. I trotted along behind as we climbed to the second floor, where we emerged into another long corridor. So far we hadn't seen a single soul. Bertie found the door she wanted and pushed it open. We walked into a small, dark, crowded room, with one desk, one visitor's chair, and rows of overstuffed filing cabinets topped by dusty, dying plants. A fold-up table in the corner held a kettle and an assortment of stained mugs, most of which had some pithy comment printed on them. Four closed doors ran off the central room.

A woman sat behind the desk, presumably guarding the inner sanctums. She looked up from her computer and peered over the frames of her horn-rimmed glasses at us. "Can I help you?" she asked in a tone indicating that she had absolutely no intention of doing that.

"I'm here to see Professor McClanahan," Bertie said.

"Do you have an appointment?"

"No, but I expect he'll see me. Tell him B. James is here."

B.?

The receptionist suppressed a yawn and reached for the phone on her desk. She needn't have bothered. One of the inner doors flew open with such force it hit the wall with a loud crack before bouncing back. The depth of the dent in the drywall showed that this wasn't an uncommon occurrence. A man stood framed in the entrance. He was in his late fifties, with a shock of curly white hair, a huge salt and pepper mustache, and rimless glasses. He was about six feet tall and as thin as the skeleton of the fish lying on my plate last night after I'd finished dinner.

"B!" he cried.

"Eddie," my boss replied. Her voice was cool and composed, but something beneath it cracked.

"Come in, come in!" he shouted. "Judy, cancel all my appointments for the rest of the day."

"That won't be necessary," Bertie said. "We won't take up much of your time."

"Tea! We'll have tea!" he cried.

He gestured Bertie into his office, and I followed. The professor made space for her to sit by simply lifting up a chair, turning it over, and dumping the contents onto the floor, where it joined the other debris. Papers spilled out of open cabinets and were piled on side tables nearing collapse. I assumed the professor had a desk. Something had to support the computer as well as the stack of books and tumbling towers of student essays. A plant, sadly neglected, sat on the windowsill.

"B!" he said. "After all these years." He made a buzzing sound and poked Bertie in the arm with his index finger.

His nickname for her was "Bee," not "B."

"As beautiful as ever!" he said. "No, I take that back. You're even more beautiful than I remember. I am so delighted to see you."

She gave him a smile. "You haven't changed one bit, Eddie."

"Which is why you've finally agreed to marry me. Fortunately, I recently separated from my third wife. Or was she my fourth? Never mind. I am available once again."

I tripped over a copy of Winston Churchill's *A History of the English Speaking Peoples*, Volume I.

Professor McClanahan noticed me for the first tame, "Careful there, young lady."

"I'm fine."

"Don't damage my book. It's signed."

"By Winston Churchill?"

He didn't bother to answer me, but turned back to Bertie. He took both her hands in his, and his eyes studied every detail of her face. "How have you been, my dear?"

Her smile grew. "Well, Eddie. Very well. Healthy and happy."

"I'll get Judy to make a reservation for lunch. Something special, I think. Your daughter can amuse herself on campus while we catch up."

"I'm not here for old-time's sake, Eddie. And Lucy isn't my daughter. She works with me."

"A librarian then?"

"Yes."

Bertie removed her hands from his and settled herself in the recently emptied chair.

The professor sighed and took a seat behind the desk. He peered at us over the top of a stack of magazines. I couldn't read the writing on the top one, but I guessed it was Greek. "Very well, if you have not come to fulfill my fondest dreams and run away with me at long last, how can I help you?"

I leaned up against a bookshelf. It shifted beneath my weight, and I quickly moved away. A swift scan of the books in the room and the framed diplomas on the walls told me that Edward James McClanahan was a professor of Latin. I wondered if Bertie spoke Latin. She'd shown no sign of it. He was around her age, a year or two older perhaps. If he'd been married three—or four—times since knowing her, it was likely they'd been at college together.

"I'll come straight to the point, Eddie," Bertie said.

"I have no expectation that you would do otherwise, Bee."

"Tell me about the history department at this university."

"Not my field, as you know, but we're a small school, so I have contact with most of the faculty, whether I want to or not. The head of the modern history department is Professor Elizabeth McArthur. A competent woman, although rather too serious for my liking. She has not the slightest sense of humor. Makes it dreadfully easy to bait her, of course. Her and her equally dour henchman, Professor Norman Hoskins. They loathe being called Norm and Lizzie, by the way. Keep that in mind if you are speaking to them, and remember to use it constantly." His light blue eyes twinkled.

"What's the state of the modern history department itself?"

The twinkle faded away. "Why are you asking, Bee?"

"I've had contact with them lately. I like to know who I'm dealing with."

He leaned back in his chair. "You are the director of the Bodie Island Lighthouse Library."

"You've been keeping tabs on me."

"Not at all. I simply put two and two together. The late Jay

Ruddle has a collection of North Carolina historical documents. A valuable collection, I understand, which he was in the process of granting to a recognized institution when he suddenly passed away. The reason I know this is because, prior to his death, Lizzie spoke before the budget committee, which I am on, and told us that we, meaning the college, had only one competitor for obtaining the Ruddle collection: the Bodie Island Lighthouse Library. Lizzie was, I have to point out, highly dismissive of your chances, Bee. *Sneering* is the word that comes to mind."

"Why would she bring this to the budget committee," I asked. "if the bequest wasn't finalized yet?"

He looked at me. "A good question." Back to Bertie: "Because the budget committee was voting that very day on a recommendation that the entire North Carolina History Department be shut down. I myself was planning to vote yea. There are other institutions that do a far better job of teaching and researching our state history than us. Let them do what they do, and we will do what we do so well. *Ne in vobis?*"

"It doesn't matter," Bertie answered, "if I agree or not. Would the bequest save their department?"

"It would. We would get not only the collection, Lizzie told us, but funds to properly house it and to hire staff to maintain it. And, we were given to believe, a tidy bit extra for the college as well."

"The head of any department will fight for their department," Bertie said, "or they shouldn't be in the job. Beyond that, did you get the feeling there was anything, say, personal about Professors Hoskins and McArthur's discussion with the budget committee?"

"If they leave this institution," he said, "both Norm and Lizzie would be lucky to get jobs teaching history at a technical college."

"Is that your professional opinion, Eddie? Or personal?"

"Both. That's always convenient, isn't it? Norm is Blacklock alma mater. His parents were major donors to the university. Ergo, he kept his job when anyone else as inept as he would have been told to move on. His mother died about two years ago, his father before her, and it turned out there wasn't much of an estate left, so those funds dried up. Elizabeth has a good head on her shoulders. She might have made something of herself in her chosen field, but she got comfortable here at Blacklock. Too comfortable. That and her abrasive personality ensured that she doesn't have the type of friends who might be able to help her if she needs to make a professional move."

"Are they lovers?" Bertie asked.

He shook his great mop of hair. "That has never so much as been rumored. I don't think they like each other much, but they do have something in common."

"The need to keep the North Carolina History Department alive," Bertie said.

"And that means get the Ruddle papers," I said.

Professor McClanahan nodded. "I assume your library is still in the running for the collection?"

"The race ended without a winner," Bertie said. "Mr. Ruddle had not publicly announced a decision, so it's up to his heirs to decide what to do next. That could take years."

"You're investigating as to who killed Mr. Ruddle."

Bertie's voice stayed calm. "What makes you think that?"

"If the race has been called, there's no need to investigate your opponent's weaknesses. The man died in your library, and I know you well enough, even after all these years, to know that you intend to find out why. Why and who. The question, my dear Bee, you are asking is, *Cui bono?*"

Even I knew what that meant: "Who benefits?"

"Perhaps," he said, "Lizzy and Norm weren't aware the race was ending."

"It had ended, Eddie; only the prize ceremony was cancelled. They hadn't been informed, but shortly before he died, Mr. Ruddle had made up his mind to give his collection to our library, simply because we were the best choice. It's possible his granddaughter will want to keep it in the family."

She got to her feet. "Thanks for this, Eddie."

He leaned back in his chair and made a steeple of his fingers. He peered at Bertie over them. "Now that you've tracked me down, Bee, keep in touch."

She gave him a smile. "I think I will."

We left.

Bertie thanked Judy for her time. There were no signs that the receptionist had done anything toward making tea as the professor had ordered.

Classes were breaking up as we left the office, and we fought our way through surging crowds of undergraduates. We stepped out of the dark building into the sunlight of the quad, and I pulled my sunglasses out of my bag. "Okay, talk."

"As I suspected, Elizabeth and—"

"I don't care about them. At least not at the moment. Tell me about you and the professor."

Bertie sighed. "We did our postgraduate degrees together at the University of Virginia. Him in Latin and Greek, me in library science. We dated for a long time. We were in love. That is, I was in love with him. Eddie? I was never entirely sure."

"He had other girlfriends?"

"No. But he had other loves: Latin, Herodotus, Winston Churchill, reading Homer in the original. Everything in his studies excited Eddie."

"Sounds like a virtue, not a fault," I said.

"Any virtue carried to an extreme becomes a fault," she said. Her voice was wistful, and I sensed she was looking back through the years. "Dates were forgotten because he'd found a new interpretation of the *Aeneid* he had to start reading that night. My big news about what my doctoral supervisor had to say was shoved aside in favor of a treatise on a fresh biography of Winston Churchill. Our relationship ended the night he failed to get to the bus station for a trip to visit my parents. It would have been his first time meeting them. I left the station and ran back to town, worried he'd been in an accident. I found him at home, watching a program on PBS about Pompeii. He was sitting on the floor directly in front of the TV, trying to read the writing on buildings or documents in the background. He hadn't caught the bus, he said, because he wanted to watch the show. He'd forgotten to tell me his plans had changed, and brushed that off as a triviality.

This was in the days of VCRs. I told him he could have taped the show to watch another time, and he said he was afraid he'd make a mistake and set the timer wrong. I stormed out, spent the night in an uncomfortable chair at the bus station, and caught the morning bus. He continued watching the destruction of Pompeii."

"And that was it," I said.

"It was. I'd moved out of my apartment, as it was the start of summer break, and I was going home. I hadn't given Eddie the phone number at my family's house, assuming we were going there together."

"Ah, yes, the glorious days before cell phones and constant communication."

"It had its benefits. He could have tracked me down, but he was accompanying his professor to do research in Italy over the summer, and they were scheduled to leave in a few days. No contest as to which task was the more important to Eddie. When we returned to school in the fall, he wanted to pick up where we'd left off, but I told him I'd found someone else, although that wasn't true."

"He's carried a torch for you ever since."

She sniffed. "He's been married four times."

"Maybe three. And that proves my point. He never found true love again."

She smiled at me. "You're such a romantic, Lucy. If we'd married, I would have been but wife number one. The charm of the brilliant but scatter-brained intellectual soon wears off when there are groceries to buy and meals to cook or children to pick up from day care. If he'd missed his TV program to catch that bus, he wouldn't have been the dazzling Edward McClanahan. Give me a second, will you? I have a stone in my shoe."

Bertie dropped onto a bench and pulled off her right shoe. I stood beside her, glancing around. On the third floor of the liberal arts building, a curtain moved. A shape stood in the window, looking down onto the quad.

"We passed a coffee shop on the way into town." Bertie got to her feet. "Let's grab something for the road."

When I looked back at the building, the person watching us had disappeared.

Chapter Fifteen

We picked up our coffees and then drove back to the library in silence. Bertie kept her eyes fixed on the road ahead, and when I peeked at her out of the corner of my own eye, she appeared to be wrapped in thought. Whether she was remembering her long-lost youth and a tempestuous but ill-fated relationship with a single-minded Latin student, or thinking about what certain members of the Blacklock History Department might have to gain from the death of Jay Ruddle, I couldn't tell.

I sat back in my own seat, sipped my latte, and stared out the window.

What we'd learned from Professor McClanahan had put Professors Elizabeth McArthur and Norman Hoskins at the top of my mental suspect list. College teachers were supposed to be mild-mannered people, wrapped in the clouds on top of their ivory tower. I'd worked in the libraries at Harvard, and I knew that stereotype was nowhere near the reality. No one would fight harder over a slight, imagined or otherwise, to their field than a university professor.

Under threat of the closure of their entire department, essentially negating their life's work, I had no doubt academics could resort to extreme measures.

How extreme was the question.

Elizabeth and Norman (I must remember to refer to them as Lizzie and Norm) had been at the library for Louise Jane's lecture. Did one, or both, of them come into the lighthouse unobserved? Did he or she silently climb the back stairs and confront Jay? Demand he award them the collection?

Did Jay refuse? Did he tell them he'd made up his mind, and Blacklock College was not the winner?

Did he, she, or both of them lash out in anger and then slip out again and join the throngs on the lawn to sip tea and lemonade?

Before I realized it, we were turning off Highway 12 and onto the lighthouse grounds.

"Are we going to tell Detective Watson what we learned?" I asked Bertie.

"I think we should. As the good detective continually points out, we are not officers of the law and thus don't have powers of coercion or legal resources to reply upon. What we do have is our knowledge of the people involved."

"True," I said.

"It might not occur to Sam to specifically ask about the state of the History Department at Blacklock College. Institutions can be notoriously closemouthed to outsiders, although there's nothing academics like better than to gossip among themselves. Even if Sam does learn that the History Department needed the collection to stay afloat, he might not realize how much Elizabeth and Norman need their jobs. Most people are under the impression university professors live a rarified existence of study and teaching with guaranteed-for-life jobs. Give Sam a call, Lucy."

"Why me? Can't you do it? He gets mad when I interfere."

She switched off the engine and turned to me with a smile. "He respects your instincts and your drive to uncover the truth, Lucy. Although he'll never say so."

"I doubt that very much. The man can't stand me."

She simply smiled at me again, and we got out of the car and went to work

* * *

Inside the library, the fake spider webs and wobbly tombstones caught my eye. "Are we still going to have Halloween?" I asked Bertie. We had a full day of activities planned tomorrow for children, teens, and adults, but in light of Jay's death, I wondered if Bertie might want to cancel it all.

"Louise Jane's insistent on doing two more lectures, as scheduled. Not that I much care what Louise Jane wants, but Ronald pointed out to me that the children have been excited all week about the events he has planned for tomorrow, and he doesn't want to disappoint them. They know nothing about the death of Jay Ruddle." Bertie looked around. "So I gave in. If Jay had died here, in the main room, I would have refused, but . . ."

"But," I said, "who can say no to Ronald?"

"He's not the best children's librarian in the state for

nothing," Bertie said. "I didn't hire him to turn down his recommendations."

"They are looking forward to it," Charlene said from behind the circulation desk. "I've had a few phone calls this morning, checking that everything is still on."

"Anything else while we were out?" Bertie asked.

"It's been fairly quiet." Charlene reached under the desk for her ever-present iPhone and earbuds. She could hardly wait to get back to the peace and quiet of the research library and crank up her music. Why she wanted to destroy that peace and quiet with the likes of Jay-Z and Nicki Minaj, I never did understand.

But Charlene was brilliant at what she did, and although she sometimes tried to impose her musical taste on the rest of us, everyone liked her too much to object (too strongly, at any rate). "Ronald told me you went to Blacklock College this morning."

"We were doing a bit of sleuthing," Bertie said.

"Did you learn anything?"

"Only that they were desperate to get their hands on the Ruddle collection," I said.

"I . . . uh . . . I have something I should probably tell you." Charlene's eyes flicked from Bertie to me to Charles, sitting on the returns shelf, listening intently.

"What?" Bertie asked.

"Elizabeth McArthur came into the library on Saturday when Louise Jane's lecture was going on."

I sucked in a breath. Bertie's eyebrows rose. "Did you tell the police?"

"I told Detective Watson she was in here, yes, as they were trying to determine who was where when, but it has nothing to do with Jay. Not with his death anyway. She came to talk to me and didn't go upstairs. As far as I know anyway. I told him that."

"Talk to you? Why?" Bertie said. "And why didn't you tell me this before now?"

"I was going to tell you, but then Jay Ruddle died, and it no longer seemed relevant. Ronald didn't say why you were going to Blacklock College this morning, but"—her eyes slid to me—"as you and Lucy went together, I assumed you were asking questions about the death of Jay Ruddle."

Bertie nodded.

"McArthur offered me a job."

"Did she indeed?" Bertie said.

"She said if they got the Ruddle collection, which she assured me was as good as done, the college would hire me to manage it."

"I don't think Elizabeth McArthur is in the position to offer employment to anyone," Bertie said.

"But she can strongly recommend," I said, "if her department secured the collection."

"If," Bertie said.

"I didn't turn her down outright," Charlene confessed.

"If the collection came here, you'd be in charge of it, Charlene," I said. "You know that."

"McArthur offered me a considerable increase in salary over what I get here at the library, as well as a generous signing bonus."

"Dependent on . . . ?" Bertie said.

Charlene grinned. "Dependent on me sabotaging the Lighthouse Library's bid and keeping them informed as to what we were up to."

"Of all the nerve," I said.

Bertie huffed.

"Aside from the fact that I love everything about working at this library, I'm not a snoop, even if I had some incentive to spy. Blacklock College would mean an extra hour's commute, and I don't need that in my life. No matter how much money they offered."

"As you say, it's irrelevant now, Charlene, but thank you for telling me," Bertie said. "We know Professor McArthur desperately wanted the Ruddle collection. If she'd go so far as to attempt bribery, I have to ask what else she might have been prepared to do. I'll be in my office for the rest of the day, if anyone needs me."

I went into the break room to put my purse away and used the landline to call Sam Watson. I got his voicemail and said I had something to tell him. It would be up to him if he returned my call or not. I wasn't as sure as Bertie that he didn't sometimes consider throwing me in jail for interfering with the police.

When I returned to the main room, a young mother was dumping a pile of books, so high she had to peer over the top of it, onto the circulation desk. Charlene gave the books an approving look. "The twins' reading must really be coming along, Sue."

Charles settled himself on top of the stack. Sue laughed and gave him a pat. "I can't take out books fast enough to keep up with them. Ronald has been a miracle worker. I can't imagine what those two would do without this library. Hang around the back of the convenience store, most likely."

I eyed her books. At Ronald's suggestion, Sue had started her sons off on books for reluctant readers—short, fast-paced stories aimed specifically at teenage boys, many to do with the world of sports or adventure travel. Their taste was now expanding, and the stack included a few young adult detective novels. The topmost book was *You* by Charles Benoit. Exactly the thing that would appeal to potentially rebellious boys like Sue's two. She plucked the latest Barbara Early cozy mystery off the returns cart. "And one for me. The day has finally arrived when I actually have time to read." She sighed happily. Charlene gave Charles a nudge. He didn't move, so the nudge turned into a shove followed by another, stronger one. He stood—or rather sat—firm.

"Come here, you." I picked him up, thus giving him exactly what he wanted. If he could grin, I'm sure he would have.

When the door closed behind Sue and her pile of books, Charles went in search of someone else to admire him, and Charlene headed upstairs.

One of our library regulars, Mr. Snyder, an elderly man whose wife had died some months ago and whose children lived out of state, sat in the comfortable wingback chair in the magazine alcove, reading. Charles leapt onto his lap and curled himself into a purring ball. We knew Mr. Snyder came in for the company, under the pretext of reading magazines, and he was always welcome to do so. A man in his mid-forties, dressed in grimy jeans and a flannel shirt, with broken nails and work-worn hands, typed slowly and awkwardly with two fingers on the public computer.

"Are you finding what you need, Mr. Jones?" I asked him.

He looked up and gave me a grin that showed two missing teeth. "Slow and careful, Miss Lucy. Like you told me. This here machine's not so scary once you get the hang of it."

"Let me know if I can help with anything."

The role of libraries is changing rapidly in these modern times, and one of the things we're most proud of is providing a community for the lonely and a place to access public resources for the down-on-their-luck.

I'd barely settled myself behind the circulation desk, when we had unexpected visitors. Julia Ruddle came in, followed not only by Greg and Theodore but Anna and Dave. Anna wore a knee-length, tight-fitting, neckline-plunging red dress. A heavy gold necklace was around her throat, and matching earrings in her ears. She tottered across the marble floors in red stilettos with four-inch heels. Dave was dressed in a rumpled, pale blue shirt and beige trousers that had not seen an iron since they'd left the factory.

Julia looked at me. She jerked her head and opened her eyes wide, sending me a signal of some sort, but I failed to read it.

I stood up. "Hi. Welcome everyone. What brings you here today?"

"I thought Anna and Dave would like a tour of the light-house," Julia said.

I snuck a peek at Anna. She looked as though she would like nothing less.

"Did you get moved into the Ocean Side okay?" I asked.

"Yes, we did." Anna stifled a yawn. Charles leapt onto the desk, and she fell back with a screech. "Good heavens, what on earth is that creature doing here?"

"This is our library cat, Charles," I said. "He's very friendly." As if to prove me a liar, Charles arched his back and spat.

"I cannot abide cats," Anna said.

"Looks like the feeling's mutual," Julia muttered under her breath. She gave Charles a hearty pat.

"I hope I am not going to get home and find my clothes covered with cat hair." Anna sniffed. "I am highly sensitive."

"Wow!" Dave said. "That's quite the model ship you have there." He hurried over to the *Rebecca MacPherson*. "Look at this incredible detail, honey."

Theodore suppressed a shudder as he turned away. I wasn't the only one who noticed: Greg's eyebrows rose.

"If I must." Anna tapped her way across the floor and peered at the little model. "It's full of holes. Good heavens, are those skeletons?"

"Fantastic, isn't it?" Dave said.

"Dave and Anna would love to see the view from the top," Julia said.

"I sure would!" Dave said.

Anna said something in Russian. It might have been "Are you kidding me?"

"It's not as high as it looks," Julia said. "Only two hundred or so steps."

"The first hundred and ninety are the worst." Greg said.

"Allow me to escort you." Keeping his eyes firmly away from the model ship, Theodore gave Anna a small bow. "I myself am well acquainted with the history of the lighthouse and this stretch of the coast." His fake English accent was back, and he'd tied a paisley cravat at his throat. I suspect the look he was attempting was jaunty, but instead the cravat threatened to choke him.

"Greg'll go too," Julia said.

"I will?" Greg said.

"Not necessary," Theodore said.

"Off you go, everyone," Julia said.

Theodore held out his arm and, with a roll of her eyes and a mighty sigh, Anna slipped hers through it.

"Last one to the top's a dirty rotten egg." Dave set off. "Come on, Greg, race you."

Eight feet clattered on the iron stairs, some with considerably more enthusiasm than others. Four additional feet, of the feline version, followed, faster and much quieter.

"Teddy!" I called, "don't let Charles onto the walkway." He was a cat, yes, but I still worried that he'd leap off the railing after a passing bird.

"There's a walkway!" Anna's voice faded away as she made the first turn.

Julia let out a long breath. "Anything for a moment's peace."

"How'd your breakfast go?" I said.

"Fine. Why do you ask? Oh, you mean breakfast with Anna. Didn't happen. I wasn't going to wait until ten at any rate, so I ordered room service when I got up at six. Just as well. The lawyer my grandfather's company arranged for me arrived this morning, and I spent some time with him. Anna called around noon, apparently having totally forgotten about meeting me. She didn't forget to move into the Ocean Side, though."

"Why did you bring them here?"

"I have to do something with her. She wanted to meet for lunch, and I countered by suggesting an outing. At least Dave's keen."

I glanced around the library. Mr. Jones stabbed at the computer and printed off reams of paper. Mr. Snyder had finished with his sports magazine and had gone on to *Country Living*. A few patrons browsed the shelves, but no one needed my attention at the moment. Bertie was in her office; Ronald, upstairs in the children's library, preparing for today's after-school program; and Charlene had buried herself in the rare books room.

"Do you want to talk about it?" I asked Julia.

"About my mother?" She gave me a wan smile. "She and my grandfather didn't see eye to eye on raising me."

"Last night she said he kept her away from you. Is that what happened?"

She nodded. "Nothing was ever said, and I was too young when my father died to understand, but children have a way of finding these things out eventually. My grandfather was absolutely furious when my parents married. He wanted my father to take over the business from him, and my father wanted to be a musician. Granddad indulged him for a while, or so I've been told by some of the staff over the years . . ."

I assumed she meant maids and gardeners, chauffeurs, and the like.

". . . thinking he had to get it out of his system. But, instead of eventually settling down, my father married Anna, and he lived the rest of his far too short life in her wake. Then he died. My grandfather blamed her for that."

"Why?"

"My father was killed in a car accident. They were in London. Anna had been fired from her latest gig that afternoon, and she went on a huge bender. My father drove around the city trying to find her. He eventually did, and he managed to talk her into coming back to their hotel. Where I, apparently, waited with a hotel babysitter. After I turned twenty-one, I managed to get a copy of the police report, unknown to Grandfather. There's no suggestion my father had been drinking that night, but he suddenly pulled out of his lane straight into oncoming traffic. Grandfather was convinced he'd been fighting with Anna, and either she distracted him or grabbed the wheel. And so my father died. My mother was unharmed. Underlings were sent to London to retrieve both my father's body and me. Anna had to travel back to America in economy class. We never lived under the same roof again, but Grandfather gave her an allowance for many years. I suspect that allowance was conditional. The condition being that she'd stay away from me. Which is what happened. She sent me presents on my birthday and Christmas, usually arriving late. We met a handful of times, but always as part of an organized outing. A Broadway show, a trip to the zoo, or an art gallery, followed by lunch in a restaurant. Grandfather's driver would take me to meet her and pick me up after. She'd kiss me on the cheek and say how beautiful I was becoming, and then walk away."

"That's incredibly sad."

Julia's eyes wandered to the spiral iron staircase. "Just as well. I don't think Anna's the mothering type."

"Still, she came to be with you when she heard that your grandfather died."

"Maybe I'm the suspicious sort, Lucy, but I have to ask why. Two years ago, when I turned twenty-five, the allowance he was giving her ended. I don't think she has much in the way of financial support. Her career isn't going well, to say the least. I follow her activities on the Internet sometimes. She's incredibly talented. They say when she was a teenager, she was considered the most promising violinist of her generation, but she can't get much work anymore. No one in the classical music world will trust her. If she does happen to land a gig, it usually ends in tears and temper tantrums."

"What about Dave? Can he support her?"

She shrugged. "I'd never even heard of him before last night. He doesn't look like a man with money, but these days you can't always tell, can you?" She stared off into the distance. A tear formed in the corner of her eye. "It would have been nice to have had a mother." Her voice was very low.

Charles returned from the climb to the top and leapt onto the desk. He gave a soft meow and stretched out a paw toward Julia. She wiped her eyes and scooped him up. She held him close, and he comforted her.

I felt myself smiling. If Charles believed in Julia, then I would too. "Your parents were both musicians. Do you play?"

"Oh, no. Perish the thought. You can be sure Grandfather never let me anywhere near an instrument. I know now that he was terrified I'd follow in my father and Anna's footprints. When the other girls at school were in music class, I had an extra art or French lesson. I enjoy classical music, though." She put Charles down and then lifted her hands and let her fingers dance through the air. "I sometimes find myself playing the air piano, although I've never so much as touched a key. I wonder if I inherited some sort of musical talent. Better not to find out; it never did either of my parents any good."

Footsteps sounded on the stairs as the rest of the group descended. Anna clung to Theodore's arm with one hand, and in the other she carried her shoes. Greg and Dave followed, talking football.

"Wasn't that interesting?" Theodore said.

"Most interesting." Anna turned to Julia. "Such a nice young man."

"He is," Julia said.

Theodore beamed. "Have you been to the Wright Brothers Memorial, Mrs. Makarova? It's very interesting."

"No, I have not." Anna slipped her shoes back onto her feet. "But I'd love to see it. Is it far to go?"

"Not at all. Julia and I were planning to go there one day soon, weren't we, Julia? No time like the present."

"Wonderful. Let's do that. David, darling, why don't you and Gordon here—"

"Greg," said Greg.

"—go back to the hotel. There must be some tedious sports game or other on the television."

"I'd like to see the Wright Brothers too," Dave said. "First in flight and all that."

"No, you wouldn't." Anna tucked her hand through Julia's arm, so she had Teddy on one side and her daughter on the other. Dave and Greg were pointedly left out of the circle. "Perhaps a little lunch on the way. I'm sure you know the absolute best places, Theodore."

"I do."

"That's settled then. We'll all meet later for dinner. Lucy, you will join us, of course."

"Me?"

"Consider it a command performance. Come along, everyone."

Julia gave me a "what can you say?" shrug.

"I have another engagement tonight," I whispered to her.

"That's fine. Anna will soon forget she invited you."

"Did you know that the entirety of the Wright Brothers' inaugural flight covered less distance than the length of a modern passenger jet?" Theodore asked.

"Is that so! That is fascinating," Anna exclaimed. "I love an educated man, don't you, Julia?"

"What do you think of the Yankees' prospects for next year?" Dave asked Greg.

The door swung shut behind them. Charles leapt off the desk and went upstairs to see what Ronald was up to.

I wondered at Anna's sudden fondness for Theodore and her abrupt dismissal of Greg. Was she thinking Teddy would be a better match for Julia? Better for Julia as in able to be influenced by Anna?

Entirely possible. Teddy, if he thought Anna had any influence over Julia in matters of the heart, would leap at the chance to get the mother in his camp. The resumption of the fake accent and bookish attire might be an attempt on his part to impress Anna.

When it came to *cui bono* from the death of Jay Ruddle, Anna obviously did. She had Julia back in her life; she might have expectations that Julia would inherit and thus help her mother return to the lifestyle to which she wanted to become accustomed. It was possible, likely even, she hated Jay for his attempts to control her and limit contact with her daughter. Anna had good reason to kill Jay Ruddle.

But she had not been in the Outer Banks when he died. I suppose it was possible she'd lied about being in Europe and snuck onto the library grounds unobserved, climbed the stairs, killed Jay, and crept out again.

I had trouble seeing it. I didn't think Anna could do unobserved.

The phone on the desk rang, bringing me back to the here and now.

"Lighthouse Library. Lucy speaking."

"What is it, Lucy?" growled Sam Watson.

For a moment, I thought he'd reached down the phone line and plucked thoughts about Anna straight out of my head. Then I remembered Bertie and my trip to Blacklock College. "I uncovered something you might find of interest. In the Ruddle case."

He sighed. "I suppose I have to hear it."

"Only if you want to. It's about Blacklock College. The other institution in competition for the Ruddle collection."

"Lunch?" he said.

"What?"

"I haven't had lunch yet. Josie's in fifteen minutes."

"Okay," I said, but he'd already hung up.

After our trip this morning on non-library business, I hadn't planned to take a lunch break. On a previous occasion, Bertie had told me I could take time off to investigate a killing that affected the library community. I called her office now. "Sam Watson wants to meet me for lunch."

"See what I told you, honey? He values your opinion."

"He values my cousin's baking, but that's beside the point. Can someone watch the desk for me?"

"I'll do it myself. We have a meeting of the library board this evening. Perhaps if I tell them I don't have the budget ready, they'll cancel."

"I can ask Ronald."

"I'm joking, Lucy. I have the budget fully prepared and ready to be torn apart. I also have all my counterarguments mustered." She put on her world-weary library director voice. " 'No, Curtis, we cannot resume meeting at a restaurant, with lunch at the library's expense. No, Diane, we are not going to install a Jonathan Uppiton memorial fountain. Not now, not ever.' It'll be a nice break to take the desk."

"I doubt I'll learn anything," I said. "Watson is of the opinion that information flows in one direction only. Me to him. If I do, I'll let you know."

I went into the break room for my purse and drove into town to Josie's.

* * *

In the height of summer and around the holidays, Josie's Cozy Bakery can be a madhouse. But in late October, as the Outer Banks settles into the off-season, several tables were empty, and the lineup at the counter was only three deep. Watson and I arrived at the same time. He held the door for me and said lunch would be on him. He told me to grab a table in a quiet corner while he got our orders.

I found a place at the back, nearest the doors to the kitchen. I peeked inside and saw my cousin, elbow deep in pastry dough.

I called out, and she gave me a wide grin and a wave of floury fingers. I sometimes thought that heaven must smell like Josie's Cozy Bakery. Hot pastry, warm fruits, melting sugar, freshly ground cinnamon and nutmeg, rising bread. The espresso machine hissed as it emitted clouds of fragrant steam. Josie's bakery was rapidly becoming *the* spot for coffee, baked goods, and light lunches in Nags Head, and I was pleased to see it. My cousin worked hard to make it a success, so hard that the very thought of her schedule made me want to go for a nap.

I knew Watson, like all police officers, liked to sit with his back to the wall, facing the room, so I took the other chair. He soon arrived and handed me a sandwich and a cinnamon-topped latte. For himself, he had a large coffee, black, and a ham and Swiss sandwich with a coconut cupcake on the side. He dropped into a chair and unfolded his paper napkin. "Okay, Lucy. What do you have to tell me?"

Not one for small talk, Detective Watson.

Josie made *the* best cupcakes. I eyed the thick white frosting and sprinkle of toasted coconut enviously. If I wasn't careful, regular meetings at my cousin's bakery would put twenty pounds on me before I knew it.

"Don't tell CeeCee," Watson said.

"Huh?"

"About the cupcake. She's after me to watch what I eat. I can't continue to put the groceries away the way I did when I was a police recruit, or so she tells me. I know that, but I pretend not to." He bit into his sandwich. "What have you learned?"

"Two things. First, Bertie spoke to a friend who's a professor at Blacklock College." I didn't say that we'd gone to the college ourselves, and I didn't mention Bertie's past history with our informant. I just laid out what we'd been told. "Charlene told us that the people from Blacklock tried to bribe her. They said if she spied on us, they'd give her the job of curator of the collection. If they got it, that is."

"When did this happen?"

"Saturday. At the lecture. She says she told you Elizabeth McArthur was in the building, but not what they talked about."

He nodded. "I bet that went down well."

"As well as could be expected. They obviously don't know Charlene."

"That's all interesting, Lucy." He finished his sandwich, wiped his fingers on a paper napkin, and carefully peeled the paper away from the cupcake. I tried not to stare as the cake, as white and fluffy as a cloud upon which angels rest, came into view. "You're telling me the folks from Blacklock College wanted the Ruddle collection, and they wanted it badly. Fair enough, but that's no motive for murder. Killing him has the opposite effect, and anyone should have known that. The man's estate has to be settled, and there are no guarantees as to what his heirs plan to do with it."

"Agreed, but I'm pointing out that the Blacklock people were desperate to get it. Maybe one of them went up to the rare books room with Jay, and he told them he'd made his decision, and it wasn't in Blacklock's favor. Hearing that, did Norman or Elizabeth strike out at him in anger?"

Watson broke off a huge piece of cupcake, tossed it into his mouth, and chewed. "Want some?"

"What? Oh, no, thank you." I patted my sandwich, still

untouched. Talking to Watson makes me far too nervous to eat. "I've got plenty here."

"If you say so." He took a bite of pure icing. I thought I might swoon.

"I'll keep your information in mind," he said. "I hadn't considered this collection to be worth killing over, but if someone's job's on the line because of it, that's another matter altogether."

I felt as I had back in school when my mother praised me for getting ninety-three percent on my seventh-grade Civil War essay. My father had asked what happened to the other seven percent.

"You said two things." The last crumb of cupcake disappeared. "What's the other?"

"Julia's mother's in town. She got in yesterday."

"I didn't know that, but that's natural enough, isn't it? Her father-in-law died, and she wants to be with her daughter."

"It's not exactly a normal mother–daughter relationship. Were you aware that Jay Ruddle paid Anna—that's Julia's mother—an allowance on the condition that she stay away from Julia while she was growing up? The allowance began when Julia was three years old, after her father died in an accident for which Jay blamed Anna, and it ended when Julia turned twenty-five. That was only two years ago. It's possible Anna has recently run out of money."

Watson's eyebrows rose, and for the first time ever, I thought I'd surprised the detective. "I was not aware of any of that. Was this Anna in town at the time in question?"

"She says she was in Europe. She's a musician."

"I'll check into that," he said. "Is her last name Ruddle?"

"It's Makarova. Anna Makarova. But that might be a stage name. She's a classical musician."

"Easy enough to find out." He pushed his chair back.

"Wait!" I said. "What's happening with the case against Julia? I've told you about two possible suspects—three if you consider two people from Blacklock College were at the library when Jay died. There must be more. The man was a ruthless businessman. He would have had enemies."

"He made some enemies over his lifetime, yes. Quite a few it would appear. But all that happened a long time ago. He was retired. He was eighty-two years old."

"Some people carry a grudge for a long time."

Sam Watson stood up. He placed his hands on the table and leaned toward me, looming into my space. I braced myself, determined not to be intimidated. Around us people came and went, drinks were made, and food served. A woman laughed, and in the kitchen someone yelled, "Hey, watch that!" The busy bakery fell away as Watson stared into my eyes. "Thank you for bringing that information to my attention, Lucy. I shouldn't have to remind you once again—but I will—not to interfere in my investigation."

"I'm not interfering," I said firmly. "I am helping."

"If you're gathering information specifically designed to take attention away from your friend, that's interfering. Do you understand?"

"Yes," I mumbled, intimidated.

"You and your book club should read a Sherlock Holmes story next."

"I suppose we could do that." I wondered why he'd changed the subject so abruptly.

"Perhaps *A Study in Scarlet*. Pay particular attention to the line 'It is a capital mistake to theorize before you have all the evidence. It biases the judgment.'"

"I . . ."

"You've decided Julia Ruddle did not kill her grandfather. You then began to gather evidence to support that hypothesis. Meaning, Lucy, you are working backward. It's a good thing you're not the detective, and I am. Sherlock Holmes also said, 'I wish you simply to report facts to me, and you can leave me to do the theorizing.' *The Hound of the Baskervilles*."

"I didn't know you were a Sherlock aficionado."

He straightened up. "Stay out of it, Lucy."

He walked away, and I watched him go. Watson was right. I was not a detective. I didn't want to be a detective. But I believed in Julia's innocence, and for her sake as well as Theodore's, I wanted to do what I could to help.

Josie slipped into the recently vacated seat. "You're having lunch with Sam Watson? What's that about?"

"I'm trying to help the police. Like the good citizen I am." I unwrapped my sandwich and took a moment to admire it. A bakery-made baguette stuffed with thick layers of beef tinged a slight pink, runny cheese, glistening onions, and a handful of bright green herbs. I knew from past experience it would taste as good as it looked.

"Did he appreciate your help?" Josie asked.

"This time, I think he did. Although it would kill him to admit it."

"A bunch of reporters were in here earlier. I couldn't help but overhear them talking. They say the granddaughter did it."

"She didn't."

"If you say so, sweetie."

"I do, but unfortunately, as Detective Watson recently pointed out, what I say is totally irrelevant." I took a bite of my sandwich. It was so yummy, I momentarily forgot all about murder and the dark cloud of suspicion hanging over Julia.

Josie started to get to her feet, and that brought me back to earth. "Josie?"

"What, sweetie?"

"You ever hear about any of the wild horses from Corolla making their way this far south?"

She laughed. "Heavens no. They're totally protected. If they got out of their sanctuary, they'd be hit by a car the first time they tried to cross the road. Or fed cheeseburgers and fries, almost as fatal, although slower. Even if they stuck to the beach, someone would be sure and call the police or the wildlife authorities if they saw a horse strolling past. Why do you ask?"

"No reason. Have wild horses ever lived around here?"

"Long ago, maybe. But not these days. There are horseback-riding outfits in Nags Head who take people for a ride in the woods and along the beach. Do you want to go riding? Aaron can suggest some places. He worked at a stable one summer when he was in junior high. I don't remember which one, though."

"Just wondering," I said.

My cousin gave me a look. Then something in the room caught her attention, and her eyes widened. "Speak of the devil."

I whirled around, half-expecting a spectral gray horse to have wandered into the bakery. Instead, I saw Julia Ruddle and Theodore Kowalski. Anna wasn't with them.

A small smile touched the corners of Julia's mouth when she saw me, and she waved. She said something to Theodore, and they changed direction. "Hi, Lucy," Julia said. "Fancy running into you."

"Julia, do you remember my cousin, Josie O'Malley? You met at book club on Friday."

"I remember." Julia noticed Josie's flour-dotted apron, blue and white, with the bakery's logo of a croissant curling around a lighthouse. "Josie? Is this your place? It's lovely."

"All mine." Josie stood up. "And I'd better get back at it. Nice seeing you again, Julia. My condolences on the death of your grandfather."

"Thank you," she said, and Josie slipped away.

"Do you mind if we join you?" Julia asked me.

"Please do." I'd scarcely taken two bites out of my sandwich. I rolled it back up in its wrapping to enjoy at work later. "I thought you were going to the Wright Brothers. Where's Anna?"

Julia dropped into the seat recently vacated by Detective Watson and then Josie. The table was for two, but Teddy dragged a chair over and squeezed himself in.

"We didn't get any further than the outlet shops," Julia said. "As soon as she saw them, Anna let out a mighty yell."

"I thought I'd hit something," Theodore said. "Gave me quite the fright."

"She mustn't have noticed them earlier," Julia said. "Anyway, nothing would do but we had to pull in. We hit Sunglasses Hut and then Coach. She's now trying on dresses, and that got a bit too much for Theodore."

"Not at all," he said. "I was happy to offer her the benefit of my advice. A man's point of view is always appreciated, as your mother pointed out."

"Okay, I'll confess. The steady parade of clothes was getting too much for me," Julia said. "We arranged to go back and pick her up in an hour. I shudder to think what this is costing me."

"Costing you?"

"I gave her my credit card. Anna"—Julia made quotes in the air with her fingers—"forgot hers at the hotel."

"Can I get you something, Julia?" Theodore asked.

"Just a latte, please."

He went off to join the line without asking me if I wanted anything.

"I didn't like to talk about it earlier, when we were in the library with everyone around, but have you heard anything more from the police?" I asked Julia.

She shook her head. "Questions. More questions. Watson didn't come himself, but he sent someone to the hotel this morning. Another round of the same questions I've answered a hundred times already. I don't think that Detective Watson's at all competent. He's got a bee in his bonnet about me and won't let it go."

I shifted uncomfortably. Good thing Watson had left before Julia arrived. She wouldn't have continued to be friendly with me if she'd seen me having lunch with him. Never mind that I was trying to help her. And the best way to help Julia was to find the real killer.

Theodore put the drinks on the table. A latte for Julia and a hot tea for him. "If you're talking about Detective Watson, I'm thinking of paying a call on him myself. I can tell him Julia had nothing to do with her grandfather's death."

"I don't think that would be wise," I said, "unless you have solid evidence. Watson doesn't like what he sees as people interfering in his cases."

"It's so nice of you to care." Julia smiled at Theodore. "But I have to agree with Lucy. He's not going to listen to you. You scarcely even know me."

Theodore puffed up his chest. "I know you well enough, Julia, to know that you have a kind and loving heart."

"You're so sweet," she said.

He puffed up some more.

"I want to go home," she said with a heavy sigh. Deep smudges lay under her eyes, and I suspected she hadn't slept much, if at all, last night. "I need to take my grandfather back to New York to make funeral arrangements. I need to mourn properly."

"I have to get to work." I gathered up the remains of my sandwich. "Call me if you need anything."

"Thank you," she said. "I'd like to spend some more time at the library, if I may."

"Of course you can."

"I like your library. I like it a lot. I'd love to have a look through your rare books room. My grandfather might not have wanted me to take control of his collection, but he did insist on me having a firm knowledge of East Coast nautical history."

"You're welcome any time," I said. "Charlene would be delighted to talk about it with you. Tomorrow's Halloween, and we're having a variety of festivities. As well as children's parties upstairs, Louise Jane will be speaking again, telling different stories from the ones on Saturday, no doubt less child-friendly ones, and we'll have refreshments after." Theodore hid a shiver under the pretext of adding sugar to his tea. "The teenage party is at five, and the adult one, at seven. If you're free, why not come? Some people will be in costume, but many won't."

"I'd like that."

"I hope you don't mind that we're still celebrating Hallow-een. After the death of your grandfather, I mean."

"Why would I mind? Life goes on, doesn't it? And you have your jobs to do. Granddad would have approved. He liked your library because it was a vibrant community center."

"Excellent idea." Theodore gathered his courage around him like a cloak. "I hadn't been planning to go the library tomorrow evening, as I find Halloween excessively childish, but if you are going to be there, Julia, I'll also participate in the festivities. If you're interested in the history of the area, my family has lived in the Outer Banks since . . ."

I stopped at the counter on my way out. "One coconut cup-cake to go, please."

Chapter Sixteen

I put the remains of my lunch in the fridge to have for supper and took the circulation desk from Bertie.

"I wish I could cancel tonight's board meeting," she said. "We have such a busy day tomorrow."

"I'd offer to help," I said, "but I'm canvassing for Connor tonight."

"Far more important than a board meeting," she said.

"Did you hear anything about Doug Whiteside's radio interview? Connor was expecting him to attack the library over the death of Jay Ruddle."

"Eunice Fitzgerald called me to report on it. The usual Doug nonsense, implying that the library brings murder and destruction down upon itself. Eunice said he didn't sound as though his heart was in it today, and he got easily distracted when the interviewer asked him what his plans were, should he win, for that plot of land where the Mega Mart was supposed to go before they pulled out. Connor was given a chance to respond after the show, and he reminded everyone of the importance of the library to the community. I'm glad we have Connor on our side."

"Me too," I said.

The library was steadily busy for the rest of the day. Many of the children who came in for the after-school programs seemed more excited than usual. Pre-Halloween enthusiasm was building. I was glad we'd decided to go ahead with Halloween.

We closed at six, and I was scheduled to be at the campaign office at six thirty. I would be door knocking with Connor himself tonight, provided no emergency took him away, and I found myself looking forward to it.

Good thing I had a ready-made dinner. I gobbled the remains of my sandwich and the coconut cupcake, standing at the kitchen sink in my apartment. That had been a mistake, I thought, as I nipped into the shower. My stomach protested at the speed with which the cupcake had gone down. What a waste of a million calories.

I put on a plain black dress with a thin red belt and a red sweater, and slipped my feet into black ballet flats. I studied myself in the mirror. Suitable for a political campaign, I decided.

I locked the door to my apartment behind me and hurried downstairs at six twenty. Charles had not come up with me, preferring to supervise Bertie as she set up for the board meeting.

The meeting was scheduled to begin at six thirty, and to my surprise, Diane and Curtis were standing at the door when I opened it.

"Good evening." I was about to slip past them when I had a thought. Instead, I held the door and ushered them in. "I noticed your store in Kill Devil Hills is going out of business," I said to

Curtis. "Are you expanding elsewhere?" That sounded politer, I thought, than asking if the chain was in dire financial straits.

"I wish," he said. "Times are tough everywhere. Tourism is down, competition is up."

"I'll have a coffee, Lucy," Diane said. "I still don't understand why we had to stop having luncheon meetings. It was so much more convenient for everyone. Six thirty! We can hardly have dinner at five, and by the time this meeting is over, everyone will be starving." She walked away, somewhat unsteady on her sky-high heels.

"You have other stores," I said to Curtis. "I'm sure they're doing well."

"If I can hold on until next season we might be able to recover. Thing is, Lucy, it's not enough to be a sharp businessman anymore."

Not that Curtis, from what I heard, had ever been a sharp businessman. He'd inherited the chain of stores established by his father and had plenty of ideas of expanding. But ideas, so the gossips said, were all Curtis had. Not the drive to succeed—or even the ability to hire the right people to succeed on his behalf.

"Not with the sort of cutthroat business people out there these days. I'll have a coffee too, thanks." He started to walk away. Diane had stopped at the magazine rack and was reaching for a copy of *Martha Stewart Living*.

"Haven't there always been cutthroat business people?" I said quickly. I hadn't planned on interrogating Curtis, but now that the opportunity had presented itself . . .

"My father and his contemporaries might have been tough, but they conducted business like gentlemen."

"Is that so?" I refrained from telling him I had some knowledge of business history. And it wasn't pretty.

"These days, people think they can get away with anything." Curtis's gaze moved upward, as though he could see through the ceiling to the rare books room where Jay had died. "Men like Jay Ruddle. Out to make a buck any way they can, fast as they can, and they don't care who they step on."

"Mr. Ruddle was of your father's generation," I said.

"My father died a long time ago. The end of an era. Jay Ruddle died on Saturday. No loss to anyone."

"I've heard he made enemies when he was first expanding his business, but that was a long time ago, and he retired recently, didn't he?" It was absolutely none of my business, but I've found that when people have a grievance, sometimes all they want is to tell someone else about it. Whether it's their business or not.

If we'd been outside, Curtis would have spat. As it was, he looked as though he was considering it. "Ruddle let go of hands-on management, yes, but he kept control of the board. He still made the big decisions, and some of the small ones too. Like to undercut my business. Earlier this summer, right out of the blue, that big store of his in Kill Devil Hills started stocking beach furniture. Folding chairs, packable shelters, folding tables, coolers. That's my core business. It always has been. He set his prices so low, there's no way I can compete and still make a profit. He did it with the specific goal of driving me out of business, and it's working. I've had to close one outlet this year. I don't know if I can hang on until next summer." Curtis was building up to a full-blown rage, but suddenly he deflated. A small smile touched the edges of his mouth. "Doesn't matter now, does it, Lucy? Jay Ruddle will no longer be making any decisions. The new chairman will be horrified at his business practices. There's no place for a personal vendetta in the corporate world."

"Vendetta? What do you mean? Why would Jay Ruddle care about your stores, Curtis?"

"Because he was a miserable, bitter old man who carried a grudge all the way to his grave, that's why."

"I don't understand—" My words were cut off as the door opened and Eunice Fitzgerald, chair of the library board, came in, followed by a cluster of other members. "Good evening, Curtis," she said. "It's unlike you to be early."

Curtis appeared not to realize that had been a dig. "Diane wants to get started on time. We have dinner reservations after."

"Of course you do, dear. Mustn't let our little library business interfere, must we?"

"I'm glad you understand," he said.

"Are we going to stand here all day, people?" Diane shouted. "Let's get on with it. Lucy, why aren't you making coffee?"

"Because I'm off the clock," I muttered.

"I'm very much looking forward to tomorrow, dear," Mrs. Fitzgerald said. "I'm glad Bertie decided to go ahead with the scheduled events. Halloween has always been one of my favorite holidays. When my children were young, I went to so much trouble to make their costumes. These days, my granddaughters grab something premade from the dollar store." She shook her head sadly.

"Are you planning to dress in costume?" I asked.

She put her finger to her lips. "I might be. I might not be. Come along, everyone—let's not dawdle. Curtis and Diane have their dinner to get to."

They headed for the hallway and the break room for their meeting, and I lost my chance to ask Curtis what he meant about a vendetta.

I checked my watch. I was going to be late for canvassing.

As I drove into Nags Head, I used the Bluetooth on my phone to make a call. "Hi, Aunt Ellen. Lucy here."

"Lucy! How nice to hear from you. I've just come in from helping at a tea for Connor at the seniors' residence. I can assure you he has the old-lady vote wrapped up. Most of them don't care much about local politics, but they all think he's very handsome."

I laughed. "We'll take whatever we can get."

"They also think it's a shame he's not married."

I was not going to go there. "Did you learn anything about Jay Ruddle? You were going to look into his past and see if you could think of anyone who might have wanted to see him dead."

"I did a bit of poking around, dear, but learned nothing worth telling you about. Some of the older people remember him, and not necessarily fondly, but he left the Outer Banks a long, long time ago. Memories die and grudges are slowly forgotten. Some of the folks I talked to said they were surprised to hear he was still alive. Until he wasn't, that is."

"I'm wondering about something Curtis Gardner said to me. He seems to think Jay was on a vendetta against him."

Aunt Ellen sighed. "Someone is always out to get poor

Curtis, at least according to poor Curtis. Covers up a world of incompetence on his part."

I waited to turn onto Highway 12. Traffic was heavy going north, bringing people back to Nags Head for the night. To the south, there wasn't much other than the small ocean-side communities of Rodanthe and Buxton, and the ferry to Ocracoke at road's end.

"But," Aunt Ellen went on, "as in most conspiracy theories, there lies a grain of truth. Jay Ruddle and Ed Gardner were both in love with Margaret Duncan. That was well before my time, and pretty much everyone forgot all about it until Jay's recent return and then his untimely demise put it back into folks' mind."

"Who's Margaret Duncan?"

"These days she's better known as Margie Gardner. Curtis's mother."

The traffic broke and I pulled onto the highway. "Is that so?"

"Margie was apparently a great beauty back in the day, and her father had a fair amount of money, or so folks say. Ed and Jay were local boys. Ed was from a fishing family, and Jay's father owned a furniture store. Neither of them had much in the way of expectations. Everyone figured Margaret would marry a man chosen by her father, but nope. One day it was announced that she was going to marry Ed Gardner. They say Jay Ruddle was furious. So furious he threw himself into running his father's business. And we know how that turned out."

"Was there a reason for this sudden engagement?"

"If you mean was she expecting, that was the gossip at first, but nothing came of it. Curtis wasn't born until some years after the wedding. Margaret and Ed had two daughters after Curtis. The girls moved away when they married in turn."

"Is Margaret still alive?"

"Very much so. She used to keep the books for Curtis, but I don't think she does that any more. She lives in Duck and is quite active in the community. My sources tell me it was money from Margaret's father that enabled Ed to start his own business. Gardner Beach Wear. Initially it was a clothing store, selling bathing suits and clothes and shoes to wear on vacation, but they soon expanded into beach and patio accessories."

"Sounds like the plot of *The Legend of Sleepy Hollow*. One eligible woman, two suitors." I slowed as I reached Whalebone Junction. Time to get off the phone and pay attention. "Thanks for this Aunt Ellen."

"Do you think it means anything?"

"Probably not. Oh, one thing. Was Margaret Gardner at the lighthouse on Saturday?"

"I didn't see her."

"Catch you later," I said.

That, I thought, *was very interesting.* I honestly couldn't see a man like Jay Ruddle seeking revenge on the son of the man who'd won the girl all those years ago. As Aunt Ellen had said, Curtis saw enemies under every bush without realizing that his biggest enemy was himself.

But that might be irrelevant. Whether or not Jay Ruddle lay awake at night plotting vengeance on the son of Ed Gardner and Margaret Duncan, Curtis thought he did. Whether Jay had deliberately undercut Curtis in order to drive him out of business didn't matter. Not if Curtis thought he had.

He hated Jay Ruddle and was glad the man had died.

Everyone else I'd spoken to about Jay's business practices had told me the man had made enemies, but it had all been a long time ago. These days everyone believed Jay was a retired man with an interest in North Carolina history and the money to indulge his hobby.

Everyone but Curtis Gardner.

I arrived at Connor's campaign office twenty minutes late. "Sorry, Lucy," the volunteer co-coordinator said when I ran in. "Connor left with the first group. He couldn't wait any longer. You can go out with Melody here. She has your package."

I forced a smile at Melody.

* * *

I spent the evening touring the streets of Nags Head with the taciturn Melody. When we got back to the campaign office, I was told that Connor had gone out again. I said my good-nights and went home alone.

Before switching off the engine and getting out of the car, I sat for a long time, peering intently out the windows. Finally, I summoned my courage and switched off the headlights. No mist. No colored lights bobbing above the ground. I felt no urge to wander into the marsh.

I got out of the car and ran up the path, keys firmly in hand. I unlocked the door, ran in, and slammed it shut behind me. I let out a long breath.

Charles stood on the table next to the *Rebecca MacPherson*. His spine was arched, and the long hairs along his back stood at attention. He hissed.

My heart sped up again. "What are you looking at?"

I walked over to the table, and Charles's body relaxed. The ship was as I had left it. No, something had changed. The captain was not on the quarterdeck, and the miniature cat, George, perched high in the rigging.

"How did that get there?" I plucked the little figure off. I held it out to Charles. He hissed at it. "Just a toy." I put the tiny cat back in its place next to the man standing at the wheel. Someone must have touched the model when we weren't looking and rearranged the figures. I'd have a look for the captain tomorrow. I ran my fingers through Charles's long tan and white fur. He purred. "Let's go to bed. Halloween is tomorrow, and then we can get this thing out of here."

* * *

When I hesitantly opened my curtains the next morning, I wasn't greeted by the sight of a ghostly horse.

Clearly, my imagination had been in overdrive the last few days. I vowed to put those supposed sightings out of my mind and never think about them again.

Chapter Seventeen

L ibraries continue to have the reputation as staid, no-nonsense places where thin, middle-aged women with gray hair tied in stiff buns, dressed in overly large, tattered sweaters and sensible shoes, hiss at anyone who dares to utter a whisper, and where patrons tiptoe around in deadly fear of turning pages too loudly and thus falling under the wrath of the *librarian*. I sometimes think of the movie *It's a Wonderful Life*, when, in the alternate universe, Jimmy Stewart recoils in horror when he hears that poor Donna Reed has, with no man to marry her, become "a librarian." This announcement is made to the accompaniment of fearsome music.

Anyone who thought we still lived in Bedford Falls would have had a considerable shock as they stepped through the front door of the Bodie Island Lighthouse Library on the afternoon of October 31st.

The preschool children's program had just ended, and a pack of highly excited, wildly costumed toddlers descended the stairs in a rush, clutching their Halloween treat of juice boxes and homemade cookies decorated and cut into ghost shapes by Ronald and Nan. Parents gathered up their noisy offspring and headed out to their cars. A group of women wearing tall, pointed black hats over purple and pink wigs chatted by the magazine rack. A high school–age boy was coming down the stairs from the research room, dressed as Darth Vader (carrying his helmet so he could watch his footing), and Charity, the oldest Peterson daughter, followed wearing a loose white dress tied with a thin gold belt, her long dark hair wrapped in cinnamon-bun loops around her ears. Louise Jane had arrived in ship-wrecked-sailor costume and was arguing—loudly—with Bertie about the placement of her ghost ship. She was being supported by Diane Uppiton, who some might incorrectly think had come in costume as a politician's wife. Incorrectly, because a pink Chanel suit with pearls was her regular getup. Mrs. Fitzgerald, in poodle skirt, black and white loafers, and ponytail wig, was arguing on Bertie's side. Louise Jane was scheduled to be the entertainer at the teenage-focused party at five and then the later adult one.

Charles sat on a bookshelf high above the fray, eyeing the cat on the deck of the *Rebecca MacPherson* and following the conversation with much interest. I hadn't been the first to arrive this morning, and when I looked at the model ship, the captain was in his correct position on the quarterdeck. Someone must have found him on the floor and picked him up.

Ronald, black eye patch in place and stuffed green parrot bobbing on his shoulder, saw the last small child out the door and then joined the group. "Be sensible, Louise Jane. We'll have overstimulated children running through here."

"Isn't it your job, Mr. Children's Librarian, to keep them under control?"

"I do the best I can," he said. "But I can't do anything about the overstimulated adults coming in later."

"Enough!" Bertie said. "The ship cannot occupy the center table, and that is that. Put it on the small table in the alcove."

Diane opened her mouth to continue arguing, but Louise Jane, clearly realizing which way the wind was blowing through her tattered sails, huffed loudly and did as she'd been told.

The group began to disperse, and Louise Jane was the first to notice that I'd come in. "There you are, Lucy. I'd been wondering when you were going to show up. Must be nice to have such long lunch hours."

"Everything all right?" Bertie asked.

"Fine," I replied. "No new developments." We'd been so busy this morning, I hadn't had a chance to talk to Bertie about the murder investigation. Not that I had anything to report. I was dying to find out if Watson had managed to confirm Anna's location at the time of Jay's death, but I didn't dare phone him and ask. I wanted to talk to Greg about his employment situation, but I couldn't think of a way of politely finding out what I needed to know, which was how desperate he was to keep the curator job. And Lizzie and Norm were unlikely to confess to murdering Jay Ruddle in a disappointed rage, if I did call them.

Once again I'd come to a dead end.

"Developments in what?" Louise Jane and Diane chorused.

I didn't reply, and Louise Jane said, "No matter. Now that you're finally here, we need to get the chairs arranged for my lecture. Good thing we decided to move the ship off the center table and get it out of the way. We'll be able to get more chairs in. Ronald and Lucy, you can do that while Diane's fetching the chairs from the third floor."

"Chairs?" our board member said. "I'm dreadfully sorry, Louise Jane, I have an important appointment. I'm going to be late as it is, but I wanted to pop in and make sure everything was under control." She bolted for the door. "It'll be tight, but Curtis and I will be back in time to hear you speak. You've arranged for someone to pick up the cookies and tarts?"

"Cookies?" I said.

"Diane and Curtis," Bertie said through gritted teeth, "thought it would be nice to splurge on refreshments for the Halloween parties. No packaged treats this time."

"That was thoughtful of you." I'd eat Louise Jane's ship, sailors and all, if Diane and Curtis would be putting their hands in their own pockets. "I hope it didn't cost you too much."

Diane laughed lightly. "What are library budgets for, if not indulging ourselves—I mean, our patrons—now and again? Don't forget, Bertie, to send someone around to Josie's to pick them up at three."

"I thought you were doing that, Diane," Bertie said.

"No time. No time." Diane Uppiton bustled off, a flurry of pink busyness.

"I've just come from town," I said. "I could have brought them with me."

"She wanted us to serve wine and beer also," Ronald said. "But I pointed out that these events include children and teenagers, so maybe we don't want to set a bad example."

Louise Jane clapped her hands. "This room isn't going to get itself organized, people. Let's get to it. Lucy and Ronald, move the *Rebecca MacPherson*, and be careful with it. Then you can bring out the chairs."

"We can, can we?" Ronald muttered under his breath.

I ran into the staff room to toss my purse into the closet, and came back to give him a hand while Charles and Louise Jane supervised.

* * *

At four thirty, I was standing outside on the steps, getting a breath of air before the teenaged patrons descended.

"Where's your costume?" a voice said to me.

I blinked and glanced down. Batman, a very short, very small Batman, was looking up at me.

"What?"

"Today's Halloween. Where's your costume? Everyone wears a costume on Halloween."

"Now, Bobby, don't bother Ms. Richardson." A flapper—fringed dress, hair in a bob, long string of pearls, elbow-length white gloves—took him by the hand.

"This is my costume," I said. "I'm dressed as an undercover police officer."

"Cool," he said. His mother gave me a wink.

I laughed and went back inside. Our library was looking more like a haunted mansion than a public library. A few more gravestones had appeared out of nowhere, more spider webs had been wrapped around the iron staircase, and more skeletal sailors added to the wreck of the *Rebecca MacPherson*.

Bertie had gone to Josie's to pick up the Halloween-themed treats, and they were arranged on the circulation desk, looking devilishly tempting indeed. Ronald had called Nan and asked her to bring a metal ice bucket made to resemble a skull, into which we'd put cans of soda. He really did have some strange things. The paper plates and napkins continued the theme, decorated with orange pumpkins on a black background.

Bertie stood in the door to the hallway, studying the preparations. Instead of a smile on her face, her mouth was turned down, and a fine line ran between her eyebrows.

"Everything okay?" I asked.

"Tell me this isn't disrespectful and tacky. A Halloween party so soon after someone died one floor above this very room. I notice you're not in costume."

"I'm okay with doing the events for our patrons, but dressing up myself didn't seem all that appropriate somehow."

"No, it doesn't."

"Don't worry about it," I said. "I mentioned our plans to Julia yesterday, and she wants to come. She says her grandfather liked to see a library that was the center of the community."

Bertie broke into a smile. "That does make me feel better. Thank you, Lucy." She glanced toward the door. "Looks like your guests are here now."

Julia was accompanied (no surprise there) by Greg and Theodore.

I hurried across the room to greet them. "I'm so pleased you came, Julia."

"I wouldn't miss it." She studied the room. "Everything looks great."

"Why don't you help yourself to refreshments and then take a seat. Be sure you try one of Josie's justifiably famous pecan squares. The sugar cookies are fabulous too. Louise Jane will be beginning shortly. You're welcome to stay until seven, when we've planned a second event for the adults, with all different stories." Additional baked goods and drinks were stored in the break room, waiting for round two. At the moment, Louise Jane was also in the staff room, preparing herself.

Theodore and Greg tripped over their own feet gathering cookies and squares for Julia. Theodore presented her with a glass of lemonade, and Greg brought her tea. She gave them both a smile and said, "Good heavens, I can't eat all that. You gentlemen go ahead." They plopped themselves down on either side of her with their paper plates and plastic glasses.

"Boys and girls, ladies and gentlemen, please take your seats," Bertie said. "We'll be starting in a moment."

The last rush for the treats table began, and then everyone found a seat. Mrs. Peterson had brought all five of her daughters, and they were all in some sort of costume. The Darth Vader boy I'd noticed earlier with Charity plopped down beside her, tossing his black cape over the back of his chair. They wiggled their seats closer together. Mrs. Peterson gave the boy a piercing look, to which he paid not the slightest bit of attention. "Dallas," she snapped, "change places with Charity."

"Why?" Ten-year-old Dallas said around a mouthful of chocolate-chip cookie.

"Because I said so," Mrs. Peterson said.

"Oh, Mom," Charity groaned.

Grumbling, the girls did as they were told. The boy's

disappointment was written all over his face. I caught Ronald's eye, and he winked at me. I smothered a laugh. Poor Mrs. Peterson had some hard years ahead of her. Five daughters who were not likely to wait for their mother to arrange suitable suitors in the traditional, genteel Southern manner.

"Lucy," said a hissing voice from the hallway. "Lucy!"

"What?"

"I told you to turn out the lights at five after."

"Oh, right." I flicked the main switch, leaving the room softly lit by a gentle glow from the lighting over the shelves and in the alcove. Louise Jane swept into the room.

I knew that some of these teens would be here under protest. They'd rather be out throwing eggs and dispensing toilet paper, not sitting in a library under the watchful eye of their parents. At the beginning of Louise Jane's talk, there was a lot of shifting in seats, nudging with elbows, and surreptitious checking of phones, but they soon settled down as she wove her spell. Nothing teenagers love more than ghost stories. Even I found myself enraptured. She talked mostly about the legend of the *Rebecca MacPherson*. As this audience wasn't only teens but also younger children like the smaller Peterson girls, she kept the tale light as she drew out the story of the doomed ship, fated to wander the seas for all time when the cowardly actions of its captain and crew brought about the destruction of a companion ship. I was pleased that she didn't talk about Frances, called the Lady, who supposedly haunted my apartment, and glossed lightly over other tales of haunting of the lighthouse.

I glanced at Theodore to see how he was reacting to the stories. He didn't appear to be too bothered by the ghostly tales.

After all, this was just Louise Jane, who he'd known most of his life. Judging by the way he was sneaking glances at Julia, seated next to him, he probably wasn't hearing a word anyway.

Louise Jane finished to considerable applause and smiled happily.

"Thank you so much, Louise Jane," Bertie said. "Please, everyone help yourself to more refreshments. The library is still open if you'd like to take out some books."

"I'd be happy to answer questions," Louise Jane said.

But there weren't any questions, and as interesting as the teenage boys had found the lecture, nothing could compete with cookies and squares. Soon all that remained on the platters were crumbs, and not many of those.

"I enjoyed that very much," Julia said to me, after taking a moment to thank Louise Jane. "Thank you for inviting us. You've all been so kind to me since Grandfather died."

"Allow me to see you back to the hotel," Theodore said. "You must be tired."

"Oh, no. I'd like to stay for a while. Louise Jane said she has different material in the next talk."

"Don't take anything Louise Jane says as fact." Charlene joined our little group. "She has been known to embellish on occasion."

"Ghost stories." Theodore laughed uncomfortably. "All nonsense."

"Isn't embellishment the heart of good storytelling?" Julia said.

"Not if it's supposed to be nonfiction. Hi—we haven't met yet." My colleague put out her hand, and Julia accepted it. "I'm

Charlene, the reference librarian here. Nonfiction is my bread and butter, so I get defensive when people think history needs to be improved upon."

"Julia Ruddle. Your work must be fascinating. I'm familiar with some of the history of this coast, and I agree with you that it needs no embellishment."

"Is history an interest of yours?" Charlene asked.

"Naval history in the Age of Sail in particular, but only as an enthusiastic amateur. I might not be leaving your lovely town for a few more days. Can I come around tomorrow and talk to you?"

"I'd enjoy that," Charlene said. "We have a substantial collection of rare books and private papers that I'd be happy to let you have a look at."

"Lucy!" Mrs. Peterson trilled. "Lucy, we're waiting to check out books here."

I hurried to the circulation desk. Mrs. Peterson had a death grip on her eldest daughter's arm. The younger girls held books, and Charity was gazing across the room into the adoring eyes of the boy who'd tried to sit next to her.

"Did you enjoy the presentation?" I asked Dallas.

"It was great. They should make a movie of that story about the ship. It'd be awesome."

"They could film it right here in Nags Head," Primrose, age twelve, said. "Maybe I could have a part. I'm going to be an actress, you know."

"As if," Dallas snorted. "You need to be *pretty* to be in movies."

Primrose stuck out her tongue.

"I wasn't at all pleased," Mrs. Peterson said. "Louise Jane should know better than to be telling such graphic stories in front of children." I wondered if Mrs. Peterson had any idea what was going on in movies and TV these days.

I checked out the books, handed them to the girls, and they left, Mrs. Peterson dragging Charity along behind. I helped other patrons, and when I again looked up, Julia was still deep in conversation with Charlene. Theodore and Greg stood at opposite sides of the room, alternately watching Julia and eying each other suspiciously.

Gradually, most of the teens and their parents departed, and a new round of guests began coming in. Ronald and Bertie brought out more refreshments. Louise Jane had disappeared, presumably to once again prepare herself. No one had turned the lights back up, and the room was full of a delightfully gentle glow, which I found not at all spooky. Diane arrived and immediately hit the replenished trays of baked goods. "Mr. Gardner won't be joining us," she said to me as she bit into a raspberry tart, although I hadn't asked. "A last-minute business emergency."

More likely, I thought but didn't say, *he decided not to come when he heard we were not providing free beer.*

"I hope everything's all right," I said. "It must be stressful managing a successful chain of stores."

"You don't know the half of it, Lucy. Curtis is responsible for the livelihood of his employees and their families. A responsibility he takes seriously."

I nodded. I'd heard the staff turnover was high at Gardner Beach Wear. Any local teenager who could get a better summer job didn't stay working for Curtis for long. "How admirable."

She sighed, and then she leaned closer to me. I caught a whiff of heavily applied perfume. "It's hard enough running a successful company without *other people* trying to force you out of business."

"Is someone doing that to Curtis?" I asked, all innocence.

She tapped the side of her nose. "Let's say, Lucy, that sometimes death is not entirely undeserved."

Diane wandered away, leaving me gobsmacked. Had Diane Uppiton just confessed to killing Jay Ruddle to save Curtis's business?

One thing I know, from a lifelong reading of mystery novels, is that killers, those who aren't total sociopaths or professional criminals, often get caught because they have to confess—or brag—to someone.

I'd considered that Curtis might be the killer. I hadn't even thought about Diane. But she'd been at the lecture on Saturday. She knew her way around the library.

I couldn't keep this to myself. I'd have to give Detective Watson a call, whether he wanted to hear from me or not.

While all these thoughts were running through my head, I was trying to keep my distance from the refreshments table. Josie's pecan squares were the definition of heaven on earth, but since coming to live in the Outer Banks, I'd enjoyed a few more of them than I should have. My wobbling resolution to remain strong was saved when Theodore noticed me standing alone and slid up beside me. He'd given in to pecan square temptation, and I gestured to him to brush the crumbs off his sweater. He did so. He hadn't come in costume tonight, but wore his new jeans and a collared blue shirt under an oatmeal sweater. Other than when he'd escorted Anna yesterday, I hadn't seen him in his English-scholar getup since he'd first met Julia. Even the fake British accent was gone. I was pleased he'd realized he didn't need the pretense to impress her. "Nothing to report, I'm sorry to say, Lucy."

"Report?"

"On Greg's job prospects. Unfortunately, I don't have the resources the police do, but an intense survey of the Internet didn't reveal any cases of embezzlement, being fired for cause, or criminal activity, petty or otherwise."

"I didn't expect anything like that. Jay wouldn't have hired him if he had a criminal record."

"That sort of man can pull the wool over people's eyes, Lucy. You don't . . . uh . . . think Greg's handsome, do you?"

I glanced over to the fiction shelves, where Greg was pretending to read the back of an Andrew Pyper book while keeping an eye on the fair Julia. He lifted his hand and brushed at a lock of hair. Greg was strikingly handsome. I'd never dare say so to Teddy. "What on earth makes you ask me that?"

"I overheard heard one of the teenage girls talking to her friend. They seemed to think so."

"Teenage girls. What do you expect?"

He grinned. "That's exactly what I thought, Lucy. Have you heard anything more about the situation? Anything that might help Julia, I mean?"

"The police have other suspects, and they're working hard on it."

"Not all that hard, it would appear," he said. I turned to see Sam Watson and his wife CeeCee arrive. She was in costume, but he was not. Somehow that didn't surprise me.

"He's allowed some time off," I said.

"He shouldn't be." Theodore spotted Eunice Fitzgerald, seated stiffly in a wingback chair, with her cane at her side, like Maggie Smith in *Downton Abbey*. Her poodle skirt was spread out around her, and her ponytail moved as she spoke. Our board chair was chatting with my aunt Ellen, and Theodore went to join them.

CeeCee caught up with Butch and Stephanie, in their Laurel and Hardy costumes, who'd arrived minutes before, but Watson took a spot against the wall. A spot, I couldn't help but notice, where he could keep an eye on everyone. Julia Ruddle included.

The room was filling up fast. This library is small, but it seems to be able to stretch at the seams to accommodate everyone it needs to. I wasn't expecting the next people to arrive. Elizabeth McArthur and Norman Hoskins stood in the doorway, blinking in surprise.

I looked quickly around for Bertie. She was trapped against the wall by Diane Uppiton. I hurried across the room to greet the newcomers. "Hi, welcome."

"What on earth is going on here?" Elizabeth said.

"A Halloween party."

"In a library?" Norman said.

"Where better?" I gestured to the guests. "Many people have come as characters from books." Did I detect the slightest of smiles touch the edges of Elizabeth's mouth? "What are you doing here, if you didn't come for the party? As you can see, we're pretty busy right now."

The door opened again, and in came Anna and Dave. The violinist swooped down upon me and wrapped me in a deep hug that pretty much expelled all the breath from my lungs. "I invited these nice people to come along to your little library, *moya dorogaya*. I knew you wouldn't mind."

"You know each other?"

"We do now." Anna slipped her hand through Norman's arm and gave him a radiant smile. He blushed to the roots of his thick black hair, and the edges of his mustache twitched.

"Oh, look," Dave said. "Cookies. Those look great. I haven't had dinner yet." He wandered off.

"We met these lovely people at the hotel." Anna said. "We were walking through the lobby when I overheard them ask the receptionist to put them through to Julia's room."

Elizabeth shifted from one foot to the other. Norman studied the bookshelf behind my head: Roberts to Zelazny. "Naturally, I introduced myself," Anna said. "They're from a university, and they want to talk to Julia about Jay's tedious little collection. Apparently, it contains some important artifacts. Isn't that interesting?"

Julia spotted us and came over. After she freed herself from one of Anna's enthusiastic hugs, she was introduced to Elizabeth and Norman. "It was nice of your mother to invite us," Elizabeth said. "We were hoping to catch you at your hotel before you went out to dinner, but this is much more convenient."

Julia didn't return her smile. "I'm not going to discuss my grandfather's collection here. This is a party."

"You are so right, my darling," Anna said. "But it never hurts to meet the interested parties, does it? These nice people would like Jay's collection to come to their university. It seems he was going to *give* it to them, but he died before the papers could be signed. I told them they must have been mistaken, as Jay would never give something of value away. You and I will be negotiating a fair price."

"I'm sorry." Julia looked directly at Elizabeth. "You've come all this way for nothing. My mother is not my business advisor. My grandfather's estate has not been settled, and if I should be bequeathed his collection, I intend to manage it myself."

We smiled awkwardly at one another. All except Anna, who let out one of her light, tinkling laughs. "That sounds more like Jay Ruddle. I found it hard to believe he'd give anything away. No, that was nothing but an opening ploy on his part." She patted Elizabeth's shoulder. "Leave it with me."

Julia shook her head.

"There's your nice young man." Anna took her daughter's arm. "You mustn't leave him standing all by himself, *moya dorogaya*. You never can tell what men will get up to when they are left to their own devices."

"He's not my young man," Julia protested. Anna paid no attention and dragged her daughter away. She was heading for Theodore, but Julia managed to pull herself free and stop next to Charlene.

I was left with Elizabeth and Norman. "As long as you're here, you're welcome to stay for the program and have some refreshments."

"You were at Blacklock College yesterday," Norman said. "I

saw you and Ms. James poking about. If you came to accept our generous offer, why didn't you come to our offices? We were in."

"We were there on library business," I said.

"Spying, more likely." Elizabeth couldn't help stealing a glance at Anna. "Now, more than ever, you can forget about us paying you to withdraw from bidding for the Ruddle collection."

"Whatever." I left them standing by the door.

Charles was sitting on the windowsill, watching the festivities. Earlier he'd checked out the food offerings. Clearly dissatisfied to find sugary baked goods rather than thin slices of salmon or a bowl of smoked trout dip, he'd looked almost as disappointed as the teenage Darth Vader when Mrs. Peterson had ordered Charity to change seats with her sister. I gave the big cat a rub on the top of his head. He purred and together we watched the partygoers. Greg was filling a glass with lemonade and ice, and Theodore watched the other man like Charles might eye a mouse, ready to pounce if Greg made a move toward the fair Julia.

I bent over Charles and whispered into his ear. "I want you to keep an eye on everyone. Give me a signal if you identify the killer." Since coming to work at the library and being adopted by Charles, I'd come to realize that he was an excellent judge of character. I glanced at Detective Watson, standing with Butch. Watson might be talking to the other man, but his eyes never stopped moving around the room. He was, I realized, working.

I could imagine what he'd have to say if I told him I'd solved the murder based on Charles's reaction to one or another of the suspects.

The door opened, and a handful of last-minute guests came in along with a wave of cold damp air. Charles leapt off the

windowsill and went to find a warmer place to observe the festivities. He found it in Mrs. Fitzgerald's lap and settled in for a
good long pat.

If Charles wasn't going to be any help, it might be up to me.
I joined Butch and Watson.

"Good evening," I said. "No costume, Detective?"

"I've come as an undercover police officer."

I laughed. "I used that line myself earlier. If that's your costume, it's a pretty poor one. You might as well have 'cop' tat-
tooed on your forehead."

Butch grinned.

People swirled all around us, and I lowered my voice. "That's
Julia's mother over there. The woman in the red cloak. That's
not a costume, by the way—it's how she dresses all the time."

"I know," Watson said.

"You do? Did you meet her?"

"I am a police officer, Lucy. That means I have sources. And,
as you are obviously still curious, I'll tell you that my sources say
Ms. Marakova was on a flight from Rome to the United States
that left early Sunday morning Italian time."

"Meaning she wasn't here, in the rare books room of the
library, Saturday afternoon East Coast time."

"Meaning precisely that. She appears to have caught a flight
as soon as she heard the news about Jay Ruddle's death."

"Have you given any thought to Curtis Gardner or Diane
Uppiton?"

Watson's piercing gray eyes studied me. "Why would I do
that?"

"Curtis believes, and through him Diane, that Jay Ruddle

was out to destroy his business. His stores are more than simply a business to him. His father started the company, which means a lot of emotion is involved. I heard that back in the day, Curtis's father and Jay were rivals for the hand of the same woman. She married Mr. Gardner, and Jay left the Outer Banks."

"And he held a grudge for something like fifty years? Really, Lucy, your imagination carries you away some times."

I bristled. "So? It seems as though some imagination is needed to get to the bottom of this case."

To my surprise, Watson grinned at me. Butch said, "I'm not getting involved in this," and left us.

"It's not common knowledge, Lucy, but not confidential either," Watson said. "Gardner's business is in serious trouble. Not through the machinations of some evil millionaire with an ancient grudge, but changes in the tourist economy as well as sheer incompetence on the part of management. Ruddle Furniture saw an opening and took it. I doubt Jay himself was involved in the decision."

"Oh," I said. "But Curtis and Diane think—"

"Yes, Curtis thinks Jay was responsible. And that is worth keeping in mind. Anyone else you want me to keep an eye on?"

"As a matter of fact, yes. See those two over there? Standing by themselves, not exactly taking part in the fun? They're the ones from Blacklock College that are after Jay Ruddle's collection of historical documents." I glanced around the room. Except for Curtis, all the suspects were here, I realized.

"Hope I'm not late," a voice said in my ear, pulling me out of my thoughts. I felt a rush of pleasure as I turned and looked up into Connor's smiling blue eyes.

"You're not late, although I fear you've missed the pecan squares and ghost cookies."

"I'll have to live with that."

"I'm glad you could make it."

He pulled at his tie and stuffed it into his pocket. "Meeting with the chief went overtime."

"Any developments in the Ruddle case?" Watson asked.

"Not that he told me. We were talking about budgets. Never my favorite topic." Connor glanced around the room. "Nice crowd."

"CeeCee's waving at me," Watson said. "She's saved me a seat. Talk to you later, Mr. Mayor."

Most of the chairs were taken, or places saved with bags or books. About half of the guests had come in some sort of costume, and the dim lights from the bookshelves and the alcove cast a charming glow over the room. People ate and drank, laughed, and chatted with their neighbors.

"Give me a minute to say hello to Bertie and the board," Connor said. "Then I'll come back and join you."

"Okay," I said.

I watched him work the room. He moved quickly, going from one person to another, smiling, exchanging greetings and handshakes. He was back with me in a few minutes. "Now that that's over, have you got a minute to talk in private?"

My heartbeat went from normal to end of a marathon in a second. "Yes."

His smile was warm: his real smile, not the politician one. "Let's step outside. Any minute now old George Delahunt is going to spot me and come rushing over to remind me that they want speed bumps installed on their street."

Talk. Connor wanted to *talk.* I didn't know if I liked the sound of that. Had he grown tired of my evasiveness and intended to dump me? Or maybe he was going to propose? Either option filled me with dread. We walked to the door, my thoughts rolling like a dinghy cast adrift in a hurricane. He couldn't be proposing. He was too old-fashioned to do that in the middle of a party. On the other hand, this was a good situation in which to dump me. I wouldn't throw a fit and burst into tears, not surrounded by my coworkers and friends.

I never did find out what Connor wanted to *talk* about. He opened the door, and a bright white light hit us full in the face. "Mr. Mayor," a woman's voice called, "do you think it's proper to be attending a Halloween party in the Library of Horror?"

Chapter Eighteen

"Turn off that blasted light," Connor said, "so I can see who I'm taking to."

The light shifted to one side. The woman who'd spoken was the thin blond TV reporter who'd been here earlier. The man with her had his camera mounted on his shoulder. Several others were gathered around them, armed with more cameras and microphones.

"Hampton Hitchcock. *Raleigh Daily Bugle*," a man called out of the darkness. "Care to make a statement, Mayor McNeil, on the suitability of having a party at the site of a recent tragic death?"

Like Superman dashing into a phone booth, Connor changed before my very eyes. His whole body stiffened, his posture straightened, his head rose, and the soft blue eyes I loved so much darkened.

Soft blue eyes: he wouldn't have been looking at me in that way if he'd planned to dump me. Would he?

The eyes I loved so much: If I did love them, and him, it was time I remembered that. Before it was too late.

"The Bodie Island Lighthouse Library is a public place," Connor said, his words clipped, his voice formal, "as well as a beloved Outer Banks institution and a place of great historical importance. We're deeply sorry that a visitor to our magnificent seaside died here, and our heartfelt condolences are extended to his family."

Shutters clicked and the TV camera was back in our faces. I didn't know what to do. I should probably step away, but might that look as though I, a library employee, was distancing myself from Connor and his statement? I forced out a smile and then dropped it. I didn't want to look happy as we talked about Jay Ruddle's death. I was glad I wasn't wearing a ridiculous costume.

"You don't consider a Halloween party to be at all inappropriate?" the TV woman asked.

"The residents and visitors of Nags Head, North Carolina, are welcome to continue to enjoy the beloved holiday as they see fit, at one of their favorite places, if they so choose. I have nothing further to say. Thank you, ladies and gentlemen."

"Doug Whiteside, mayoral candidate, released a statement a short while ago, calling this party tasteless."

"He would," I muttered.

"What's that, Madam?" The cameras and microphones swung toward me. "May I ask your name?"

"No," Connor said, his calm beginning to snap. "You may not."

"Lucy," called a voice from the back of the pack, "can you make a statement on behalf of the library?"

"Uh," I said.

"Let's get some shots inside," the TV woman said, "of party-goers celebrating at the death scene."

"You can't come in," I said. "Fire regulations. The building's at capacity. Mayor McNeil and I were stepping outside to ensure no other patrons are arriving. Sorry."

"We'll choose a pool reporter then," someone said.

"You will not." The door had opened so quietly I hadn't heard Sam Watson come out. "The library is closed, and this is a private party. You people have not been invited."

"Detective Watson, do you have a statement to make to the press?"

"Any updates on the case?"

"Is an arrest imminent?"

"As I am with my wife, enjoying an evening out," Watson said, "I'm not taking questions at this time. Good night. Your Honor, Ms. Richardson, why don't you folks come back inside."

More pictures were taken of our retreating backs. The door slammed shut behind us.

A few people had been aware of what was happening outside, but not many. The refreshments were finished, and the seats were filled, leaving standing room only. The buzz of conversation filled the room.

"What's going on?" Bertie asked.

"Doug Whiteside causing trouble," I whispered.

"I saw the pack when I left the office," Connor said. "I told them I had nothing to say. They must have followed me here. I'm sorry."

"Not your fault," Bertie said. "Vultures, the lot of them."

"I told them not to come in," Watson said. "But I can't order them to leave the property, and even if I could, they'd lay in wait on the road."

We all grumbled.

"Bertie, are you doing the introductions?" Watson said. "Maybe you should get started."

"Yes, of course," she said.

"Sorry about that," Connor said to me once they'd departed.

"Not your fault."

"We can talk later," he said.

Together we found a place by the window. Charles jumped up to join us, and he rubbed himself against Connor's arm. Connor rewarded him with a scratch under the chin. I trusted Charles's instincts, but I already knew he liked Connor. Tonight, Charles was falling down on the job: he was doing nothing to help identify the killer.

Louise Jane's second set of stories was much darker than the first. She talked briefly about the *Rebecca MacPherson* and other seafaring ghostly legends, mentioning that it was rumored that the *Flying Dutchman* itself had been seen in these waters. She then went on to talk about hauntings (supposedly) in the very building in which we were having our party. Bertie, I knew, would not be happy. Neither would Theodore, who was beginning to shift uncomfortably as the mood of the stories darkened.

"This lighthouse has a long and troubled history. Many of

you are familiar with some of the stories. Perhaps the best known is the tragic fate of Frances, known as the Lady."

I sucked in a breath. If Louise Jane dared to imply in front of all these people that the Lady or any other of her imaginary friends had caused the death of Jay Ruddle, I wouldn't be responsible for my actions.

As Louise Jane related the tragic tale of the post–Civil War bride, I glanced at Julia. Her face was in profile, but she showed no hint of distress. She leaned over and whispered to Theodore. Relieved at the interruption, he smiled at her. The Lady, Louise Jane told us, had been forced into marriage to a cruel, old lighthouse keeper, who kept her locked in the upper levels until she was driven mad and threw herself out the fourth-floor window. The very window, apparently, in the apartment where I now lived. Frances, according to Louise Jane, was not an evil spirit. As kind in death as she had been in life, she only wanted to help women she believed to be trapped as she had been.

By helping, she tossed them out the fourth-floor window.

"Are you okay with this?" Connor whispered to me.

"Bertie will be furious that Louise Jane's saying the building's haunted, and I hope she doesn't try to link the ghost of Frances to Jay's death in public. But if you're asking about me personally, I don't mind her silly stories." That was true. When I'd first come here, Louise Jane had tried to chase me away by repeating legends of hauntings of the lighthouse. I'd never once experienced anything even remotely threatening—in a non-human way, that is—and perhaps more to the point, neither had Charles. I froze.

"What is it?" Connor said. "You've gone as white as a sheet."

"Nothing. Just a sudden chill. Don't you feel it?"

"If anything, it's warm in here. Take my jacket." He whipped off his suit jacket and placed it lightly around my shoulders. Charles meowed. I tried to give them both a smile. I failed.

I had never experienced anything. Until this week. The ghostly horse, watching me from the mist. The candle lights in the marsh, beckoning to me to follow.

"You're freezing," Connor said, his hands light on my shoulders, his voice low. "You need to sit down."

"I'm fine. Really. She's almost done."

Louise Jane switched to a story guaranteed to bring tears to her audience. A lighthouse keeper's small son, playing on the forbidden upper levels, climbing the rail, and plummeting to his death below. "To this very day," Louise Jane said, "children visiting the library have reported seeing a boy, dressed in old-fashioned clothes, asking them to come upstairs with him and play."

"Ronald and Bertie aren't going to be happy about this," Connor muttered. "Hasn't Bertie forbidden Louise Jane from repeating that story?"

"To no avail, obviously. About the last thing we want is parents to be afraid to send their children to the library in case they're lured away by a ghostly child." The sudden chill had passed, and I was warm in Connor's jacket. But I didn't give it back. It felt very nice.

Bertie was standing next to the shelf marked "Morrison–Proux." She stepped forward, but Louise Jane ignored her. "The War Between the States saw the destruction of the lighthouse. It was rebuilt . . ."

Bertie might want to wrap things up, but the audience

continued to be enthralled. You could hear the proverbial pin drop when Louise Jane paused for breath and spread her arms out, inviting everyone into her circle. I had to admit, she looked (and sounded) marvelous, her voice deep and full of emotion as she stood there draped in shadow, wearing her tattered sailor's suit, the model of the *Rebecca MacPherson* lit by the single light in the alcove.

"The press have given up," Connor whispered in my ear. "I saw a line of cars moving down the road."

"Good riddance," I said.

He slipped his hand into mine. My heart did that marathon thing again.

At last, Louise Jane said, simply, "Thank you." She took a deep bow, and the audience burst into applause.

Bertie joined her at the front of the room. "Wasn't that entertaining? You almost had us believing you for a few minutes there, Louise Jane. If anyone wants to learn about the *real* stories of the Outer Banks, Charlene, our reference librarian, would be happy to direct you to some good books."

Charlene waved to the crowd.

People began gathering up bags and chatting to their neighbors, but before anyone could get away, Anna leapt to her feet, clapping enthusiastically. She swept to the front of the room and grabbed Louise Jane's hands in hers. "Music! You need musical accompaniment, my darling. We will take this show on the road, yes? You can speak to the masses, and I will play my violin. I know the perfect score." She let go of Louise Jane and lifted her arms. She imitated playing the instrument, eyes closed and body swaying, her face a study in concentration. I swear, I could almost hear the slow plaintive notes. Louise Jane stared at her, open-mouthed. Everyone in the room was frozen into place except for a few who fell back onto their chairs.

Anna dropped the violin with a crash. "No! I have a better idea. We will call these spirits to show themselves. Now! You will call their names, and my music, playing the notes of the great Russian composers, will draw them forward."

"Who the heck is that?" Connor asked.

"Julia's mother," I said. Julia had slithered lower in her seat and dipped her head, trying to turn invisible. Greg looked confused. Theodore looked terrified. Dave looked amused.

"Okay . . . I guess . . . ," Louise Jane said. "I suppose that might be fun."

"Fun!" Anna cried. "We are not looking for fun. The mysteries of life and death are not fun. David! Where is David? I will send him to my hotel to get my violin. I will play now. The scene is set, the audience is waiting."

Dave got to his feet. "I didn't drive—remember, babe? We got a lift with those people from the college."

"Then Gregory can go," Anna said.

"Not me," Greg said.

Bertie resumed her place at the front of the room. "I'm sorry, but the library is closing shortly. If you manage to get this act together, Louise Jane, please do let us know. Some of us might like to come if we are free that evening. Thank you, everyone, for coming, and good night."

No one made a rush for the doors.

"You can keep the library open a while longer," Anna declared. "I cannot play on the lawn. It's damp, and my violin is too valuable to be exposed to the night air. Julia. Where are you? Tell your young man to go to my hotel. Quickly now."

Julia scrunched herself into an even smaller ball. From behind, I could see the tips of her ears turning red. Theodore, realizing Anna had referred to him as Julia's young man, leapt to his feet, fear forgotten, clearly eager to stay in Anna's good graces. Julia reached out a hand and pulled him back onto his seat. Bertie stepped in front of Anna. Anna feigned moving to the left, and then took a sharp swivel to the right, but Bertie was too fast for her, and the violinist was blocked again.

"I haven't seen footwork like that since I last played basketball," Connor said.

"The audience will no doubt have further questions for you, Louise Jane," Bertie said. "Why don't you take a place by the refreshment table?"

"Uh . . . okay." Louise Jane turned to Anna and said, "I love your idea. Let's talk later." She took a small bow, received another round of applause, and then left the stage.

"A few cookies are still on the table," Bertie said. People got the hint and stood up.

"That was surprisingly entertaining," Sam Watson said to Connor. "And I don't mean just the encore." He peered out the window. "Looks like the press has left."

"They tend not to like standing around in the cold and dark," Connor said. "Good thing no one told them Josie had done the catering."

Watson laughed. "Anna will be disappointed to hear she missed them. What a flake she is."

CeeCee slipped her arm through his. "Ready to go, honey?"

"I guess so. Night all."

"Good night," we said.

"I want to talk to Bertie for a moment," Connor said to me. "How about a drink once everyone's left?"

"That would be nice," I said.

I noticed Julia getting up and hurried over to her. "I am so sorry. Are you all right? That must have been dreadfully embarrassing."

"My mother. What can I say?" Julia glanced over to where Anna was handing out business cards to a circle of what were probably classical music lovers. "It was a lovely evening—up until the end anyway. I loved hearing Louise Jane even more the second time. Thank you for inviting me, Lucy."

"Any time."

"Are we still on for tomorrow?" Charlene asked.

"I wouldn't miss it. I'll be here at ten, as we arranged," Julia said. "Good night."

"Night."

"Allow me . . . ," Theodore began.

She put her hand on his arm. "You're so kind, but I'll go back to the hotel with Greg. I'm dreadfully tired all of a sudden." She sighed. "I suppose we have to offer Anna and Dave a lift."

Not without difficulty, Julia managed to round up her mother and drag her toward the door. "I am at the Ocean Side Hotel," Anna shouted. "Call me tomorrow, Mary Jane, and we can continue with our plans. Fortunately, my schedule is temporarily empty for the foreseeable future."

To which Louise Jane replied, "It's *Louise* Jane."

Greg couldn't help throwing a smirk over his shoulder at Theodore as he left the library with the fair Julia and her mother.

"Nice to see Anna and her daughter getting on so well again, isn't it?" Dave said to me before running after them.

The library was thinning out, and I joined Louise Jane.

"That went well, I thought," Louise Jane said, waiting for compliments.

I gave them. She deserved them.

Bertie broke away from the circle of people she was chatting to and headed toward us. She didn't look as though offering compliments was the main thing on her mind.

"Will you look at the time?" Louise Jane said. "Public performances are so exhausting. I've got to run. I'll be back tomorrow to get the *Rebecca MacPherson*. Bye all." She dashed out of the library.

Ronald and Charlene began gathering empty glasses and crumpled napkins, and I hurried to help them get the room back to normal. It took us a long time—all those chairs to carry up three flights of twisty, winding stairs—and when we finished, other than the library employees, only Teddy and Connor remained. I'd given him back his jacket, but he hadn't put it on, and he was sweeping the floor, shirtsleeves rolled up.

"Nothing I love more," Charlene said, peering over the second-floor railing, "than a man with a broom."

We went down to join the others.

"I'd say tonight was a big success," Ronald said.

"The audience loved it," Bertie said. "But when I get my hands on that Louise Jane . . . Imagine, telling the story of the lighthouse keeper's little boy!"

"Is there any truth to it?" Connor asked.

"Certainly not!"

He held up his hands. "I don't mean the ghost. I mean the boy falling."

"Like most legends, it has a basis in fact," Charlene said. "The child didn't die. He was where he wasn't supposed to be and tripped and fell down the stairs. He didn't go over the railing, but broke both his legs. This happened sometime in the 1890s. The boy took over as lighthouse keeper from his father, and he was greatly admired because the breaks left him with a lot of pain in his legs. He had trouble with the stairs, but he knew how important the light was to ships at sea, and he was dedicated to keeping it lit. Back in those days, the job involved climbing all two hundred and seventeen steps several times a day."

"I find that a more inspiring tale than a disobedient little boy plunging to his death," Connor said.

"But not for Halloween," Ronald said. "I tell the true story to the children when I explain why we have a gate over the stairs leading up from the second floor that's kept locked when the library's open, and why adults have to ask permission to go up."

Charlene yawned mightily. "Time I was going. I enjoyed meeting Julia, Lucy. She's very keen on naval history. She didn't say so outright, but she gave me the impression she's going to take control of the Ruddle collection herself. If we can't have it, then I'm glad it'll be in good hands. Did you notice the people from Blacklock getting mighty chummy with Julia's mother?"

"If they think Anna has any influence over Julia, they are going to be sadly disappointed," I said.

"Most certainly," Theodore said. "Julia is a woman of

independent mind. Highly admirable. Although, I suppose that means she'll continue to employ the odious Greg."

"Odious?" Charlene said. "Why do you say that? I think he's quite nice. Doesn't hurt that he's soooo good-looking either."

Theodore looked as though he were sucking on a lemon.

"You can worry about that tomorrow," I said.

"Good night," he said.

"Good night," we chorused.

"See you all tomorrow." Ronald walked out with Charlene and Teddy, and Bertie went to her office to get her purse. Charles, who'd managed to disappear while the cleaning up was in progress, jumped onto the wingback chair by the magazine rack.

Connor smiled at me. I smiled at him and shifted my feet uncomfortably, trying to control my blushing.

Bertie was soon back. "Connor. Something came up earlier, and I've been wanting to talk to you. Why don't you give me a lift into town, and we can discuss it. I can get Ronald to pick me up in the morning."

"I . . ." Connor took a quick glance at me.

Heat rose into my face. Charles meowed.

Bertie looked at Connor. She looked at me. "Never mind. Just remembered. Appointment in the morning. Need my car. Another time." She sprinted for the door.

I absolutely love living in the lighthouse, but sometimes it can get a bit uncomfortable residing at what is also my place of work. Hard to keep secrets.

Not that my relationship—or whatever it was—with Connor was a secret. Although *whatever it was* still seemed to be a secret from me.

"Why don't you make yourself comfortable, and I'll run up and get a bottle of wine," I said, once we were alone.

"That would be nice. So, Charles," Connor said as I slipped up the stairs, "did you enjoy the evening? You'd tell us if there were ghosts in here, wouldn't you?"

I grabbed a bottle of Sauvignon Blanc out of my tiny fridge, took two long-stemmed glasses off the shelf, and ran back down. Connor had not yet been in my apartment, and I wasn't ready to suggest we go there. Even if nothing happened, it would take our relationship (that word again!) to a whole new level. A level I wasn't ready to climb to yet.

I was no longer worried that he was planning to dump me. Not tonight anyway. He'd been giving me little smiles during the lecture, and placing his hand on my shoulder or taking mine in his.

I stopped on the second-floor landing and looked down. Connor was bent over the *Rebecca MacPherson*, examining it carefully. Charles sat beside the model ship, also studying it. *Looking for tiny skeletal mice,* I thought with a smile.

I had to get over my former boyfriend, Ricky, the man I'd dated for almost as long as I could remember, the one I'd left Boston to get away from. Not *over* in the sense that I still had feelings for him, because I didn't, but *over* in the sense of realizing that exciting things awaited me if I'd only open myself to them. I'd been raised in a moderately wealthy, stable family environment. My parents' greatest expectation of me had been that I do the accepted thing. I'd been with Ricky since I became aware of what boys were (other than annoying older brothers). My big act of rebellion had been to go to Simmons for a master's degree in library science. Not exactly on the level of running away to sea to become a pirate, but my mother seemed to think so. In the nick of time, I'd realized how incredibly bored I was with my life, and I left Ricky on bended knee (diamond ring in hand, champagne chilling, restaurant patrons gaping) and fled into the night. I was working at Harvard, and I loved it there, but Harvard meant Boston and the social whirl of the Richardson and Lewiston families, so I quit and came to the Outer Banks.

Here I was, happy and content. Now, it was time to make another leap.

Although not literally. I walked down the stairs, moving quietly in ballet flats. Connor continued to be engrossed in the model ship. I came up behind him and wrapped my arms around him. I leaned my cheek against his warm, strong back.

"Nice." He turned and kissed me. The bottle and glasses were in the way, and the kiss was nothing more than a peck, but the joy in his eyes settled all my doubts.

He took the bottle, and I put the glasses on the table. Connor twisted the cap off and poured. We silently toasted each other. "This is quite the model ship," he said. "The detail is amazing. Every time I look, I notice something I missed earlier. Did you see this?" He indicated a black creature, crossing the deck near the bow. "I'm sure that wasn't there earlier, but Charles pointed it out to me."

Charles groomed his whiskers.

"That cat does seem to move around," I said. "I'm positive that man there—I assume he's the captain by the trace of gold on what's left of his epaulettes—was looking to the left earlier. It's almost as though he's watching us."

"I wonder where Louise Jane got this."

"I don't know. She just showed up with it last week."

"Let's sit," he said.

I took the wingback chair, and he pulled the office chair out from behind the circulation desk.

"Any updates about the election?" I sipped my wine. "You said the last polls were promising."

"They still are. It didn't reflect well on Doug when his campaign manager started spreading rumors that I'd been responsible for the death of Will Williamson and Doug lost a lot of support over that. But I'm not counting my chickens yet. I learned very quickly that nothing is as it seems in this racket. I'll be glad when it's all over and I can forget about the campaigning nonsense and simply be the mayor. Or, if that doesn't work out, go back to my dental practice full time. I'm fine with either of those options."

"Do you have any political ambitions after being the mayor?"

"Absolutely not. To be honest, Lucy, I hate it. I don't mean I hate being the mayor. I enjoy the job, and I do it because I care about the future of Nags Head and its people, and I like to think I have something to contribute. But I hate the political part of it. Would I consider moving up the political stage to state or federal level?" He shook his head firmly. "Never."

Charles curled up in my lap and purred. Connor and I drank our wine and chatted comfortably, enjoying each other's company amid the quiet of the library at night.

I offered Connor a second glass of wine, but he put his glass on the table and said, "Much as I'd like to, I'd better not. I have yet another day of campaigning tomorrow." He stood up, and I also got to my feet. He took me in his arms, and we met in a long, deep kiss, which seemed to go on forever.

But nothing lasts forever, and he eventually pulled away. "Good night, Lucy."

"Good night, Connor,"

"Do you know," he said, glancing at the *Rebecca MacPherson*, "I'm pretty sure the captain's moved."

Our chairs were on the other side of the alcove table from where we'd earlier been standing to admire the model ship. Connor was right: even though we'd moved, the sailor's head was still turned toward us. The empty holes where his eyes should be stared into mine. I felt their black depths calling to me.

"The cat too," Connor said. The small black figure was now on the quarterdeck, next to the captain.

Charles jumped onto the table. He swatted at the model cat, and it toppled over. It made no attempt to get up, and the captain didn't react. Once again, the *Rebecca MacPherson* and her tiny crew were nothing but a toy.

"Charles has been fooling around," I said. "But I have to say, there's something creepy about that ship. I'll be glad when Louise Jane picks it up tomorrow."

"It's almost midnight," Connor said. "What do they say about Halloween? The night when the veil between this world and the next is at its thinnest."

He'd begun to turn away and didn't see me shiver.

"Good thing I have the mighty Charles." I tried to keep my tone light, although my throat had gone dry.

At the door, Connor bent and gave me a light kiss and then walked into the night. It had been bright and clear earlier, the air cool and crisp with the hint of winter soon to come. A fog had come up while Connor and I were talking, rising out of the marsh, drifting across the white face of the moon. The mist swirled around Connor's legs, and it looked as though he were floating.

He unlocked his car, turned, and gave me a wave. I waved back and watched until the rear lights were disappearing down the long driveway.

The mist was thick at the edges of the marsh, but overhead the moon was still visible. The great light far above me went into its twenty-two-point-five–second dormancy as I took a deep breath of salty air. It stuck in my throat, and I was suddenly chilled to my very bones.

At the edges of the marsh, the mist swirled and separated. A shape stood there. It tossed its long, graceful white neck, and its strong front legs pawed the ground.

It was the white horse. And it was watching me.

Chapter Nineteen

"*Come. Come and ride me.*" Unbidden thoughts swirled through my mind. "*We can ride across the seas. We can be free. Come.*"

I ran into the library, slammed the door shut, and twisted the lock. Eyes fixed on the door—did I see the door knob move?—I backed into the room, gasping for breath, my heart racing.

What had Connor said about the veil between the worlds? That Celtic legend is the origin of Halloween. People traditionally dressed in costume on the night before All Saints Day to scare away spirits who were able to move among the living when the veil was at its thinnest.

I almost leapt out of my skin at a crash from the alcove. I whirled around. A group of skeletal sailors lay in a jumble on the floor. Charles jumped off the table and came to me. He twisted himself around my legs.

I bent down and picked him up. Something was in his

mouth. "What have you got there?" He dropped the model cat into my palm.

"You eat that," I said, "and Louise Jane is not going to be happy with you." He didn't appear bothered by the threat in the least. He jumped out of my arms and headed for the stairs, telling me it was bedtime. I gathered up the fallen sailors and laid them on the table, and then I tossed the throw kept behind the circulation desk, in case it gets cold, over the *Rebecca MacPherson*. "That," I said to Charles, "should keep them from wandering."

Instead of turning the lights off before going upstairs, as I usually did, I went around the main room, switching them all on. Not that I expected the sailors to get up to anything. But it was the night when the veil was thin, and the horse was out there.

*   *   *

I also kept my bedside light on, but I needn't have bothered. I slept well, comforted knowing that Charles lay peacefully at my side. If Charles wasn't afraid of skeletal sailors or ghostly horses in the marsh, then I had no reason to be either.

I rose early the next morning. The only daily chore I performed was to fill Charles's bowl with fresh water and to lay out his breakfast. Then I pulled on track pants, a sweater, and sneakers and hurried downstairs. I glanced at the throw on the table as I passed, but nothing had moved in the night. I opened the front door and stepped outside. The sun was rising in a clear sky, and the breeze off the sea was soft and cool. Two cars were parked at the edge of the lot, hikers or birders getting an early start on the day. I crossed the grass to the edge of the marsh and began searching. It didn't take long to find what I was looking for: the imprint of hooves in the wet ground. The depression was round, with a triangle in the center. I'd done a lot of horseback riding when I was a teenager, and I recognized this as an unshod hoof. Highly unlikely to be a horse that had escaped from a stable offering beach rides to tourists. I snapped a couple of quick pictures with my phone and returned to the lighthouse, full of thought. I'd seen something. And that something had been out there on Saturday during Louise Jane's lecture, Monday morning, and again last night. But was it a ghost horse?

Did ghosts leave hoofprints?

What else could it be?

An escaped wild horse? A figment of my overactive imagination? And then there were the strange lights I'd seen in the marsh and the moving figures of the *Rebecca MacPherson*'s crew. I consider myself to be a practical woman. I do not have visions or hallucinations, and I am not subject (I think) to being overly impressionable. Ghosts, equine or otherwise, do not exist. Model pieces do not move on their own. And that is that! I went upstairs and called the police to let them know a horse was loose on the marsh.

The operator told me they'd had no reports of one missing, but she would pass my information on. I then set about getting ready for my day. The weather report was for temperatures in the low sixties, so I decided on a black and white striped dress worn with a thin black belt and a black shrug. I laid out the clothes and hopped into the shower. The phone rang as I was drying my hair. Wrapped in a towel, I made a dash for it.

"Lucy, its Louise Jane."

"Good morning," I said.

"What's Bertie's schedule for today?"

"Why do you want to know?"

"I'm coming in to get the *Rebecca MacPherson*, and I'd rather avoid her if I can. She seemed to be awful cross last night."

"I wonder why that would be, after you expressly disobeyed her orders and told tales about the lighthouse."

"As everyone keeps telling me, Lucy, honey, I'm not a library employee. Bertie is not my boss; therefore she cannot give me orders."

"True," I said.

"I'm wanting to avoid any potential . . . shall we say, unpleasant words."

"Fair enough. She knows where you live if she's in the mood to hunt you down. She has meetings all morning at the library in Manteo and isn't due in until after lunch."

I heard a click. Louise Jane had hung up without thanking me.

I should have lied.

* * *

Today was November 1st, All Saints Day, and the veil between the worlds had closed. Sunlight streamed in through the east windows, and dust mites danced in the beams. Feeling rather foolish, I switched off most of the lights before pulling the throw off the *Rebecca MacPherson*. In the clear light of morning, it was nothing but a model ship, albeit somewhat unusual. I placed the captain on the quarterdeck, the cat at his feet, and arranged the sailors as though they were performing their duties.

Louise Jane burst through the door the minute I opened up, a box in her arms.

"Good morning, Louise Jane," I said. "Looks like it's going to be another lovely day."

"You're sure she won't be back until this afternoon?"

"That's what her schedule says." I cleared my throat. It wouldn't kill me to be gracious. "Your presentation last night was very good. Everyone enjoyed it."

She preened and with great effort forced the words over her lips. "Thank you, Lucy." She began packing the *Rebecca Mac-Pherson* into its box. None of the sailors or George, the ship's cat, tried to escape.

The door opened again, and Julia and her ever-present entourage came in. "Hope I'm not too early," she called, "but I'm so excited to talk to Charlene again, I couldn't keep myself away any longer. Is she in?"

"She isn't due until ten," I said.

"No problem. I can wait. No better place to wait than a library."

"I said that," Theodore announced proudly. Greg grumbled. I wondered if Julia was starting to feel a mite crowded with those two always tripping over each other in an effort to help her. Perhaps she enjoyed their support while things were so difficult for her.

Today she'd added a splash of color to her usual browns and tied a blue and yellow scarf around her neck. She smiled at me, and I could see that some of the darkness had been lifted from behind her eyes. "As long as I'm here, I plan to take total advantage of this library. I got a call from Detective Watson first thing this morning."

"Good news?" I asked.

"My grandfather's body will be released soon, and I'll be allowed to take him home."

"So you're not under suspicion any longer?" I said. "That is good news."

"He didn't quite say that. He did tell me that I need to keep him informed of my movements, but I think it's a promising step, don't you?"

"Definitely."

"My lawyer's already packed and heading for the airport," she said.

Only Teddy didn't look pleased at the news. I gave him an encouraging smile. Julia had to go home sometime. It would be up to him, and to her, if they were to keep in touch.

"I loved your lecture yesterday, Louise Jane," Julia said. "Perhaps I can talk to you some time about legends of the Outer Banks. Charlene is going to tell me the history, and you can tell me the myths."

"I'd be happy to," Louise Jane said. "I'm looking forward to making plans with your mother. I sense a kindred spirit. We'll use the music of the spheres to—"

Julia cut her off. "Please don't get your hopes up about touring with her. Anna is somewhat . . . that is, she can be sporadic in her enthusiasms."

Louise Jane tried not to look too disappointed. "I didn't mean *plans* as in working with her. I prefer my lectures to be unaccompanied by cheap theatrics. Much more impressive that way, don't you agree, Lucy?"

"Me? Oh, yeah, totally."

"I'm not a showman, but a scholar of the supernatural world."

"Speaking of myths," I said, "I was talking to . . . uh . . . Mrs. Fitzgerald last night. She started to tell me something about a ghost dog that's sometimes spotted in the area around Coquina Beach. We were interrupted before she could finish. I don't think any of your stories feature animals, do they, Louise Jane?"

I tried to approach the topic obliquely, knowing that if I came right out and asked Louise Jane if a ghostly horse or corpse candles had been seen in the marsh, she'd say yes. She'd never admit that there might be a supernatural presence she (or her grandmother or great-grandmother) didn't know about.

"Dog?" she said. "Oh, yes, that dog. It's a minor story. The dog, so the story goes, came off a wrecked vessel, and some say they hear it when the wind is strong from the south, howling for its lost master."

This morning, as the sun filled the room with light, and the scent of the coffee I'd put on to brew wafted in, Louise Jane's ghostly tale had no impact. It was just the story of a lost dog.

"I know of a handful of stories of animal spirits like that one," Louise Jane said with a dismissive shrug, "but my grandmother taught me that humans trapped here on earth are more deserving of my attention. And"—she turned her eyes on me—"more dangerous to the living."

I smiled to myself. I could foresee Louise Jane scurrying off to another library branch to start a search for ghost dogs.

"I find the idea of spirit animals terrifying," Julia said. "In a story, I mean. Look at the ghostly horse in Bracebridge Hall. That's the part that chilled me to the bone. Even more than the *Flying Dutchman* or the tale of the Wild Huntsman."

"All this nonsense about ghosts makes for a fun way of scaring children, but I don't have any time for it." Theodore tried to sound firm, but his voice shook slightly.

Greg threw him a glance, and the edges of his mouth turned up in a grin. "I'm not so sure, buddy." He quoted *Hamlet*: "*'There are stranger things in heaven and earth.'*"

Charlene arrived, takeout cup from Josie's in her hand, and earbuds in her ears. "Is this a private party, or is anyone welcome?"

"Good morning," Julia said. "I'm so excited about getting into your books and papers, I came in early. I hope you don't mind."

Charlene pulled the buds out of her ears. "Don't mind a bit. Believe me, after all the work I do with bored high school students and college kids taking compulsory courses and hating every minute of it, I'm delighted to have someone who's actually interested. Would you like a coffee or something first?"

"No thanks—I had an early breakfast."

"I'm heading back to the hotel," Greg said. "I've some business calls to make. Phone me when you're ready to be picked up, Julia. Coming, buddy?"

"I need to talk to Lucy," Theodore said. "Library business."

The curator gave the book collector a long, dark look, but he could hardly say he'd changed his mind and decided to stay.

Everyone headed off in their own direction, and soon Teddy and I were the only people in the main room. "What sort of library business?" I asked.

He put his fingers to his lips and tiptoed somewhat theatrically to the door. He threw it open and peered out. No one was

269

standing there, ear to the door or otherwise. Julia and Charlene's faint voices drifted down from the upper level. We had no children's programs scheduled until after school. The library would be quiet this morning, and I'd been looking forward to it, thinking it would give me the chance to get caught up on paperwork and do some research into next year's book purchases.

"I found something important," Theodore said.

"What's that?"

"You notice how interested Julia is in talking to Charlene about North Carolina history?"

"What of it? It's fascinating stuff."

"Greg doesn't seem to share her enthusiasm, but he's supposed to be some sort of hotshot historian. Julia's considering taking over management of the collection herself. It's possible she told him he was going to be surplus to requirements once they left the Outer Banks."

"That's nothing but speculation."

"An educated guess. I've been . . . ahem . . . spending a lot of time in his company of late. He's shifty. He doesn't seem to have much money. He takes all his meals at the hotel and charges them to his room."

"What's that got to do with anything?"

"The hotel bill is being covered by Jay's accounts. Probably through Julia. He didn't even pay for a round of coffee at Josie's."

"I wouldn't read much into that. Maybe he likes having his expenses paid. I know I would."

"As a gentleman and a scholar, I would never stoop so low. The facts will eventually speak for themselves, but in the meantime, I'm concerned for Julia's safety."

"You mean from Greg? Surely you're joking." Judging by the intense look on his face, Theodore was deadly serious.

"If someone killed Jay to get the Ruddle collection," he said, "Julia might be next."

"Your logic isn't working, Teddy. Greg isn't going to get the Ruddle collection in any event."

"We don't know the contents of Julia's will."

"No, we don't. Nor are we ever going to. Drop that line of thought before it gets you into trouble."

In asking Theodore to help me with the investigating, I'd made a serious mistake. Watson had accused me of having a predetermined conclusion—that Julia was innocent. But Theodore was far worse. He'd decided, for his own reasons, not only was Julia innocent, but Greg was guilty. And nothing would dissuade him from that fact.

"Why don't you have a word with Detective Watson about Greg, Lucy?"

"Sure. I'll call him right away. Soon as you've left." I had no intention of doing any such thing. Watson would take Teddy's fingering of the culprit as seriously as he'd take Charles's.

"Good. I'll pop upstairs to see how Julia and Charlene are getting along. Unfortunately, Outer Banks history isn't one of my areas of study, so I am unable to offer much help. Perhaps it is time I learned."

While we were talking, Charles had taken his place on a nearby shelf to best follow the conversation.

"Leave Julia alone," I said. "You weren't invited to join her and Charlene, so don't."

He let out a long sigh. "If you say so, Lucy."

271

"I do. How did you get here anyway? Did you drive yourself?"

"I did. Greg asked me to check with reception as to checkout time, and when I got outside, they'd driven off. I told you he was underhanded."

"Go home. I'll tell Julia to call you or Greg when she's ready to leave."

"Don't offer Greg. I'll come."

"Goodbye, Teddy."

As Theodore headed out the door, Charles raised one eyebrow at me and wiggled his whiskers.

"*When a woman first begins to love, life is all romance to her.*" I quoted Washington Irving. "We can change *woman* to *man* in this case."

Charles meowed his agreement.

Two women came in with armloads of books. I exchanged greetings with them and went to work.

* * *

I spent the rest of the morning engrossed in publishers' catalogues. What a fantastic bunch of mysteries were due to be released in the spring. Our budget didn't stretch to buying everything we might want (nor did space on our shelves), and it would be difficult to choose.

Several of our regulars were perusing the stacks, when Julia clattered down the stairs, her face glowing. "My, but that was interesting. Charlene's a font of knowledge. I'm thinking of buying a vacation home in Nags Head so I can come in every day. Maybe I inherited some of that Outer Banks blood after all."

"That would be great," I said.

The smile faded, and a cloud settled over Julia's face. "For a moment there, I was about to call Grandfather and ask him to recommend a realtor for me. I'm going to miss him so very much. For my whole life it's been me and Grandfather. Us against the world, he used to say." Julia stared into the space above my head. "What am I going to do without him?"

Charles leapt onto the returns shelf, and Julia gathered him into her arms.

"I get the feeling your mother would like to have a relationship with you." I said.

"Anna? We've been apart for so long. We're so different."

"Give it time," I said. "Give her time." I slid a box of tissues toward her and then lowered my head and busied myself on the computer, giving Julia what bit of privacy I could.

Eventually, she put Charles on the desk and wiped her eyes. "Perhaps I should get a cat."

Charles meowed his agreement, and Julia smiled. Trust Charles to know exactly how to lighten the mood.

"I'm sorry, Lucy. You don't need to hear my life story."

"I did ask," I reminded her. "Don't be sorry. I'm happy to do what little I can to help."

She smiled at me. "Everyone here's been so nice to me. I called Greg to come and get me. I'll walk up to the road to meet him."

* * *

By seven o'clock, Bertie, Ronald, and Charlene had left for the day, and only one patron remained in the library. As soon as she was finished, I could lock up.

She dropped a stack of books onto the desk. "This is all proving to be far harder than we were expecting."

I read the spines of the volumes she'd chosen. All were variations of legal titles *For Dummies*.

"The house is far too big for us now the children have moved away," she said. "We want to sell it and get something smaller. My husband insists we can do everything ourselves without a realtor. I'm not so sure."

"You've got a lot of reading here," I said.

She grimaced. "More than I can get through. Too many now that I see them all in a pile like that. I'll only take this one, thanks." She pointed to *Home Buying for Dummies*.

I checked the book out, handed it to her, and said good night. I followed her to the door and was about to lock it, when I saw Theodore hurrying up the path.

"I've come to collect Julia," he said to me.

"Oh, Teddy. You should have called. She left hours ago."

Hangdog was the expression. "I suppose that Greg collected her."

"She didn't want to bother you." I gave him what I hoped was an encouraging smile. "Greg is her employee, remember. He worked for her grandfather, so I assume she inherited him. Natural enough she'd call him to run errands for her."

Theodore looked dubious. Charles wound himself around the man's legs. "It's just . . . you see, Lucy . . . I . . . I don't have a great deal of experience with women. I like Julia. I like her very much. I was hoping we could be friends . . . more than friends, I mean."

I tried to look surprised at that news. "Give her time, Theodore. Don't rush her."

He threw up his hands. "I don't have time, Lucy. That so-called curator is constantly lurking about. He'll be taking her back to New York now that Watson says they can leave."

"New York's not on the far side of the moon. Naturally, she'll want to go home as soon as she can. If nothing else, she has arrangements to make for her grandfather. Let her know you'll call her in a few days, perhaps come up for a visit to see how she's doing."

His big smile showed his browning teeth to full effect. "You're so wise, Lucy."

I was saved from having to reply when the door opened, and Julia came in.

Teddy's face filled with joy. Poor Theodore. Julia would go back to New York, and her life would change now that she was in control not only of the Ruddle money but the historical collection. She'd be busy settling her grandfather's estate. She'd probably forget all about the Lighthouse Library and our research room and her plans to buy a vacation home here. Charlene kept piles of original material, but they did have libraries in New York City. Once away from Theodore, Greg would make sure Julia would only remember what an unattractive, uncomfortable man the book collector was.

Then again, maybe I wasn't giving Julia enough credit. Maybe she did like Theodore exactly the way he was.

"Julia!" he said. "What brings you out this evening?"

"I'm glad to find you still here. Both of you. I'm going home tomorrow morning, and I wanted to say goodbye."

The joy died, and Theodore's face became a study in disappointment. He truly was as readable as a book. "So soon?"

"Watson called to tell me he's finished the paperwork to release the . . . my grandfather, and I'm free to leave. I have to take Grandfather home and make the funeral arrangements. We'll be on our way first thing tomorrow."

"Do you need a ride to New York?" Teddy said with as much eagerness as a puppy begging her to throw the ball one last time.

"That's so sweet of you, but Greg's arranged a plane for us."

Charles leapt onto the nearest shelf and rubbed himself against Julia's arm.

Julia laughed and gave him a pat. "Hello, you. I'm glad to see you too. I've made up my mind, and the first thing I'm going to do when I get home is get a cat. I've never had pets, because Grandfather said they were nothing but a nuisance, but I'd like to get myself a cat just like this one."

"Excellent idea," Theodore said. Julia smiled at him.

The smile she gave the man was the exact same as the one she'd given the cat. Julia liked Teddy, I realized, but in the same way that I like him. I'd happily accept a lift into town, but I wouldn't want to date him.

Poor Teddy. Shy, awkward, sometimes foolish, but good-hearted Theodore was going to have his heart broken.

"I'll be back," Julia said. "I'm determined to spend a lot more time here."

"Excellent. I'll be waiting." Theodore cleared his throat and shifted his feet. "Before you go, how about a walk on the board-walk? It's a beautiful evening."

"I'd enjoy that," she said. "It's been a long, emotional day."

I waved them out the door. Expecting them to pop back in to wish me a good night, I didn't lock the door behind them.

Charles went off in search of sustenance, and instead of going upstairs while waiting for Julia and Theodore to return, I sat at the desk and logged onto Facebook to check up on news from friends back in Boston.

The door opened as I was wondering if my sister-in-law was aware that Facebook is a public forum. My eldest brother had apparently been so drunk last night, he'd fallen asleep in the car and couldn't be woken when they got home. She'd left him there to sleep it off.

Instead of Theodore and the fair Julia returning from their walk, the new arrival was Dave. He wasn't accompanied by Anna. Charles leapt onto the desk, and the fur along his back rose.

"Hi," Dave said. "Sorry to bother you. I see the 'Closed' sign on the door, but I'm looking for Julia. I ran into Greg back at the hotel, and he told me she'd come here to say goodbye and to thank you for your help."

"She went for a walk."

"I suppose that annoying man is with her."

"Theodore? Yes, but he's not annoying. He's fond of Julia. Nothing wrong with that, is there?"

Dave sighed. "I don't know, Lucy. I've seen guys like that before. I can tell them a mile away. He's trouble, pure and simple. I told Anna to keep an eye on him, but Anna's not exactly level-headed when it comes to men." He laughed awkwardly. "She's married to me, isn't she?"

"I'd hardly call Theodore trouble. He means well."

"They always mean well. Until they don't. Julia told Anna she's going back to New York tomorrow. I'm worried that guy'll do something he might regret when she tells him she's leaving."

Charles hissed.

I shook my head. "Theodore's not like that."

"I'm glad to hear it. Perhaps I'm worried about nothing. Comes with living with Anna, I bet. Always on the lookout for high drama." He ran his hands through his hair and gave me a tight smile.

"Sure," I said.

"I'll leave you to it then. We'll be leaving tomorrow with Julia and Greg. In a private plane no less. How the other half lives, eh?"

"Have a safe trip," I said.

He smiled at me, but the smile didn't reach his eyes. "It's been nice meeting you, Lucy, and getting a look at your lighthouse. I popped in to have a last look at it. It's pretty impressive." He shifted from one foot to another. His eyes darted around the room, but he avoided looking directly at me. "Maybe if Julia buys that vacation home she's talking about, I'll see you again sometime." He fiddled with something in his pants pocket, and I got a glimpse of a black leather glove. "'Course if she's anything like her mother, any plans she makes will be forgotten the next morning. Bye."

"Goodbye," I said. He left and I went back to Facebook.

Charles swatted my hand.

"Hold your horses," I said. "We'll go up after Julia leaves. She might want to say goodbye again. Wow! Look at this. She really has no sense of privacy." My sister-in-law was telling the world that if my brother didn't sober up, she'd leave him. One of her friends replied that she knew the top divorce lawyer in Boston.

My mother kept a keen eye on family goings-on via Facebook. She'd be having a fit right about now. More about the airing of laundry in public than a potential divorce from a daughter-in-law she never liked. She'd also be on the phone to her lawyers, determined to keep every cent of Richardson money out of any looming legal battles. These things could get mighty expensive.

My attention was torn away from the computer when Charles dropped his entire body on top of *Estate and Trust Administration for Dummies*. He swatted at my hand again, this time with claws outstretched.

It hurt. "Hey! Don't do that. What's gotten into you? Don't sit on that book." I started to pick him up.

Inheritance. Wills.

Jay Ruddle had been a wealthy man. Julia was his only living descendent. I knew nothing about the rest of Julia's life, but I thought it significant that no one had come to the Outer Banks to be with her after her grandfather's death. What had she told me Jay always said to her? *Us against the world.* If she had no close friends or extended family, then who was most likely to be Julia's heir? Anna. No matter the distance of their relationship. Anna was still Julia's mother.

Julia wasn't going to be convicted of killing her grandfather and go to prison. Watson had pretty much dropped that line of inquiry.

Because she hadn't done it.

If Julia had gone to prison, that would have meant someone else would either inherit the money or manage it in Julia's absence.

I looked at Charles. He'd moved off the book and was now sitting beside it. His intense blue eyes studied my face as if saying, "*Finally*, she gets it."

I'd considered the idea that Anna, instead of being in Europe playing the violin, had been in North Carolina and had sneaked into the library during Louise Jane's lecture to murder her father-in-law. I'd dismissed that argument because I couldn't see Anna melting into a crowd. Nor could I see her calmly reappearing to comfort her daughter. Anna was the sort who wouldn't be able to resist comments like "He deserved it, *moya dorogaya*," or "You're better off without him. Now that he's gone, we can be together."

Watson told me Anna had been in Europe when Jay died. I had to believe the police knew what they were talking about.

Therefore Anna Makarova had not killed Jay Ruddle.

Anna had *said* Dave was with her on her violin tour. But that didn't mean it was true. Had he told her it was easier to say he was and avoid difficult questions? I could see Anna waving her hand and saying, "Of course, darling." Watson hadn't said anything about Dave's whereabouts, and I hadn't thought to ask him to check.

Dave, unlike Anna, could easily blend into an Outer Banks crowd. No one knew him. No one had any reason to remember seeing him. If he wore a ball cap, like so many men his age, and pulled it low over his forehead, even if I'd seen him, I would be unlikely to recognize him later. Nothing about Dave's clothes would make him stand out in a crowd.

His clothes.

It wasn't summer any more, but the weather was pleasant tonight. Dave had been wearing baggy jeans with a shirt and a denim jacket, normal clothes for such an evening. Normal, except for the leather gloves stuffed in the pockets of his jeans. Why would a man go to the trouble of bringing gloves he wouldn't need?

To keep his fingerprints off the murder weapon.

Charles leapt off the desk and headed for the door.

I jumped to my feet. Knowing Theodore as I did, I'd dismissed everything Dave had implied a few minutes ago about my book collector friend and his feelings for Julia. Dave had said the other man couldn't be trusted, not only to me, but to Anna. Could that have been an attempt to put the idea into our heads that awkward, eccentric Theodore would lash out if Julia told him she didn't want to see him again?

Dave couldn't just kill Julia. Her death, following so closely on that of her grandfather, would focus police attention on potential heirs. But what if the guilty party was found at the scene? Perhaps with a smoking gun clutched in his hand and a dead woman at his feet?

I ran.

"Call 911," I shouted to Charles, before remembering that he couldn't do that.

Chapter Twenty

F our cars were in the parking lot. My teal Yaris, Teddy's rat-
tletrap, Julia's rented Escalade, and a compact rental car. No
one was in sight.

I tried to envision Julia as she came into the library. She'd
been wearing a knee-length skirt, pantyhose, and pumps with
one-inch heels. Not suitable footwear for venturing into the
marsh itself. I ran around the lighthouse. The boardwalk is well
maintained, winding through the long lush grasses, climbing
onto stilts that extend into the water, and ending at a small dock
and viewing platform overlooking the marsh. It's a popular spot
for family groups and birders.

The sun had set over Roanoke Island and the mainland. A
thin red line marked the horizon, and the fresh, salty air shim-
mered with a fading golden light. The 1000-watt bulb at the top
of the lighthouse tower flashed in its rhythm.

Highly romantic.

I sprinted toward the boardwalk, and three figures came
into view. Two of them stood at the edge of the dock, watching

night settle over the wetlands. Theodore's tall, skinny frame and Julia's much shorter one. The man took a step closer to the woman and, after considerable hesitation, lifted his arm and placed it on her shoulders. Her head turned toward him.

I might have slipped quietly away and gone back inside if not for the third person, the one running fast toward them. He'd put on the leather gloves, and, as I watched, he reached into a jacket pocket.

I ran across the boards. I yelled, but the wind was blowing toward me, and it snatched my voice away.

Theodore and Julia heard Dave approaching. Teddy dropped his arm, and they separated and turned to face him.

"No!" Dave shouted. "No!" He rushed at Julia. When he was within a foot of her, he pulled his arm back.

Theodore leapt between them. Julia screamed. To my horror, I saw Theodore clutch his right arm. He staggered backward, collapsed into the railing, and slid to the ground. Julia reached for him, but Dave swung again. I screamed and kept screaming as I ran forward.

Dave heard me and whirled around. The last rays of sunlight reflected off the gleam of the knife in his hand. "Thank heavens you're here, Lucy. That maniac attacked Julia. Run to the library and lock yourself in. Call the police. I've got this."

"I'm fine right here," I said. I reached the viewing platform but kept my distance, my eyes on the knife and my hands in the air. Julia crouched at Theodore's side, and her arms were around him.

Dave's eyes flickered, but the knife didn't move.

"Why don't we go up to the library and make ourselves

comfortable," I said. "I can put the kettle on or open a bottle of wine if you'd prefer, and we can talk things over." I felt in my pocket for my phone. My fingers closed on its solid bulk, but I didn't dare take it out. I cursed myself for not calling for help before chasing after Dave.

"I'm all right," Theodore groaned. "You go with Lucy, Julia."

"Don't be ridiculous," she said. "I'm not leaving you here with him. I don't know what you're playing at, Dave, but you're the one who attacked me, not Theodore."

"You're understandably confused. Let me help." He stepped toward Julia and Theodore.

"Don't move another inch," I said. "You're wearing gloves and holding a knife. I see it. Julia sees it. We will not let you put it in Teddy's hand."

Dave turned around, his back pressed against the railing so he had all three of us in sight. He swung the knife from side to side. "No harm done here. Your word against mine. Go back to your library. Take these people with you."

I took a quick glance at Theodore. He was pale faced and breathing in short gasps. Blood covered his shirt. The cut was to his upper arm, but he needed to have it seen to, and quickly. Julia pulled off her scarf and tied it tightly around his arm above the wound. "You tried to kill me," she said to Dave. "Did you kill my grandfather? It must have been you. Why? What did we ever do to you? What do you want from me?" The last rays of daylight disappeared, and the world turned gray.

"Your grandfather kept you away from your mother all these years," Dave said. "It broke Anna's heart to be separated from you. She's so happy that you're together again. You can be happy now too, Julia. Mother and daughter together, like it should be."

What a lot of nonsense. Dave wanted nothing but Jay's fortune. He wouldn't even have to get rid of Anna to get it. She didn't seem the sort to know much about handling money. She'd hand control over to her husband and be happy with a nice fat spending allowance.

I refrained from saying so. The man still held the knife. Thanks to Teddy and me, his plan to kill Julia and make it look like Teddy had done it had failed.

But that wouldn't be the end of it. *How far over the edge was Dave?* Would he attempt to get rid of all the witnesses? Meaning me as well.

I glanced at Theodore. His shirtsleeve was soaked in blood. His face was very pale, and he struggled to breathe.

"This is obviously all a misunderstanding." I tried to keep my voice calm. I failed. "Teddy needs help. Let's go back to the lighthouse and make the call." I kept my eyes on Dave. "Why don't you throw that knife into the water? Get rid of the evidence, and we can all calm down."

"You should do something about security in your library," Dave said. "Anyone can simply wander in. Anna was in Italy last weekend, pretending she had a concert to give. In reality, she was knocking on doors, trying to find work. Her situation was getting pretty desperate. She burned through all the money Jay Ruddle had given her over the years, and she'd burned her bridges with most musical companies. Her father-in-law was a wealthy man. I've been following his movements for a long time, waiting until the right time to get involved. I intended to tell him to let bygones be bygones and remember that Anna's the mother of his beloved granddaughter. But before I could arrange a meeting, I heard he was going to give away his historical collection. If he wanted to give it away, why not give it to me—I mean to Anna? Not to some public library. I drove down to Nags Head to have a chat. Man-to-man sort of thing." He glanced at Julia. "I was only thinking of you."

"Yeah, right," she said. Theodore groaned. His color was not looking good. I didn't want to stand here talking all night, but as long as Dave had that knife and was in striking distance of Julia . . .

"I heard your library was likely to get the collection and figured I'd check it out first. Who knew you'd have a couple of hundred people hanging around that afternoon? I saw Jay and Julia arrive, and then Jay went into the library. I started listening to that lecture, but it was—well, let's be honest—mighty boring. I figured it was a good opportunity for me and Jay to have our chat. The library was empty, so I called out. He answered, and I went upstairs. As soon as I saw him, I could tell something was bothering him. He had this gold chain in his hand and was wrapping it around his fingers. I told him who I was and what was on my mind. He laughed at me and told me to get out. I don't like being laughed at."

Eyes fixed on Dave, Julia began to slowly get to her feet.

"No one does," I said. "It must have been an accident."

"I'm glad you understand," he said. "You'll tell the cops that, right?" He began to lower the knife. I let out a sigh of relief.

Julia was small, but powered by rage. She threw her entire

body against Dave, throwing him off balance. The knife slashed through the air with an audible swish, but she'd knocked it aside, and it missed. I'd seen what she was intending to do and moved the moment Julia did. I grabbed Dave's arm before he could swing again. Julia screamed and pummeled the man while I twisted his hand, trying to get him to drop the knife. He fought back, hard, and my grip began to weaken. We were losing. Then, Dave let out a yell and staggered backward. Julia's foot shot out, and she tripped him. I let go of his wrist and he fell, hard. The knife dropped out of his hand and clattered on the wooden slats. I kicked it over the edge and heard a satisfying splash as it hit the water. Dave lay on the boardwalk, blood leaking from a cut on his head, a shattered cell phone next to him. Theodore struggled to sit up, his breath coming in harsh gasps, his face pinched with pain.

While Julia and I had been fighting with Dave, Teddy had managed to get his phone out of his pocket and use it as a weapon. Good thing it was his right arm that had been injured. Teddy was left-handed.

Julia and I piled on top of Dave and held him down. I fumbled in my pocket for my own phone, found it, and pulled it out. I didn't see how I was going to be able to use it, though—not and help keep the screaming, struggling Dave down.

"Give it to me," Teddy said through a gasp of pain. "I'll call for help. Mine is probably broken."

Chapter Twenty-One

While Theodore made the call and Julia held Dave down, I pulled my belt free of my dress. "We can use this."

I pulled the man's arms back and secured them behind him with the belt. Dave kicked and swore, but he wasn't going anywhere. I sat back on my haunches and took a look at Theodore. His face was sickeningly pale and pinched with pain, and he was sweating profusely, but the flow of blood appeared to be slowing.

We soon heard the welcome sound of sirens approaching, and red and blue lights broke through the row of tall pines lining the lighthouse driveway. Flashlights shone in the marsh, growing stronger as they approached us. At last I could move off Dave's still-kicking legs. Strong hands reached around me and jerked him to his feet.

"He killed Jay," I gasped. "He said so himself."

"It was an accident!" Dave yelled. "I told you it was an accident."

"Save it for the judge," Butch Greenblatt said. He nodded at the officers to take Dave away.

Julia crouched beside Theodore, murmuring comforting words. Paramedics arrived and tended to him. He tried to protest that he was fine, but they paid him no attention. "Doesn't look too bad, but you'll need to be checked out at the hospital." They loaded him onto a stretcher.

"Please," Julia said, "can I come with him?"

"Should be okay," one of the paramedics said.

"You go, Julia," I said. "I'll answer the police's questions."

Teddy was wheeled away. Julia walked beside the stretcher, clutching his left hand.

"You were lucky," Butch said.

"Yes."

"I've called Watson, and he's heading for the station. Who is that guy anyway?"

"Julia's mother's husband."

"He seems chatty, and Watson's keen to talk to him. Looks like he's going to claim it was an accident, but that won't stand up for long."

"No," I said. "He took down the rope that was blocking the stairs and carried it upstairs into the rare books room with him. No one would do that unless they intended to use it." I shuddered.

"You don't look too good yourself, Lucy. You need to sit down. Officer Franklin, help Ms. Richardson inside."

"I've got her." Connor put his hands on my arms and looked into my face for a long time.

"What are you doing here?" I said.

"I am the mayor, remember? It has its privileges. The 911 operator has instructions to alert me whenever there's a call to the lighthouse. You don't seem to be able to keep yourself out of trouble."

"I'm fine." I took a step, and my legs collapsed beneath me. I would have fallen had Connor not swept me into his arms.

"Sorry," I said. "I don't go looking for trouble, you know. It seems to find me all on its own."

He kissed me. "I guess that's why I love you so much."

Chapter
Twenty-Two

Julia and Greg's plans to return to New York were cancelled so she could make a formal statement to Detective Watson and fuss over Theodore. He'd spent the night in the hospital and was released in the morning with plenty of stitches, his right arm in a sling, and a prescription for painkillers.

I went down to the police station first thing in the morning to make my own statement. Connor insisted on picking me up and driving me into town.

Last night, he'd taken me into the library, sat me in the wingback chair, told Charles to stand guard, and then made a cup of hot, excessively sweet tea. I'd begun to shake by the time the tea was served, and so Connor simply sat with me and chatted about nothing in particular for a long time. When my eyelids began to droop, he took me upstairs, scooted me into the bathroom with my pajamas, and then tucked me into bed. When I awoke, it was daylight, and Connor was asleep in a chair, hair mussed, tie askew, shoes off. Charles was snoozing on the arm of the chair, one paw stretched out and resting on Connor's chest.

Man and cat started awake as I put the coffee on.

"Morning, Your Honor," I said. "You don't look very comfortable."

Connor stretched his shoulders. Charles stretched his entire body. "I don't want to make a habit of it," Connor said, "but I thought someone should be here in case you had nightmares."

"Slept like a baby," I said. "Safe and sound. Don't you have campaigning to do?"

"After I ran out of the Rotary meeting mid-speech last night, I probably should start making amends. But some things are more important. I told Dorothy to cancel all my appointments this morning."

We smiled at each other. Charles purred.

Sentiment over, Charles leapt down and demanded to be fed.

Detective Watson called to tell us that David White had been charged with the murder of Jay Ruddle and the attempted murder of Theodore Kowalski.

* * *

Other than that, it was a normal day at the Bodie Island Lighthouse Library. I thought we all might need some closure before Greg and Julia left, so I called Julia in the afternoon and invited them to the library, after closing, for a drink. I also invited my coworkers, Butch and Stephanie, Josie and Grace, Connor (of course!), Theodore, and Louise Jane.

Theodore came with Greg and Julia, as he wasn't able to drive. Julia fussed over him, making sure he was comfortably seated and had a drink at hand, while Greg threw poisonous looks across the room.

I took Julia aside and spoke to her quietly. "How's your mother doing?"

"After an initial attack of the vapors at the news that Dave was being charged with Grandfather's murder, she settled down. She might have forgiven him for that, but she says she will never forgive him for attacking me. She's at the hotel, not wanting company. She'll be coming to New York with me tomorrow. We're going to take rebuilding our relationship slowly."

"I'm glad," I said. We hugged each other and then rejoined our circle of friends.

"No malicious spirits at work, Louise Jane," Charlene said, "Nothing but a deranged man. You must be disappointed."

"What lead to his derangement, I might wonder?" Louise Jane replied. "Something tipped him over the edge."

Charlene rolled her eyes. "Greed. Pure and simple."

Louise Jane helped herself to another glass of wine. "Out there on the marsh, at dusk, spirits are at work. As we know, the spirits have a strong influence over those of weaker minds."

I shifted uncomfortably in my seat.

"Stuff and nonsense." Theodore tried to sound firm, but he wasn't able to disguise the slight quiver in his voice.

Louise Jane ignored him. "I've sensed activity around the marsh for some time." She leaned back in her chair and crossed her long legs. Tonight, instead of her usual sneakers, she was wearing pink and purple rubber boots.

"Some time," Charlene muttered to me. "Meaning since last

night. Why don't I put on some music? I'll run up to my office and get my speakers." And she was off before I could stop her.

It was a fun, casual party, and the mood was good. Louise Jane was the first to leave, saying she had a long day ahead of her. She got to her feet and headed out, but not before I noticed her giving Greg a long meaningful look and him nodding in return.

Strange.

"I'm off too," Connor said not long after Louise Jane had left. "Another day of campaigning tomorrow. The end is in sight, thank heavens."

"I hear the polls are promising," Bertie said. "You have a strong lead."

"The only poll that matters is the one on election day," he replied.

"I've booked the rest of the week off work," I said, "so I can be available to help out."

He smiled at me. I walked him to the door, and we kissed good night lightly, aware of everyone watching us.

"Time to go," Josie said. I exchanged hugs with her and Grace, and they left, followed by Butch and Stephanie.

Bertie, Ronald, and Charlene began to tidy up. I reached for a dirty plate, but they told me to sit down.

"The heroes of the day," Ronald said, "get the night off dishes."

"What's the next book for your book club?" Julia asked me.

"We'd chosen *Jane Eyre*," I said, "but Sam Watson suggested a Sherlock Holmes. I'm thinking of putting that to a vote."

"Excellent idea," Theodore said. "The Great Detective has inspired millions around the world with his—"

"Whatever," Greg said.

When everything was neat and tidy once again, Bertie said, "Night all."

Julia began to get to her feet.

"What's the hurry?" Greg said. "Let's have another drink."

"It's late," Julia said. "I'm sure Lucy wants to get to bed."

"I enjoy your company." I smothered a yawn. Truth be told, I wanted them all to be gone.

"Julia's more determined than ever to buy a place in the Outer Banks," Greg said. "We'll be back soon to check out property."

"Don't you have your new job to get to?" Theodore said.

The corners of Greg's mouth twitched. "Julia has asked me to stay on, to help sort things out while she makes her decision about what to do with the collection."

"Oh." Theodore's face fell.

Greg smirked.

Julia smiled at Theodore. "Perhaps you can come to visit me in New York. I'd love to show you around our home. My grandfather wasn't a serious book collector, but he does have a few nice first editions in his library."

Teddy beamed. Greg's face fell.

"You too, Lucy," Julia said. "I owe you so much."

Greg's phone beeped, and he pulled it out of his pocket. He read the screen quickly and put it away. "Never mind that other drink. Julia, it's late. Let's go."

Julia stood up, and Theodore scrambled to his feet. I walked them to the door.

Julia thanked me once again, and I reminded her to call

when she was next in town. She wrapped her arms around me, and I hugged her in return. When we separated, moisture in her eyes reflected off the light above the door. I might have had tears of my own.

I stood on the steps and watched the three of them start down the path. Then, to my considerable surprise, a low noise came from the side of the lighthouse.

"What was that?" Greg turned with a cry.

It sounded again. A horse's neigh, lost, empty, full of despair.

A shadow emerged from the deeper shadows of the lighthouse walls. Moments ago, it had been a clear night, but tendrils of mist drifted across the ground. I sucked in a breath and stepped closer to the solid wall, still warm from the heat of the day.

A few feet from me, Julia, Greg, and Theodore stood transfixed.

The mist drifted, and an indistinct shape struggled to take form. I could see a long tail, the memory of four legs, a mane. That sound again . . .

"Be gone!" Greg stepped in front of Julia and spread both arms out as though to keep the creature away from her. "Come no closer!"

The shape began to turn. Where the head should be, two red lights flared. The eyes, the horrible red eyes, focused on Theodore. The creature neighed once again.

Teddy squealed, and he ran. He bolted down the path to the parking lot, wrenched the car door open, jumped into the back seat of the Escalade, and disappeared from sight.

"Be gone!" Greg cried again. He took another step toward the apparition, still shielding Julia with his body.

The creature backed up. It disappeared around the lighthouse, taking the rolling mist with it.

Greg wrapped Julia in his arms, and she didn't pull away. "What on earth was that?" Her voice quaked.

"I don't know," Greg said, "But whatever it was, it's gone now. I frightened it away." He stroked her hair. "You're safe with me, Julia. Where's Theodore gotten to? Oh, looks like he's hiding in the car. Never mind. Let's get out of here."

I ran into the lighthouse and slammed the door shut behind me. *It was real. My ghostly horse was real.* Others had seen it too.

Charles was snoozing in the wingback chair. He opened one eye and looked at me. He yawned.

Slowly my breathing returned to normal and I mentally examined myself. That had been scary, but not bone chilling. I'd seen something, and I'd been frightened, but I'd not felt anything deep in my bones. Tonight's horse had been close to me, standing only a few feet away, but it had not reached into my mind the way I'd thought the one in the marsh had tried to do.

Animals were highly perceptive to the supernatural, or so I'd been told. Charles couldn't have looked more bored, and this creature had been virtually on his doorstep.

I took a deep breath, straightened my shoulders, gathered my courage, and went back outside. The lamp over the door threw a pool of light onto the step, but outside its range all was dark. The Escalade was gone.

High above me the lighthouse beacon flashed. I switched on

my phone's flashlight and walked to the side of the building. I played my light across the ground. No hoof prints. No marks of any sort. I rounded the building. The soft earth was grooved as though a wheeled machine had been dragged across it. Footprints—human prints—accompanied the mark of the wheels. I placed my foot next to one of them to judge the size. Only slightly larger than mine. The treads looked like they were from rubber boots.

I followed the prints for a short distance. They headed toward the far side of the parking lot.

When Louise Jane gave talks at the library, she used no props. No sound and light show. No spooky music or ghostly effects.

Did she save those for other appearances?

I wouldn't put it past her.

I remembered the secret look between Greg and Louise Jane. She'd been the first to leave, which was unusual for her. Greg had held off leaving until he got a text message, and then he'd abruptly hustled Julia out the door.

I kicked at the marks on the ground. Two suitors, one scared witless by the other. The only thing missing here was the shattered pumpkin; otherwise, this could have been a recreation of the end of *The Legend of Sleepy Hollow* when Ichabod Crane is frightened away from his pursuit of the heiress by his rival.

I went inside, locked the door, and called Charles to bed.

I'd brought a new book upstairs and was looking forward to getting into the *Garden of Evening Mists* by Tan Twan Eng, which several patrons had recommended. But first, I checked the photos on my phone. I'd forgotten that I'd taken pictures of the hoofprints on the marsh the other morning. There might not have been a real ghostly horse outside tonight, but I had seen something over the past few days. I opened the app. The first picture that came up, meaning the last one taken, showed nothing. A black screen. I'd taken the pictures outside in daylight: *something* should have been recorded. But it hadn't even picked up the marsh grasses. I scrolled backward. More nothing until I arrived at a selfie of Josie, Stephanie, and me taken in front of the lighthouse at the decorating party a couple of weeks ago.

I swung the phone toward Charles and snapped a picture. It came out okay. The tousled bedclothes, the snoozing cat, the warm light from the bedside lamp.

I put my phone on the side table and snuggled into bed. I fluffed my pillows, picked up my book, and began to read.

Chapter
Twenty-Three

Connor McNeil was reelected mayor of Nags Head by a landslide.

Before going onstage to give his victory speech, he whispered to me, "I'm glad that's over."

"Until next time?" I asked.

"There will be no next time. I promise." He kissed me lightly.

I watched him switch on his professional smile and bound onto the stage. The applause was deafening. Balloons poured down from the ceiling, and children chased after them. Dorothy, the campaign manager, stood in the shadows, beaming from ear to ear.

Connor's parents joined him at the front. I'd met them earlier in the day at the crowded campaign office as we were working the phones and getting out the vote. Connor had introduced me as his "lady friend," and his parents had been (I thought) happy to meet me. I liked them immediately. Mrs. McNeil had the same lovely blue eyes and prominent cheekbones as her son, and she spoke in a soft Southern drawl as befitted a lifetime spent on the Outer Banks. Mr. McNeil was hearty and gruff, and pumped my hand as though he were trying to start a two-stroke engine.

Connor held up his arms, asking the cheering crowd to calm down. Then he turned to me. He smiled his private smile and held out his hand. I pointed to my chest and mouthed, "Me?"

"Yes, you, dummy," Josie said, giving me a shove in the back. "He wants you up there with him."

Blushing furiously, I climbed onto the stage. Mr. and Mrs. McNeil greeted me with heartfelt hugs.

"Go, Lucy!" Josie yelled.

Connor hugged his parents and then he hugged me. A big, generous, enthusiastic hug. "Thank you for being here with me tonight, Lucy," he whispered.

"Where else would I be?" I replied.

He kept his remarks short, thanking the people in the room for coming, his tireless volunteers, his friends and family. He told us that Doug Whiteside had phoned him a short while ago to offer his congratulations.

The crowd cheered.

Connor promised to work his hardest for the town and people of Nags Head, and the crowd cheered even louder.

Then he was finished, and we all trooped off the stage.

I was at the bar, ordering a glass of lemonade, when Theodore Kowalski came up to me. He was dressed in Harris Tweed, smelling strongly of pipe tobacco, and peered at me through rimless spectacles containing clear glass.

"Good evening, Lucy," he said formally, English accent firmly in place.

"Theodore. I didn't see you earlier. Did you just arrive?"

"Sorry to be late. I was in time to hear the mayor's speech. Most inspiring."

"Can I get you something?" the bartender asked.

"I'll have a Glenlivet, my good man."

"A what?"

Theodore sighed, "Whisky, bourbon. Whatever you have."

Drinks in hand, we went to a quiet corner to talk. I hadn't seen Teddy since the night Louise Jane McKaughnan and Greg Summers set out to frighten him. And succeeded. It was a mean trick, I thought. Greg must have been horrified when he found out that his rival had saved the fair Julia from Dave's knife attack, and retaliated by trying to make Teddy look bad.

"Have you heard anything from Julia Ruddle?" I asked.

"She phoned me the other night," he said. "She wanted to tell me the good news in person."

"Good news?"

"She and Greg have announced their engagement."

He sipped his drink, and I studied his face. He didn't look too upset. I touched his arm. "Are you okay with that?"

"Why wouldn't I be? I'll admit that I entertained a certain . . . fondness . . . for Julia. She's a lovely woman, and it would have been nice for us to be friends. But I don't think I fit into her world, Lucy. She's a wealthy woman and will be moving in privileged circles." He shook his head. "In other news, she's rented an apartment for her mother in Manhattan. When Julia realized Anna was planning on moving in with her, she managed to persuade her she needed her own space."

"Did she say anything about getting a vacation home near here?"

"No." He broke into a smile. "She asked me for my postal address. Would you like to know why?"

"Yes, I would."

"Julia is going to give me, completely free of charge, access to her grandfather's entire library. I've been invited to the apartment in Manhattan to view it and pick out the volumes I want. As a teaser she couriered three books to me." His smile grew. "All first editions and all in excellent condition. An Ian Fleming, a Dashiell Hammett, and—pièce de résistance—a signed copy of Agatha Christie's *Murder on the Orient Express*. I haven't been so excited for a long time. I cannot wait to see what else is in the collection."

"It's nice of her to give them to you."

"I insisted on paying, although I knew I'd never be able to raise anywhere near enough money, but Julia was equally insistent that she wants me to have them. She says it's her way of thanking me for helping her with that unfortunate incident involving Mr. White."

"Don't sell yourself short. You saved her life. I'd say that's worth a few books."

"There's Donna Raeburn. I never did get a chance to reschedule our meeting about her Mickey Spillane collection. Perhaps we can do that now." And off he bustled.

I sipped my lemonade with a good feeling. Julia had rewarded Teddy the best way she could, and he was wise enough to know it.

I spotted Louise Jane chatting to Josie, Butch, and

Stephanie, and made my way through the crowd. It took a long time to cross the room as people kept stopping me to offer their congratulations, as though I'd done something important.

"Having a good time?" I asked when I joined my friends.

"Relieved," Butch said. "The chief would never come out and say so, but everyone at the station knew he was hoping Connor would win. Doug Whiteside had some unusual ideas about how to pay for an efficient police force."

"If I never hear the name Doug Whiteside again," Steph said, "it will be too soon. Nice of Connor to invite you up on the stage, Lucy."

"He was thanking everyone."

"I didn't hear me being asked up. And I helped with the campaign too. He was making sure everyone knows you're a couple."

"If you don't need your apartment anymore, Lucy," Louise Jane said, "I'd be happy to take it over. It shouldn't be left vacant. Mold and mice can get out of control quickly."

"If I have any plans to move—and I don't—you'll be the first person I'll call, Louise Jane."

"Good to know," she said, completely missing my sarcasm. "The spirits in the lighthouse have been quiet lately. Someone being in residence must be helping keep them calm."

"Speaking of restless spirits, that was a mean trick."

"Whatever do you mean, Lucy, honey?" She studied me over the top of her beer bottle. Her look was serious, but she couldn't disguise the trace of a mischievous twinkle in her eyes.

"Don't give me the innocent look. When did you and Greg manage to get together to concoct that ridiculous plan?"

"I don't know of any ridiculous plan to which you might be referring. Greg kindly came up to me after the Halloween night lecture and congratulated me. As I recall you did also. We exchanged phone numbers in case we had reason to talk again."

"I didn't suggest you set a trap for anyone."

"Some people believe, and some do not," she said. "Some need a slight nudge to believe, that's all. You're always telling me I'm making it all up. You're welcome to believe so. Doesn't mean that I am."

Did I believe?

No, I didn't believe Louise Jane with her magic powders and grandmother's tales and her desire to see the back of me.

But I had seen something out on the marsh. Or at least I thought I had. Nothing else strange had happened since Halloween night. No ghostly horses reaching into my mind. No corpse candles luring me to my doom. If those had been tricks played by Louise Jane on me, she wouldn't have been able to keep herself from gloating. I wanted to think that the combined influences of the Halloween preparations, stress over the forthcoming election, worry over the state of my relationship with Connor, Jay Ruddle's death, and the tales of Washington Irving had done a number on my head.

But . . . something had happened. I had seen something and felt something out there. Not old legends embellished by Louise Jane or stories handed down from her great-grandmother, but something I believed was real.

Then there was the model of the *Rebecca MacPherson*. The way the captain seemed to be watching Connor and me that night, or how George, the tiny cat, moved around apparently all by himself. Was it possible the ship itself had drawn . . . something to the marsh?

Next Halloween I'd set myself on watch. I might ask Connor to sit up with me, so I'd have a witness. If anything appeared, that is.

As for here and now: it was over. Life could go back to normal. What passes as normal at the Bodie Island Lighthouse Library anyway.

Louise Jane put her beer bottle onto a side table. "Didn't our own Teddy quote Shakespeare just the other day? *'There are stranger things.'*" She started to walk away, and then she turned. She threw me a self-satisfied grin. "Oh, I almost forgot to tell you: I won't be around for a few weeks. I hope the library can manage in my absence. I'm going on vacation. I've always wanted to go to Europe, and now I have the chance. I'm leaving tomorrow and joining a tour called Haunted Castles of England. I'm so excited. The airfare cost a lot as it was a last-minute booking, but that's not a problem. I was lucky enough to come into some money recently." She walked away.

"What was all that about?" Steph said.

"Who knows with Louise Jane," Butch said. "She likes to sound mysterious."

"She certainly looks pleased with herself," Josie said.

"Very pleased," I said. "I can only hope she hasn't found another line of work."

"What sort of work?"

"Never mind," I said.

"Here's Bertie," Butch said. "I don't recognize the guy with her."

Bertie was making her way across the room, greeting people and introducing her companion, Professor McClanahan from Blacklock College. "An old flame," I said.

"Really?" Steph said. "Do tell. Oh, not now. They're heading our way."

"Good evening, everyone," Bertie said. "Sorry we're late, but I heard the results on the radio. This is an old friend of mine, Eddie. Eddie, you remember Lucy, who works with me."

"Nice to see you again," he said.

Bertie introduced the others. Eddie smiled politely and shook hands, but didn't seem terribly excited at meeting us. I suspected he didn't remember me at all.

Formalities over, he turned to Bertie. "Can I get you a drink, Bee?"

"That would be nice, thank you. I'll have a glass of wine."

They smiled at each other. They kept on smiling. Josie looked at me, raised her eyebrows, and formed her mouth into a round O.

"Never mind," Butch said. "I'll get you something, Bertie. Eddie, what'll you have?"

"Have?" He tore his eyes away from Bertie.

"A drink," Butch said. "Would you like a drink?"

"Thank you. A beer would be nice."

"Lucy?"

"Nothing more for me, thanks."

"It's a good night." Dorothy, Connor's campaign manager, joined us. "Connor's victory was impressive. Very impressive indeed. Thank you all for your help. This night belongs to the volunteers as much as it does to Connor."

"I can't imagine Doug's concession call was terribly gracious," Steph said.

"It didn't choke him too badly. The results couldn't have been all that much of a surprise to him. I heard something you might be interested in."

"What's that?" I asked.

"My curiosity was piqued by what you learned about Jay Ruddle taking a place in Doug's administration. Should we have been unlucky enough to have had one." She shook her head. "No such thing. When Jay came to Nags Head looking for a home for his collection, Bill Hill gave him a call at his hotel. Jay said he'd been away so long, he had no knowledge of or interest in local politics on any level, and hung up. Billy, not being the sort to take no for an answer, decided to quietly spread word that Jay had been interested and was throwing his support behind Doug."

"What a sneak," Josie said.

"Bill Hill has a future in politics," Dorothy said. "I heard that before this election was even over, he was making calls to Raleigh. Oh, well. Not my problem. I've done my bit. From now on I'm devoting my life to my grandchildren and doing good works."

"Ha," Josie said. "You'll be back."

"Probably. It's like a drug. I'm off home. I've haven't had a good night's sleep for weeks. Good night."

"Good night."

"Speaking of sleep," Josie said. "Time for us to be going too. Lucy, Steph, let's have lunch one day next week and start talking wedding plans. I mean my wedding. Unless either of you have plans too?"

Steph sputtered, and I said, "I most certainly do not. Lunch would be great." We hugged, and Josie went to collect Jake, who'd spent most of the night arguing sports with Connor's dad.

Butch returned with a round of drinks and said he wanted to talk to Sam Watson for a few minutes. Steph spotted a friend. Bertie took Eddie to meet Ronald, who'd dressed tonight in a conservative gray business suit and giant yellow polka dot bow tie, and Nan.

I glanced around the room. While we'd been chatting, the party had started to break up. Only a few of Connor's closest friends, his campaign workers, and the serious partiers remained. The bartenders began putting the tops back on bottles and wiping down the counters.

Connor was surrounded by well-wishers. He'd taken off his tie and jacket, undone the top button on his shirt, and rolled up his shirtsleeves. Some of the worry lines had faded from his face, and he looked relaxed and comfortable as he laughed at something Sam Watson said. He must have felt me watching him, because his head turned and he looked directly at me.

I lifted my lemonade glass in a silent toast. The smile he gave me in return lifted my heart.

Author's Note

The Bodie Island Lighthouse is a real historic lighthouse, located in Cape Hatteras National Seashore on the Outer Banks of North Carolina. It is still a working lighthouse, protecting ships from the Graveyard of the Atlantic, and the public are invited to tour it and climb the two hundred fourteen steps to the top. The view from up there is well worth the trip. But the lighthouse does not contain a library, nor is it large enough to house a collection of books, offices, staff rooms, two staircases, and even an apartment.

Within these books, the interior of the lighthouse is the product of my imagination. I like to think of it as my version of the Tardis, from the TV show *Doctor Who*, or Hermione Granger's beaded handbag: far larger inside than it appears from the outside.

I hope it is large enough for your imagination also.

Acknowledgments

I am very grateful to the fabulous cozy community, in particular the Facebook page *Save our Cozies*, for their love of cozy mysteries and their determination to see favorite series continue.

And Matt Martz and Sarah Poppe at Crooked Lane Books, who gave readers what they wanted, and Kim Lionetti at Bookends, who facilitated it.

Thanks also to all my friends in the Canadian writing community, including Barbara Fradkin, Mary Jane Maffini, Robin Harlick, and Linda Wilken for continuing support and friendship.